SACRED DARKNESS

Levan Berdzenishvili

SACRED DARKNESS

THE LAST DAYS OF THE GULAG

*Translated from the Russian
by Brian James Baer and Ellen Vayner*

Europa
editions

Europa Editions
214 West 29th Street
New York, N.Y. 10001
www.europaeditions.com
info@europaeditions.com

Translation from the Russian by Brian James Baer and Ellen Vayner
Original Russian title: *Sviataia mgla. Poslednie dni Gulaga*
Original Georgian title: *Ts'minda ts'qvdiadi*
Translation copyright © 2019 by Europa Editions

Library of Congress Cataloging in Publication Data is available
ISBN 978-1-60945-492-0

Berdzenishvili, Levan
Sacred Darkness

Book design by Emanuele Ragnisco
www.mekkanografici.com

Cover image: Pixabay

Prepress by Grafica Punto Print – Rome

Printed in the USA

CONTENTS

IN EXERGUE (1925)

Moral talk is for the young,
While shrewd and sturdy spirits
Hear differently the rumors of the old,
As Hegel rightly claimed.

But there is other talk mid heaven and earth
Through which the great All enters conscience:
Teaching us that all things pass
And nonetheless all things remain.

As Hegel wrote: In the glow divine,
In the high filter of purest light,
Things mean so little, and so obscurely,
That a sacred darkness seems to reign.

Thought glides upon a whitish tomb
Of insatiable fire and dullened ash.
And there? A different word for talk:
Logos, the sense of that which is.

—GALAKTION TABIDZE (1892–1959)

SACRED DARKNESS

There were LCD monitors, thick cords, clamp stands, support arms, and a control panel surrounded by people dressed in white, blue, and maroon. And there was light, light everywhere, the light of a hundred thousand lumens.

"Sacred light . . . as if I were on a spaceship," I thought, then lost consciousness. I felt like I was being swiftly carried away, and that made me happy. Everything was light and speed. I was in motion for a long time and then, suddenly, I stopped. As I slowly regained awareness of my body, I heard two women talking. The light went off. Motion was light, and stillness was darkness. Complete blackness descended on me. It was total, absolute blackness—a "sacred darkness." Two women were talking in that darkness. They spoke softly in worried tones. They were discussing something, but I couldn't understand what it was. That annoyed me: Why couldn't I understand what they were saying? "In sacred light," Hegel said, "in the great abyss of sacred light . . . " I could hear women's voices, but I couldn't understand them. "In sacred radiance, in the great abyss of sacred radiance . . . So little is known, just as in sacred darkness . . . "

Finally, something emerged from the sounds, something I could make sense of. That something was a word. "In the beginning was the Word . . . " and that word was *insurance*.

"That's not an empty sound," I thought. "I even know what it means." But why don't I understand anything else? Because it's not a Georgian word—it's in a different language. It's the English word for medical coverage. Those women were speaking in English. But why were they speaking in English? Where was I? I obviously wasn't on a spaceship, but in a more earthly place. A hospital where they speak English. I was here because I'd suddenly gotten sick—it started on the plane. When we were flying over the ocean, I began shivering. Then, in the Mexican embassy, I passed out, but not before calling the Georgian embassy. What was I doing in the Mexican embassy? Oh, I remember now: I'm in Washington. From here, I was supposed to fly to Cancun, Mexico, and then, somewhere else. I ended up at Irena's house on Connecticut Avenue. Irena Lasota is a friend. "You're very sick," she told me, and she made a convincing argument to prove her point: "You haven't even touched my duck!" Those were the last words I remembered. I didn't even try her heavenly duck, and that was clear proof of my illness.

"We're worried because he doesn't have insurance. Our hospital's not Johns Hopkins, but you couldn't say it's cheap either."

"I was right, this is a hospital," I thought.

The unknown woman's voice continued:

"How will he manage to cover such a huge bill?"

"My dear doctor, this is no ordinary man. He's a member of parliament and a former political prisoner who spent time in the Soviet Gulag. Where he's from, everybody knows who he is and thousands of people would be happy to help him. Don't think there's no one to take care of him!" said my friend Irena—I would have recognized her voice and her French-accented English anywhere.

"Strange, in all of America, there's probably not even a hundred doctors who know what the Gulag is, and among them, there's probably no more than a dozen who'd be interested in anything connected with the Gulag. But you managed to run into one of them. My mother was a prisoner in the Gulag, and I was born there."

"Where were you born? What prison was your mother in?" Irena asked, excited.

"In Potma, in the Dubravny prison camp," the woman answered.[1]

"I'll pay for everything," I wanted to say, but couldn't.

"This can't be just a coincidence. This man was in the Dubravny camp too, in Barashevo."

"If my mother were alive . . . "

"All three of us were imprisoned there," Irena said. "In the whole D.C. area, we're probably the only three people who were in the Gulag, and now, all of us are here, in Sibley Hospital."

"Not for long," I wanted to add, but couldn't.

"I'm sorry, what's your name?"

"Irena. Irena Lasota."

"Ms. Lasota, what's your relationship to the patient?"

"He's an old friend. He arrived this morning from Georgia."

"I'll try talking to him. Hello," said the unknown woman in a white coat.

"Hello, Doctor," I tried to answer, but couldn't.

"It's possible that he can hear us, but can't answer. What's his name?"

"Levan Berdzenishvili. B as in Boris, E as in Elena, R as in Ronald . . . "

"That's a very difficult last name!"

"You can just call him Mr. B."

---

[1] The Dubravny prison camp, often referred to as Dubravlag, was part of the Soviet Gulag system. Located in the Autonomous Republic of Mordovia, the camp was created in 1948 to house political prisoners. Some of its more notable inmates include the poet Irina Ratushinskaya and the writer Yuli Daniel. [All the notes were added by the translators.]

"Very well, then. Mr. B. it is. I'm his attending physician, and my name is Paige, Paige Van Wirt."

"Nice to meet you, Ms. Van Wirt."

"Ms. Lasota, Mr. B. is facing two serious problems. There's a skin infection on his left leg, and his kidney function is impaired. The infection has already spread, so we'll have to use very powerful antibiotics to treat it. Unfortunately, this treatment might further damage his kidneys. I want you to know that the risk is significant. For the first three days, he'll have to stay in the intensive care unit. First, we need to manage the infection and then we'll deal with his kidneys. Does all of that make sense?"

"He has an infection, and it's possible that his kidneys will fail due to the antibiotics. We need to be prepare for the worst, Ms. Paige."

"Just Paige or, if you insist, it's Ms. Van Wirt," the doctor corrected her in a sad voice.

"Okay, Ms. Van Wirt."

"I know he has travel insurance, which is not going to help him here, but, regardless of his financial situation, we'll take care of him for now."

"Thank you very much."

"You said he's an ex-prisoner of the Gulag. Is that true?"

"Yes, it is."

"Okay, then. Whenever I'm on call, I'll ask him about his time there. Talking will be good for him and I don't sleep much at night anyway. In return for those stories, I'll do a good deed for him: I won't charge him for my services. This will save him several thousand dollars. Do you think Mr. B. will agree?"

"How could he not!" Irena exclaimed. "If only he'd come to right now! He's a real talker."

"Great," said Ms. Van Wirt. "We'll start in three days."

"If you can hear me," the doctor said to me, "please concentrate and listen very carefully: We gave you an IV with very strong medication, which is why you can't talk. For the next three days, you'll be on the brink between life and death. This will be your war, and *you'll* have to win it. They might call to you and try to take you away. Don't let them! When that time comes, you have to make an effort—remember, you can't leave now because you have debts to pay. Think of how much you owe. If you can't think of anything else, think of what you owe me—you have to tell me everything about the Dubravny prison camp and Potma because I was born there. We'll leave you alone now. Relax and get some sleep."

"Debt," I thought, "that's the right word. I can't go anywhere until I've paid off my debts. That's true. That's how it is. I have a debt, a very big debt. And my debt even has a name—Arkady Dudkin."

* * *

As with any book, my book had its own special fate—it was born by mistake.

According to the elegy by the Ancient Greek poet Solon, a human life consists of seven-year periods: in the first seven years, a child loses his teeth; in the second seven years, he reaches puberty; in the third, a man grows a beard; in the fourth, he blossoms; in the fifth, he starts a family; in the sixth, he commits to his life's work; in the seventh and eighth, he is perfected; in the ninth, he begins to grow weaker; and in the tenth—his death could not be described as premature.

I've lived through many things, but when I really think about it, I'm convinced that the most important seven years of my life were the four I spent waiting to be arrested and the following three years I spent in prison. The influence of those seven years on my life is so great that as soon as I meet someone new—whether that person is a Georgian or a foreigner—after the first few words are exchanged, I begin to explain that I used to be a political prisoner. All conversations inevitably turn to that topic, without fail.

Deep down, I try to resist the temptation to talk about it. I don't like to be described in such a reductive way. I try to convince myself that it's not such a good idea to bring up the KGB, the Gulag, prison and misfortune while talking about ancient Greece, Homer, Aristophanes, Rustaveli, Baratashvili, Galaction, soccer, Pelé, Garrincha, Ronaldo, computers, Windows, Macs, iPhones, diets, protein, Atkins, carbs, the private sector, funds, education, history, politics, Ilia Chavchavadze's murder, the Georgian people, traveling and Brazil . . . Talk about whatever you want—especially, if you're a good talker—but how can Barashevo, the Dubravny prison camp, and an incarceration that happened thirty years ago help along your conversation?

That's why I could never bring myself to write anything about the establishment of the Georgian Republican party, the investigation, the wait to be imprisoned, and the arrest itself, which happened on Vedzini Street in Tbilisi; nor could I write about the KGB detention center, which was located just a hundred steps away from my house and where I spent six months; nor about the Rostov, Ryazan, and Potma prisons or about the Stolypin prisoner transport or about Barashevo, where I spent the best three years of my life. When I say "the best years," I mean that in two ways: they were the best years of my life because at that time I was young—and what can be more beautiful than youth—but also because of the people that surrounded me, people the KGB had so zealously brought together.

I'd never written anything about Barashevo even though I'd told friends stories about the region's water, climate, environment, the prison routine and the particulars of prison life, and, most importantly, the people—my fellow-prisoners and our vigilant guards.

My friends used to tell me, "You really ought to write down

the story of your time in prison!" And I understood that I had to do it, but it never seemed like the right time. But when, in a far-off country, in Sibley Memorial Hospital, a concerned doctor concluded that my days were numbered, and her verdict was clearly reflected on the faces of my loved ones, I finally realized that, despite my one-hundred-and-four-degree temperature, "the time" had come.

I know I'm not the first person to be compelled to write by extraordinary circumstances—there's no shortage of hacks and geniuses in that category. But I set pen to paper (or rather, glued myself to a keyboard) not to write a great work of literature or to search for "lost time" (Ah, Proust!) but to rescue a character who was about to disappear. I was fighting to rescue Arkady Dudkin. If it weren't for me, Arkady would be lost, and no one would ever know that he'd existed and that his life had meaning. Some forgot about him a long time ago, and others didn't forget because there was nothing to remember—they'd never seen him in the prison camp. If I didn't describe Arkady, he'd find me in Hades and demand an answer, the same way Tiresias appeared to Odysseus. If Arkady is lost, then I will be too, and someone might mistakenly think that he knew me just because he'd attended one of my lectures, saw me on TV, or read an article of mine in a newspaper.

I'm not capable of writing like Flaubert, but if that great writer could say "I am Madame Bovary!" then I can say: I am Arkady Dudkin.

A short while later, the doctor admitted that her worst fears were unfounded, and so my departure to Hades was postponed for an indefinite amount of time. But it was already too late: The character Arkady Dudkin had been transformed into a text created in Arial Unicode OpenType font and now he was wandering across the World Wide Web beyond my control.

In the forty-first psalm, David says: "Abyss summons

abyss," and in the same way Arkady Dudkin summons Grisha (Gregory) Feldman, Grisha—Zhora Khomizuri, Zhora—Johnny Lashkarashvili, Johnny—Rafik Papayan, Rafik—Henrikh Altunyan, Henrikh—Misha Polyakov, Misha—Borya Manilovich, Borya—Vadim Yankov, Vadim—Fred Anadenko, Fred—Yuri Badzyo, Badzyo—Alexey Razlatsky, Razlatsky—Pyotr Butov, and Butov—Deinis Lismanis. All together there are fourteen of them, and all fourteen summon my brother Dato. Then my memory was illuminated in such a way that the light became darkness, the darkness settled in, and that persistent darkness began to speak.

ARKADY

He led two lives or, rather, he resided in an *institution* (after the disappearance of the Soviet Union, this word should no longer be used—it is so Soviet, proclaiming the superiority of the State over the individual), the ZhKh 385/3-5 prison, where he didn't have any life at all, though he didn't know it. He knew that he was Arkady Dudkin, a veteran of the Great Patriotic War, a hero of that war, and a man who, along with Kantaria, had raised a red flag above a church (of course, he meant the Reichstag, which he'd seen in the movies, but it seemed in his imagination that only churches could have domes) and that Gorokhov (a name he'd given to Kantaria's comrade Mikhail Yegorov, the other legendary flag-bearer) was never there at all. Arkady also knew he'd be released on May 13, but he either stopped counting the years or just existed in that one final yet eternal year in which he would be liberated. But some bad people, or villains as he called them, wouldn't let him out.

Arkady Dudkin "knew" many interesting things. For example, he knew that Leonid Brezhnev, who he called Lyonya and with whom he'd shared a prison cell in Vladimir, stole the military medals and awards he'd earned with his own sweat and blood. He knew he'd been *catapulted* from a tank ("They catapulted me," he liked to say), and he knew other things that followed the same trajectory, a naïve and unpolished myth—a *legend* in criminal slang—that he'd begun telling on the day he was arrested and had never changed. Namely, that he'd fought in the war, earned medals and awards, and raised a flag where and how he was supposed to raise it. After that, he was arrested for no reason at all.

It seemed that in creating his legend, Arkady had been greatly aided by the life of his older brother, Vasily Dudkin, who did fight in the Great Patriotic War, who truly was a war hero, and, if he didn't raise the flag above the Reichstag along with Kantaria and Yegorov, did actually take part in its seizure.

Yes, Arkady knew he was a hero, but his knowledge didn't align well with the prison administration's data, and, honestly, the rest of the camp didn't believe it either. His fellow-inmates acknowledged only one thing—that during the war, Arkady was a German policeman. When the Germans arrived at his village in Belarus, Arkady was fifteen years old. He didn't run away, or more likely couldn't run away, into the woods to join the heroic partisan resistance. However, at seventeen, the Germans put Arkady, who wasn't really up to speed on read-ing or writing and was generally a bit "out of it," in a police uniform and gave him a machine gun, ordering him to restore order in the village. Arkady walked toward the woods and fired several rounds to try out his new weapon. (In the prose-cution's closing statement, this was presented as "firing in the direction of the partisans.") Two days later, the partisans liber-ated the village and Arkady's time in the police force came to an end. The partisans didn't even think of punishing the men-tally challenged boy. Trying on a German uniform, however, ended up costing Arkady dearly. (That was the only crime listed in the prosecution's closing statement, which wasn't a surprise as there were only five families in the village and none of them were Jewish or communist, so it was unclear what kind of order Policeman Dudkin could have restored during that forty-eight-hour period.) His mind, which was already weak and had a child's understanding of the world, was adversely affected by the whole episode. He began presenting himself as if he were his brother; he started making up war stories, and in each story, he had a starring role. That's how he simultaneously broke through the Leningrad blockade, fought in the battle of Stalingrad as well as on the Kursk Bulge, and, of course, captured Berlin.

The village felt sorry for him. Everyone remembered his laughable two-day police service and knew he wouldn't hurt a flea, not to mention a human being, and so the villagers played along. Out of pity, they kept him as the village fool, and (along with an old church) he was the only local attraction.

Arkady had never received much education, but he loved the movies. After watching a new movie, he'd create his own little story, where he—not Stalin or Zhukov—was the chief military leader of the Soviet Union. And that's how his life continued until the moment he was found out by some hypervigilant, know-it-all Belorussian boy scouts, united under the general term "pathfinders," with the full and steadfast support of the Komsomol and Party leadership. They exposed his real history and brought him to justice. (He wasn't formally arrested by the boy scouts—that was done by the Soviet police force. However, several of the scouts were named in the indictment against Arkady.)

In 1972, Arkady Dudkin began serving his sentence as a traitor to the motherland and a war criminal.

It's no surprise the KGB made a traitor to the motherland out of a harmless village fool. However, every year a committee of experts would come to the prison from Moscow in response to the persistent demands of dissidents. (As soon as my brother Dato and I arrived in the prison, we endorsed those demands, which were supported by international organizations.) That committee included the biggest hotshots in Soviet psychiatry—how could they have included anyone less worthy, when their conclusions would have to earn the trust of the international scientific community? In any case, this committee worked tirelessly (one of the Communists' favorite words) to establish the following: that Arkady Dudkin was of sound mind, that he was of sound mind when he committed his crime and continued to be so, and, therefore, that his request for early release had no basis. Our people will always hold traitors to the motherland accountable for their actions with the utmost severity, especially anyone who tries to pass off a bloodthirsty policeman as a harmless child.

That's why every year, on May 13—when the Georgians in the camp celebrated the historic victory of the Tbilisi Dinamo soccer team at Dusseldorf stadium in 1981, when, thanks to the heroic performance of Daracelia and Gutsaev, they won the European Cup; while Lithuanian and Latvian Catholics prayed for the health and longevity of Pope John Paul II, who in that same year was miraculously saved from two bullets fired by Mehmet Ali Ağca of the Gray Wolves—the whole prison camp waited for six o'clock to arrive. At 6 P.M. all the prisoners would gather near the "smoke shack," waiting for the eternally running show to begin.

The play had only one actor. It was a special Barashevo version of a one-man show. In the first act, Arkady would leave the barracks carrying a stick, walk over to the administration building, and approach the windows of the very room where the psychiatric committee, made up of famed academics, was holding its meeting. Then, with intermission, he would begin the second act—beating the wall of the building furiously with his stick. Finally, in the third act, he'd recite a monologue in Belorussian that no one knew. Even the most famous Slavists in the camp, Mikhail Polyakov and Heliy Donskoy, couldn't identify the text. Apparently, he was demanding freedom in his mother tongue.

No one tried to stop him or call him to order. For an entire hour, he'd beat the wall with his stick, and the administration would say nothing. Only after an exhausted Arkady, feeling that he'd fulfilled his duty, joined the crowd near the smoking shack, would the inspectors go outside and check for any damage to the wall. In a maximum-security prison, where even growing your hair two millimeters longer than mandated would earn you fifteen days in "the hole" (solitary confinement), Arkady was never punished for this political act. The administration and prison inspectors knew perfectly well who they were dealing with. They weren't famous academics, but they could tell the difference between a normal person and a crazy one.

Like the majority of prisoners in the camp, Arkady smoked; but he never had his own tobacco, or *makhorka*, and never used the prison store. (Once a month, every prisoner had the right to make purchases at the prison store amounting to five rubles, but no real currency was used.) He was saving his money for his future life, which would begin, he believed, on May 13 of some year. This is how Arkady became a classic freeloader, a modest *makhorka* moocher. As a result, the prison's smoking population was divided into two unequal camps: those who would never, under any circumstances, share their *makhorka* with Arkady—the overwhelming majority—and the infinitely smaller number of those who might, sometimes, under certain grave circumstances, give Arkady a smoke.

The position of both groups was understandable. In prison, everything was in tight supply, and giving Arkady *makhorka* meant depriving yourself of the pleasure, which only added to your sentence. Inmates associated those moments spent smoking *makhorka* with freedom. Generally, to an inmate, the outside world seems like a place inhabited by innumerable pleasures. That's why no one quit smoking in prison and even nonsmokers were converted into smokers on occasion.

Arkady knew that a simple "Can I have a smoke?" would only help him mooch *makhorka* from two or three naïve prisoners, and so this obligatory but insufficient request was only part of his show. He performed with such artistry that it was easy to imagine why the Germans had put him in a uniform and how Arkady was able stick to his fantastical legend all his life: Arkady Dudkin was a natural-born actor.

Let's say Arkady saw the Armenian politician Rafael Papayan in the smoke shack. He'd start his show by slowly approaching Papayan and at a distance short enough to "bum a smoke," he'd begin his story: "I used to serve under Marshal Bagramyan"—the famous Armenian commander.

I should mention here that Arkady used Belorussian phrases to give his speech an Old Slavic, almost mythological, air. For example, he wouldn't say, "I once served . . . " but "Having once served, I . . . " Going back to his show, Arkady would exclaim: "Bagramyan, now that was a real commander! He really liked my tank. You know, he begged me to switch tanks with him. What a man he was! A real officer. The Armenians are excellent warriors, not like the Turks! Can I have a smoke? I wonder, does Bagramyan have any children?"

In the beginning Rafael would reluctantly share some of his *makhorka*, but with time, it became much harder to move Papayan with primitive patriotism. Unfortunately for Arkady, Rafael Aramshotovich Papayan—who held a Ph.D. in literature and was the son of a famous Armenian playwright—had excellent taste in drama and could detect a false performance in an instant, at which point the scholar would utter Stanislavsky's famous phrase: "I don't believe!" More often than not, this phrase would be uttered, leaving Arkady without any *makhorka*.

Among Arkady's immeasurable virtues, his resilient character and persistence were the most interesting. This man truly had no idea how to take a break. Even before he'd finished his show with Papayan, he'd head in the direction of a Georgian guy who happened to be in the shack and, with almost Homeric objectivity and impartiality, he'd launch into a new story. He didn't even have to dig deep—there were so many, he never had to repeat himself. He would mumble in his Belorussian accent: "Before that, I served with General Leselidze. Now that was a real officer, a father to his soldiers. I met Brezhnev over there—afterwards he stole my medals and awards, but this isn't the time to talk about that. General Leselidze used to be a very good friend of mine. You know, he used to say that I, not Gorokhov, should have raised the flag over Berlin. He used to love Georgian songs, *sakvarlis saplavs*[2] . . . Can I get a smoke? . . . *vedzebi-i-i*. I wonder if there's a Leselidze Street in Baku?"

Despite Arkady's geographical floundering (I could never convince him that the capital of Georgia was Tbilisi, not Baku), his acting never failed to impress me. And so, a good part of my monthly supply of *makhorka* unconditionally belonged to him.

Once, during one of our classic prison arguments when the theater-lovers were discussing who was the best Othello in the 1950s—Akaki Khorava, who held the title of People's Artist of the USSR and was hailed on stages from Arkhangelsk to Vladivostok (in the time of Stalin, of course) or Vahram Papazyan, who was also a People's Artist of the USSR (though Akaki Vasadge's Iago was also praised by everyone)—I joked: Fight all you want, I said, but I personally think Arkady is the greatest actor of all time. Exactly at that moment, my fellow prisoner, the psychologist Boris Manilovich, pronounced Arkady's last name in a Jewish manner, Dudkind, making it sound like the last name of the scholar Efim Gregoryevich Etkind, who was a friend of Joseph Brodsky and was highly respected among the anti-Soviet public.

---

[2] This is a reference to the famous Georgian ballad "Suliko" by Akaki Tsereteli (1840–1915), the first lines of which, "*Saq'varlis saplavs vedzebdi*" [I was looking for the tomb of the beloved], were well known throughout the Soviet Union; the song was a favorite of Stalin.

Deep down, Arkady was a poet and, unlike other poets, he was a grateful one. After scoring some *makhorka* with the help of his acting talents, he would roll it up in a small piece of paper torn from the newspaper *Izvestia* and begin to smoke, at which point he'd start telling a funny story:

> Once I was in a tank. I was a tank driver, you know! Okay, so I was sitting in my tank and I see there are three German Tiger tanks approaching. All this was happening in the outskirts of Berlin. There was a tank riding next to mine, the tank of Lieutenant Makharashvili, the old man's son, you know. The Germans were approaching in their three Tigers and shouting: "Arkady, *hande hoch!*" They were shouting in German. The Germans were in three tanks. I only had a T-34, but I was a lion to their Tiger tanks. Poor Makharashvili, the old man's son, was a wolf. They were screaming at me "*hande hoch*," which means "hands up," and I was screaming back at them: "*Ich bin Arkady, ich nicht hande hoch, ich bin killen sie, schwein fritzen, yavol!*" That means I'll kill them all, the German pigs. One German tank fires, hits my left side, and yells, "*Ya, ya!*" I fire back and kill one of the Tigers. The second Tiger was shot by Makharashvili, the son of the old man with the mustache. The third Tiger starts moving. I couldn't stop it. The tank keeps moving, and then it kills Makharashvili. The tank keeps moving, and I see that it's about to destroy me. I shoot and shoot, but it doesn't die! As it turns out, Hitler himself was in that tank. I realized there was no escape and shouted, "For the Motherland! For Stalin!" Then I released the wings from my tank, took off, and flew very high, higher than the Sun!

Arkady Dudkin was supposed to be released on May 13, 1987. He died on May 12. Following a local tradition, the prison administration took off his boots and buried Arkady in a nameless grave. And so, Arkay Dudkin went barefoot to that final meeting with his heroic brother, whose role he so successfully played throughout his life.

GRISHA

Among the hundred and fifty prisoners in our camp with whom I served time, Grisha Feldman was the most cheerful and energetic. In 1982, he was arrested for anti-Soviet agitation and propaganda and was sentenced to six years imprisonment. He was Jewish, had graduated from high school, and worked as an electrician at the hospital for railroad workers in the city of Konotop in the Sumy region of Ukraine. He hadn't committed any crime—it's just that he was a Jew, and in the war with the Arabs, he'd rooted for Israel. It was all he talked about, before his arrest and after.

If you happened to ask him how he was doing, he'd answer vigorously: "We have assault rifles, we'll get bullets, and then bang, bang, bang go the Arabs!"

That virtual assault rifle was obviously in very experienced hands, and the virtual location of the Arabs was correctly chosen from an ideological point of view: Grisha would aim at the propaganda wing of the administration building, which was covered with wise billboards—among them such pearls as "Bread is the head of everything!" (although no one could ever figure out the connection between this piece of wisdom and state criminals) and "It is better to think before than after. *Democritus.*" As a specialist in ancient literature, I can assure you that Democritus never said anything even remotely similar to that, but the prison administration, and especially our father of ideology, Colonel Ganichenko, had their own ideas. The colonel loved the name Democritus for several reasons: first, because it belonged to an ideologically acceptable materialist, as opposed to, for example, the bad and gloomy Heraclitus; second, this name evoked associations with democrats and, in the camp, this was our ironic nickname: The members of the administration mockingly called us prisoners convicted for anti-Soviet propaganda and agitation democrats. This is how Boris Manilovich, a psychologist and a respected convict, explained this pseudo-quotation: "Democritus teaches us that if you plan to collaborate with the Soviet security forces, it's better to do so before your arrest rather than after."

During evening roll call in the prison yard, Grisha always looked upward. Usually as soon as the prisoners gathered, pigeons would fly onto the roof of the barracks and start cooing, and Grisha would give them a warm and teary-eyed look. Everyone knew that he was an adventurous glutton. That's why no one was surprised when we heard that Grisha had killed and eaten a pigeon. But the technicalities interested us—how he'd snuck up on the bird, what he'd used to kill it, how he'd dressed it, and, finally, whether he'd boiled or fried it. This last detail was of special interest: Did he fry it or boil it, or did he boil it first and then fry it? None of those questions was ever answered. One group of prisoners saw this episode as clear proof of man's natural instinct for self-preservation, an attempt to save one's life, while another more intellectual group saw it as yet another sign of man's moral degradation. But most importantly, neither group believed that Grisha should be punished for his deed. Everyone felt that way until Fredrich (Fred) Anadenko, a prominent Ukrainian socialist and author of the well-known anti-Soviet treatise *From Lenin to Brezhvev*, gathered together for an evening talk those of us he considered reliable inmates, the "initiated." That conversation happened during our routine back-and-forth walk in the prison yard, when Fred, with good diction and proper emphasis, read us his letter to the State Prosecutor of the Soviet Union:

To Alexander Mikhailovich Rekunkov

Prosecutor General of the USSR

Comrade Prosecutor General of the Union of Soviet Socialist Republics Alexander Mikhailovich,

We would like to bring to your attention the fact that Grigory Zinovievich Feldman, a convict in the institution ZhKh 385/3-5, unlawfully stole and ate a pigeon or pigeons (the number of victims is unknown). This is unacceptable because it is well-known that a pigeon is a close relative of the dove, which is a symbol of peace. Taking the abovementioned facts into consideration, I hereby request that you take immediate appropriate measures.

Disrespectfully yours,

The unjustly convicted political prisoner

Fredrich Filippovich Anadenko

The discussion that followed in the courtyard was initiated by Polyakov, who, while approving the courageous phrase "disrespectfully yours," remarked with unconcealed irony that the whole idea might be lost on the addressee because the concept of a dove as a symbol of peace comes from the Bible, to which Comrade Rekunkov, as a devoted Marxist, communist, and socialist, must have a somewhat conflicted relationship. (Polyakov placed special emphasis on the term "socialist" because, as a true liberal and democrat, he did not approve of Anadenko's affiliation with socialism.) Anatoly Yankov—a mathematician and topologist, a polyglot and all around very smart man—stated that humans routinely eat symbols, as cows, pigs, sheep, birds, and various fish have assumed different symbolic meanings in different cultures. Here, Yankov was about to share more of his vast knowledge on the subject, but Anadenko got annoyed with us and, with a shaking hand, placed a stamp on the envelope. He then defiantly dropped the letter into the mailbox on the wall of the administration building. My last comment was that we shouldn't overlook the selflessness of Anadenko's action, sacrificing one whole stamp for a public act. Since there was a severe shortage of postage stamps and envelopes in political prisons, the more experienced prisoners reacted favorably to my humble comment.

We don't know whether the letter ever made it to its addressee, but Grisha Feldman got away with eating a symbol of peace, no problem. And this wasn't the end of his gastro-culinary odyssey. As a professional electrician, Feldman was always fixing his toaster oven, which he'd placed at the back of the bathroom with eight sinks, nicknamed the "smoke shack." That oven served the entire camp well until the prison administration took it into their heads to remove this invention of our modern Prometheus, who had shown such concern for his prisonmates.

Once during the New Year season, all the independent culinary-gastronomic groups in our prison were taking stock of their raw and ready-to-eat products. I should explain that the culinary-gastronomic groups were unofficial collectives of prisoners running joint gastronomic operations. For example, there was the Jewish "Kibbutz," the Christian Federation of South Caucasian Nations, or "Christofed," the Lithuanian-Latvian "Union," and the Ukrainian "Kinship." Well, during that inventory check, Rafael Papayan, a member of Christofed, fished out a two-liter jar of homemade lamb *kaurma*, or stew, that his wife had brought on her last visit a year and a half ago. The kaurma had been kept in our shared warehouse, called the "stores," patiently awaiting the moment of its consumption. Eventually, however, that endless waiting had to come to an end—it was the *kaurma*'s time. All the federation members, Berdzenishvili, Lashkarashvili, Khomizuri, Altunyan, and Papayan, anticipating a culinary miracle, were present for the opening ceremony. The two-liter jar had a screw-top lid, and when Papayan opened it on his third attempt, the jar started making scary gurgling noises. Very soon the barracks were filled with such a stench that the

WWII veteran, German policeman, and ex-hero of Socialist Labor of the USSR Verkhovin began screaming: "Watch out! Mustard gas! We're under attack! Everyone out!" And the entire barracks poured into the prison yard.

Grisha was the last to leave the barracks. He came out with the jar of *kaurma* and asked what we, the members of Christofed, were planning to do with it—throw it away, perhaps? After receiving an answer in the affirmative, he carried the jar over to the smoke shack, to his toaster oven. This was followed by a rapid exodus of prisoners from the smoke shack. Grisha claimed that his oven could reach a temperature of four hundred degrees Celsius, and that this would kill any living bacteria, never mind the bacteria in the lamb *kaurma*. He boiled that stinking *kaurma* for an entire hour, then took the pot outside, sat in the middle of the courtyard, and, in front of all the prisoners, calmly and methodically polished off the entire thing. No one, not even the camp administration, dared to approach the poisonous gas-emitting *kaurma* within a thirty-yard radius. I'm almost positive that after the *kaurma* episode, Fred Anadenko wrote the Prosecutor General a new "disrespectfully yours" letter, but he never let us read it.

Soon after the *kaurma* episode, Grisha was transferred to another camp. As we learned later, they took him to Saransk, the capital of Mordovia, and put him in solitary confinement. For a long time, we didn't have any information about Grisha. He didn't write to anyone, and there was no news about him from the outside. Four months passed, and one fine day Grisha came back—he'd put on some weight, had longer hair, and looked pale. It was very easy for us to tell how long someone had been in solitary just by the color of his skin. Feldman's facial hue suggested that he'd spent a whole four months there, and that the only contact he'd had with the sun was on his daily one-hour walk. Once the most cheerful and chatty member of our camp, he now seemed somehow faded. He no longer talked about Arabs and assault rifles, and, if you can imagine, he gave up his extreme culinary experiments. Even more surprising, he didn't even think of setting up his famous toaster oven.

A few people drew some probable conclusions about his behavior, but no one had any convincing evidence.

I must admit that Georgians make good prisoners. By that I mean that Georgians don't whine and, more importantly, they're a paragon of physical stamina. Despite this reputation, I, along with several other prisoners, came down with a high fever in the fall of 1986, when a flu virus was making its way through the prison. I lay in bed in the barracks for several days, and the doctor said that if my fever didn't drop in two days, he'd transfer me to the hospital and put me on a special diet. (In prison, diet is a very good word.) Anyway, it's nine o'clock in the evening and I'm lying in bed near the entrance to the barracks with a hundred-and-four-degree fever. There's no one else in the barracks except for Grisha and a couple of old Lithuanians. Suddenly, Zhora Khomizuri runs in with the sensational news that our Grisha would be appearing on the TV news program *Vremya*. I got up, wrapped myself in a blanket, and went to the dining room, which also served as our rec room. The TV set was high on the wall so that all one hundred of us could see it while sitting at the long tables.

First, *Vremya* informed us about a plenary session of the Communist Party Political Bureau, then, pictures of plants and factories, industrial complexes and tractors flashed by like images in a kaleidoscope. Then came the cultural news. The sports and weather forecast were about to begin when the anchor Balashov interrupted the broadcast and the entire screen was filled with Gregory Zinovievich Feldman, a political prisoner convicted of anti-Soviet agitation and propaganda. And Grisha was saying:

Israel is a scary state. They torture poor Arabs over there, shame on them! Day and night, they talk only about the Holocaust, but they're organizing their own genocide for the Arabs and Palestinians. And I can't even imagine anything worse than Zionism. As for the prison where I'm serving time, it makes me nauseous to think about the other inmates; so many criminals in one place—what a disaster! Soviet people, please, forgive me, though I can't be forgiven and don't deserve your forgiveness in the first place!

Grisha's face turned back into sports and the weather, and the stunned prisoners returned slowly to the barracks. Wrapped in my blanket, I hurried back to bed. Three yards away from me, Grisha, fully dressed and in his boots, was resting on his cot. After some commotion outside, a group of three people entered the barracks and approached Feldman. It was the "delegation of shame" led by Fred Anadenko, flanked by Misha Polyakov and Zhora Khomizuri.

"Gregory Zinovievich, what can you say in your defense?" Anadenko asked in a low voice.

"What can I say in my defense?" Grisha repeated with a phony Ukrainian accent. "Here is my defense!"

Grisha turned around and mooned the delegation, and then his ass produced a sound so thunderous that it would have surprised even Rabelais, the esteemed author of *Gargantua and Pantagruel.*

"You're not human," said a crestfallen Anadenko, and the committee left the barracks.

From that day on, Grisha became a political pariah; no one would approach him. He quickly gave up and let himself go. The prison Jews took Grisha's disgrace especially hard. They felt that this Arab sympathizer had brought shame upon them as well.

Grisha was pardoned and released on February 9, 1987. Five days later, on February 14, the last "democrat" left Barashevo Prison. Perestroika had brought the period of political prisoners to an end. For a long time, Israel refused to accept Feldman. They said that the Mossad was involved in his case. I can't rule out the possibility that his ex-cellmates prevented his Aliyah. For twenty years, Grisha tried in vain to woo his insulted countrymen, and then, in 2006, he got his wish—an exhausted and worn-out seventy-year-old man was finally allowed to enter the promised land. Upon taking his first step on Israeli soil after embarking from the plane, Grisha yelled loudly in Russian "Forgive me!"—and right there in the Tel Aviv airport, he drew his last breath.

ZHORA

Zhora—also known as Georgy Pavlovich Khomizuri, Ernest Garaev, Nekoba, Aparek Gulaguri, and Twenty-Six—was a man of numbers, just like the composer Bach in the poem by Carl Sandburg:

> He was born to wonder about numbers.
> He balanced fives against tens
> and made them sleep together
> and love each other.

In the afternoon at a quarter after two, Zhora might run up to you and, full of excitement, inform you that in one minute, you'd be exactly one million minutes away from the age of Jesus Christ! In the middle of the night, he might wake you up only to tell you the great news—in exactly forty-four seconds, there would be 44,444,444 seconds left before your release!

> He woke up twos and fours
> out of baby sleep
> and touched them back to sleep.

He smothered the entire prison camp with his calculations. He drove us insane, terrorizing us with six- and seven-digit numbers. Naturally, in order to complete such a monumental task, he was constantly scribbling calculations. He knew by heart the birthdays not only of all the prisoners, but also of their wives and children, as well as the arrest and release dates of every political prisoner (not only in our prison camp, but in all the political prisons throughout the Perm region). For example, he knew that May 21 was the birthday of Andrei Sakharov, Masha Khomizuri, Misha Skripkin, and the Georgian Republican Party; that it was the one hundred first day of the year (the one hundred second in a leap year); that on May 21, 878 AD, Syracuse was conquered by a Muslim sultan; that on that day in 1674, the nobility elected Jan Sobiesky as King of Poland and Grand Duke of Lithuania; that on May 21, 1972, a mentally ill Laszlo Toth, a Hungarian-born Australian and, by the way, a geologist (being a geologist himself, Zhora would stress this fact), vandalized Michelangelo's Pietà in St. Peter's Basilica in Vatican City, and so on. His vast knowledge had neither beginning nor end. Like a supercomputer, he was always plugged in, constantly doing calculations, running himself ragged. It's important to mention that even though his calculations were accurate, no one knew the purpose of his faultless precision. No one had any idea why it was so important to know how many minutes, hours, or seconds were left before this or that event. Though I shouldn't say no one knew—Zhora himself must have had some idea!

> He knew love numbers, luck numbers,
> how the sea and the stars
> are made and held by numbers.

He loved all numbers as his own children, but he believed that one numerical combination was predestined for him by fate. It was the number *twenty-six.*

He devoted his first significant manuscript to shattering the myth of the twenty-six Baku commissars, showing it to be a pure fantasy, a piece of Soviet propaganda.[3] That myth had left a deep and lasting impression on the still young researcher, as yet uninitiated into the world of mysticism—many facts simply didn't add up. First, of the twenty-six Baku commissars, twenty-seven were gunned down; furthermore, there were only nine commissars among them, only two were really from Baku, and so on. The more he investigated the myth of the twenty-six Baku commissars, the more he would repeat: "Shahumyan-Dzhaparidze-Azizbekov-Fioletov." (As he discovered, the leadership of Armenian-Georgian-Azerbaijani-Russian Bolsheviks was just a tribute to internationalism; the real leaders were the Armenian, Georgian, and Russian Bolsheviks: Shahumyan, Dzhaparidze, Korganov, and Petrov). From then on, Zhora couldn't free himself from that number, which, in his mind, was truly capable of inflicting disaster.

It seemed that the menacing number twenty-six was everywhere, alongside its gloomy associate, the menacing number thirteen. Even in Khomizuri's Yerevan phone number, the first two digits were two and six, and the sum of all the digits was twenty-six, and when his number was changed, the sum of the new digits was still twenty-six! When the phone number was changed again—the sum of the digits didn't change! "This is mystifying!" Zhora used to say, truly upset. My Tbilisi phone number added up to just one short of twenty-six! A calendar year consisted of twenty-six weeks multiplied by two! And Leonid Brezhnev's age was only three years short of twenty-six multiplied by three! Anyway, it's twenty-six again!

[3] The Baku Municipality was a temporary communist government established in April 1918 in the capital of Azerbaijan. The twenty-six "Commissioners of the People" who ruled the municipality were all shot on September 20 by counterrevolutionary forces in highly disputed circumstances; the story became part of Soviet mythology.

In the end, driven by an affection for Zhora, our prison community decided to reward his remarkable loyalty to the number twenty-six by creating a new numerical constant and naming it after him, one Khomizuri, which would be denoted by the capital Latin letter H. Then, following a very difficult derivation done by the political prisoner Vadim Anatolievich Yankov, a remarkable mathematician and topologist, we would designate one seventh of a Khomizuri a Zhorik, denoting it with the lower case Latin letter h. (It was my idea to use Latin letters.) The difficulty of Yankov's derivation was in the sequence—from the number twenty-six, he added the two digits $(2+6=8)$, then subtracted one from the sum $(8-1=7)$ and introduced one seventh of that $(7/7=1)$, to make one Zhorik. The major challenge here was understanding the middle step. When asked why he subtracted one in the middle of his derivation, Yankov would take out a self-made chalkboard and a huge stylus, and then for three hours straight, he would write, erase, and get into fights trying to prove this step. If we still couldn't understand even after three hours of laborious math, he would scream that simplifying it any more for laymen was beyond his capacity.

As a result, in our political prison even military criminals with a relatively low level of education knew that one year consisted of exactly two Khomizuris and one Zhorik (2H1h) weeks; that Brezhnev's age was three years short of three Khomizuris (3H-3); that according to data from January 1, 1985, Zhora, Levan Berdzenishvili, Johnny Lashkarashvili, and Rafael Papayan each had one Khomizuri of teeth, but according to data from January 1, 1986, the above-mentioned persons had only two Khomizuris of teeth among them; that the number 13 brought misfortune because it's not a full Khomizuri but only half; that the universally acknowledged champion of foul language in the camp, the creator of the Soviet multivitamins Undevit and Decamevit, Arnold

Arthurovich Anderson, was two Khomizuris old when he was arrested for passing the formula for Decamevit to his brother in West Germany and was sentenced to half a Khomizuri; that the daily quota of the work mitts that we had to sew was three and a half Khomizuris plus one (92 pairs), and so on.

According to Zhora, the alphanumerical abbreviation of our prison camp ZhKh 385/3-5 should be read as Zhora Khomizuri 1+1+ (he said those were Zh and Kh) +3+8+5+3+5=26, or in other words, Zhora Khomizuri Khomizuri as in *Homo sapiens sapiens*.

Outside our prison at that time, no one knew Georgy Khomizuri as a dissident. In rather narrow geological circles, he was known as the star of the Institute of Petroleum and Gas, as a very good geologist, and as the author of a detailed monograph about geosyncline. However, in the whole of the Soviet Union, there was not a single dissident or dissident-supporting person who did not know about Ernest Garaev and his books.

Ernest Garaev was one of Zhora's pseudonyms, which he had in abundance—starting with the anti-Stalinist Nekoba (ne-Koba)[4] and ending with Aparek Gulaguri, which, while formed from the word *Gulag*, sounded to his ear like an archaic Georgian name from the Xevsurian region. His most important works published in *samizdat* were under the nickname Ernest Garaev: *The History of the CPSS Leadership* (only facts, no commentaries), *The Myth of the Twenty-Six* (the real history of the twenty-six Baku Commissars), and *The Chronology of the Great Terror*. I used to tease him that he'd picked the name Ernest not because of his great love for Hemingway, but out of respect for Ernesto Che Guevara—a

[4] Koba, shortened from the name of the Persian king Kobades, was one of Stalin's pseudonyms, and *ne* means "non" or "not" in Russian.

reference to his Trotskyite, extreme left-wing past. He never confirmed my claim, but he didn't deny it either.

Georgy Khomizuri was a Georgian, born in Baku. As a child, he was abandoned by his mother and was brought up on Sakhalin Island by his proud and solitary Georgian father. He lived in Moscow for one Khomizuri before he was arrested in Yerevan in 1982. But most importantly, he was a fierce warrior: Not once in the two hundred eighty-three million eight hundred twenty-four thousand seconds he had to spend in prison and exile by decree of the Soviet KGB did he regret his choices. He was sentenced to six years in a maximum-security prison and three years of internal exile. His fellow dissident Rafael Papayan was sentenced to four and two years, respectively. Under somewhat unclear circumstances, their third fellow dissident, Edgar, got away. Despite this fact, Zhora always spoke with respect of his vast knowledge. It's interesting that in the Yerevan group, which consisted of two Armenians and one Georgian, the KGB unequivocally attributed its leadership to the anti-Soviet Georgian. As Zhora used to say, the KGB officers were people too, and they certainly knew Stalin's worth, so they were good at guessing who would be the leader among the Christians from the Caucasus.

We, the Georgians and Armenians, had our own friendly collective: the Christian Federation of South Caucasian Nations. Actually, there was no need to use the word "Christian," but a very bad man, Akhper Radzhabov, a spy who sold the technical drawings of the SS-20 missiles to the Americans in Yugoslavia, happened to be an Azerbaijani and, therefore, a South Caucasian. Hence, the word "Christian" served as a way to keep Radzhabov out of our Federation. And there was no possibility of exchanging him for a "good Azerbaijani" either because no one from Azerbaijan had been convicted of anti-Soviet agitation and propaganda.

In the Federation, the level of financial integration wasn't as high as in the Jewish Kibbutz (each of us could spend his five rubles as he saw fit), but once a month, when buying food in the prison store, some coordination among the members of the Federation did occur.

The Federation had its own Constitution, whose father and only author was Georgy Khomizuri. Naturally, there was a written text of the Constitution that Zhora had composed in Russian and that Rafael Papayan translated into Armenian and Levan Berdzenishvili into Georgian. (I offered to translate it into Latin and Ancient Greek as well, but this only infuriated Zhora—"It's not a toy for you to play with. This is the Constitution, a serious document!") All three texts existed only in the original versions that were in Zhora's possession, though only the Russian and Georgian versions had legal status. Because Papayan had graduated from a Russian high school and the University of Tartu, Zhora didn't trust his Armenian. According to the Constitution, an Elder was to be in charge of the Confederation (before Henrich Ovanesovich Altunyan's transfer from Chistopol Prison, Zhora was the oldest person in the Federation), and only Georgy Pavlovich Khomizuri could be elected Elder. That's exactly how it was written in the Constitution: "Only Georgy Pavlovich Khomizuri of Georgia, born February 9, 1942, in the city of Baku, qualifies as a candidate for the position of Elder. In the event Georgy Pavlovich Khomizuri should refuse to run for this position, the members of the Federation must elect him as Elder." To support this not-so-democratic principle, some evidence was presented, such as the text of the Georgian folk song "Georgian, Take up Your Sword!" (or in Zhora's translation, "Georgian, Take out Your Sword!"), and a few episodes from Stalin's biography from the Tbilisi period, especially those moments that showed the relationship between Stalin, nicknamed Koba, and the Armenian Bolshevik Simon Ter-Petrosian, nicknamed Kamo, highlighting the strict subordination between those two not-so-law-abiding citizens, along with other equally convincing evidence.

According to the Federation's Constitution, the election of the Elder should be preceded by a pre-election period, during which the candidate should bribe his voters with a cup of tea (one matchbox of black pekoe tea and one liter of water should be steeped for fifteen minutes in a thermos, then the tea should be "married"—that is, the tea should be poured into a cup and then back into the thermos three times, trying not to spill any. Only after this procedure does the tea attain its true taste) and one whole Prima cigarette, which was such a luxury the prisoners usually broke their cigarettes in two. In our prison store, Prima cigarettes were expensive—fifteen kopecks. For the same money, you could buy a box of *makhorka*, which had the ability to darken the lungs ten times faster per capita than a box of Primas. Therefore, it was a commonly-held opinion among the prisoners that *makhorka* was more efficient, more cost effective, and more practical.

Election day was on Sunday (an election was held every week or two Khomizuri times a year), and the Elder's tea party, followed by the awarding of one Prima cigarette, took place every Saturday at 8 P.M., which brought our Saturday routine even closer to heaven: work until noon (sewing heavy-duty mitts with a thumb and a rubber palm pad); then the *banya*, or Russian sauna, with bowls and buckets, *banya* ladles and soap, not with showers and shampoo, like in Western prisons; then a movie (usually about Stalin, the Young Pioneers, Komsomol members, and Communists; although once, by mistake, they showed us Bergman's *Autumn Sonata*); then the Elder's tea party; and finally, the obligatory news broadcast *Vremya*, which covered rulings by the Politburo, combine harvesters, incessant earthquakes in Japan, and endless tornadoes in the US.

In 1986, our wonderful Saturday rituals were temporarily stopped when Zhora, along with some other prisoners, was transferred to solitary confinement in Saransk, the capital of Mordovia. The reason behind the transfer was simple: It was torture by milk and eggs, i.e., erosion—the psychological testing of a Soviet man by means of luxury and comfort.

These attempts to test Zhora were, however, bound to fail because from childhood, he couldn't stand milk, and he had such a severe allergy to egg yolk that he couldn't even touch a cookie. On the first day, when they brought some milk for Zhora and his cellmate, Mikhail Tolstykh from Petersburg, Zhora returned his glass saying that he didn't drink milk. The whole next day, Tolstykh complained about Zhora's selfishness: "Okay, you don't drink milk, but I do!" Zhora acknowledged his mistake; but on the second day, he refused an egg, saying he was allergic. Tolstykh got upset once again: "You know, I don't have that allergy!" At this point, Zhora lost his patience and told him: "It's possible that for you, I might be able to 'like' milk, but don't push me about eggs. First, this is a question of principle, and second, the cholesterol from two eggs a day is bad for your health." Basically, they didn't get along with each other—a principled and emotional Georgian and a cold, not-so-principled man from the banks of the Neva. They'd never been good friends, but after returning to the prison, they barely said hello to each other.

For a long time, I hadn't known about Zhora's egg allergy, which is not surprising—how would I have known that? It's not like we were ever offered eggs or any other protein-filled crap. On October 23, 1986, I celebrated a big birthday, my thirty-third, and invited not only the five members of the South Caucasus Federation but also the "democrats"—Mikhail Polyakov from Leningrad, Vadim Yankov from Moscow, and Alexey Arenberg, the plane hijacker. The spread I managed to put together was fantastic: hot tea, five very small round candies for each guest, sandwiches with fish pâté on black thrice-baked bread, and, as Zachary, aka Johnny Lashkarashvili, would say, "the pièce de résistance of the evening"—Adjarian *khachapuri* baked in Grisha Feldman's famous oven. Instead of flour, which is the main ingredient in khachapuri, I used my portion of a special May 9 white bread, which, after being scientifically dried for months, was beaten into a powder and mixed in with the dough. For the other ingredients, I used leftover butter that Johnny Lashkarashvili had been saving from his hospital ration for even rainier days, a piece of *suluguni* cheese that came in my five-kilogram parcel from Inga Karaya (after having served half our sentence, we were allowed to receive one parcel a year), and egg powder acquired in exchange for two packs of *makhorka*. When it was time to divide the *khachapuri*, Zhora received a piece with some egg and asked Arenberg to exchange it for his piece without any egg. When the latter categorically refused, Khomizuri boldly lied, saying that this dish was traditionally prepared with pork, making Arenberg, an Orthodox Jew, run from the table (to tell the truth, Zhora had never really liked him, and later we learned that Arenberg was a scumbag who had been helping the administration add more punishments to our friend, the most honorable Misha Rivkin). That's how we learned about Zhora's allergy. And after five minutes of deliberation, Polyakov and Yankov amicably divided Arenberg's piece between themselves.

Zhora studied Georgian with a terrifying (I can't think of another word for it) and unstoppable enthusiasm, but it didn't come easily to him. Within a week, he'd learned how to read, and in a month, he was reading the Old Georgian Mrglovani and Nuskhuri scripts. The Mrglovani alphabet even inspired the creation of his own theory, in which, of course, the number twenty-six had special significance. With great zeal, he translated the Georgian poet Galaktion Tabidze, but it brought him a good deal of grief. He would often say that the translation wasn't working—and who has ever truly succeeded in translating Tabidze—but then he would add in Georgian "*Isev vdgebodi da mivdiodi*" [Again I rose and set off], and return to his translation.[5] He could recite Rustaveli in Zabolotsky's Russian translation for hours—he'd had the book since his time in the Yerevan isolation unit and wouldn't lend it to anyone. First, he would recite a passage in Russian:

> Alas, O world, what would you? Why do you whirl us round—what is it that ails you? All who put their trust in you must weep unceasing tears, even as I do. You uproot, you carry off—whence? Aye, and whither? . . . But the man abandoned by you is not forsaken of God.[6]

And then he would add in Georgian: "*Vakh, sopelo . . .*"

Zhora didn't approve of the translation by Konstantin Balmont, even though he loved Balmont's poetry. Zhora believed that Balmont's translation was too exalted, and he was mad at Balmont for pretending that his place as a translator was next to Rustaveli himself. Zhora completely denounced the translation by Shalva Nutsubidze. He used to wonder how a historian of philosophy, or even a philosopher, could translate a poet. He would get upset and say that this translation was written in the Georgian Russian language, and that Satan's hand (he meant Stalin's) was definitely involved. Once I told Zhora a long story about Shalva Nutsubidze, his sister, Simon Kaukhchishvili (my wonderful teacher who told me the story in the first place), *The Lord of the Panther-Skin*, Stalin, and, of

---

[5] This verse was taken from a poem by Tabidze of April 19, 1923, "*Me ertaderti mkonda c'ukhili*" [I only have but one complaint], which was composed at the time of the popular guerrilla war against the Bolshevik invasion that ended the short-lived Democratic Republic of Georgia led by Noe Zhordania.

[6] Rustaveli, Shota. *The Lord of the Panther-Skin*. Translated by R.H. Stevenson, State University of New York Press, 1977, p. 114.

course, Lavrentiy Beria. The most provocative part of the story was not when Comrade Stalin approved Rustaveli's Russian translation, saving both Shalva Nutsubidze and Simon Kaukhchishvili from imprisonment, nor was it when Lavrentiy Beria invited Georgian scientists, whom he'd saved from prison, to get wasted at his house. The most impressive part was when Shalva Nutsubidze, who was already quite drunk, left the manuscript of his translation of *The Lord of the Panther-Skin* at Beria's apartment and had to go back for it. When the two Georgian academics returned to Comrade Beria's to retrieve the book, a dumbfounded Beria uttered this historic statement: "I've seen a few people leave me on amicable terms, but this is the very first time I've seen people return here from a safe place of their own volition."

Zhora was a dyed-in-the-wool anti-Soviet, and so it was no surprise that he hated Stalin more than anyone else in the world. You could honestly say that Georgy Khomizuri's allergy to the greatest leader of all times and nations, the father of the world proletariat, the generalissimo himself, was significantly stronger than his allergy to eggs.

Our prison terms had one very distinct feature. We weren't serving time in the scary 1930s, during the war or at the height of the dissident movement, or even during the Brezhnev period of stagnation, but in the era of Soviet democracy, glasnost, and perestroika. While Stalinists were fighting it out on the pages of *Pravda*, the popular magazine *Ogonek* published the famous "Open Letter to Stalin" written by the well-known dissident Fyodor Raskolnikov. One day the TV would offer us the typical Soviet hogwash, then the next day, Ronald Reagan would be wishing us Happy New Year from the same screen. Experienced people said that, in those times, being in the camps was especially unbearable. I can't say anything about it because I wasn't incarcerated in that era, but I trust those more experienced prisoners.

In any case, we were doing our time in the era of glasnost and perestroika, and this era, like other important and exceptional ones, had its own liberal and enlightened heroes with a completely new image. Vadim Viktorovich Bakatin, a well-known reformer and liberal, was one such hero, whom we got to know from a very different perspective.

While giving a speech in our rec room, Comrade Bakatin, at that time the First Secretary of the Kirovsk Regional Committee of the Communist Party of the Soviet Union and later the Minister of Internal Affairs and the Chairman of the KGB, annhilated the dissidents who had been convicted for anti-Soviet agitation and propaganda but praised to the heavens the residents of our neighboring maximum security prison, who we called "stripes" (as they wore striped uniforms)—convicted felons, murderers, and robbers—saying that they were decent people, compared to us. At least, they were patriots who never uttered a word against their Motherland.

After this tirade by one of the heroes of perestroika, even the prison warden was frowning, but the holier-than-thou Comrade Bakatin stuck to his position and went on. Johnny Lashkarashvili got up first and suggested that Bakatin clean off the TV screen in our rec room, because "the General Secretary is looking very dark." Only after that should he talk about love for the Motherland. But Bakatin, who couldn't make out Johnny's accent, said that he didn't understand him. Then Zhora got up and screamed at the top of his lungs:

"Of course you feel closer to murderers and robbers—you're masters of the same trade!"

A complete transformation came over the renowned liberal's face. He turned pale (as Rustaveli would say, "went flat"), mumbled, "How dare you!" and ran out of the rec room followed by thunderous applause from the "democratic" portion of the prison. Of course, the spies, traitors to the Motherland, terrorists, and military criminals didn't applaud, but there were enough of us "democrats" to overwhelm the small room with our ovation. The administration chased after their liberal guest who was so fond of the convicted felons, murderers, and robbers in the neighboring prison camp. But this future leader of the KGB and a giant of Gorbachev's Soviet democracy, insulted and ashen, ran away so fast that neither the prison administration nor even the swift-footed Achilles could have caught him.

Comrade Bakatin hadn't managed to get out of the prison when Sureykin, the warden-on-duty, called Zhora out of the barracks and started walking him toward the hole. The entire camp poured out of the rec room and watched Sureykin escort Zhora from our bad prison to an even worse one. At this point I lost my temper and approached Sureykin.

"What's going on, Sureykin?" I asked the warden-on-duty, who was taken aback. He wasn't used to being questioned by prisoners—this level of rudeness was unheard of—not to mention being addressed by his surname rather than his title, "Citizen Warden."

The camp "democrats" surrounded us.

"I'm taking Georgy Khomizuri to isolation for punishment," Major Sureykin replied; taken off guard, he answered by the book.

"What for?" I asked.

"For rudeness," Sureykin answered.

"Major Sureykin, you and Bakatin don't know what real rudeness is. Pay attention, you will hear some real rudeness now," I warned him. "Sureykin, you're a motherf—."

Sureykin and the guards Kiselyov and Trifonov, who happened to be nearby, hurried Zhora to the hole and then hurried back to take me there as well. They were so fast that my friends didn't even have time to get my warm clothes. There were no vacancies in the hole, so they had to put Zhora and me in the same cell. The other cell was occupied by a frequent guest, Vitautas Shabonas. They couldn't put anyone else in Shabonas's cell because he was engaged in a very dangerous activity—all day long Shabonas would tirelessly and loudly pass on information about us political prisoners to Bakatin's favorite prison camp, followed by political demands: "Freedom to the Lithuanian civil right activists Algirdas Andeikas, Yanis Barkans, and Vitautas Skuodis! Freedom to the Georgian independence fighters David and Levan Berdzenishvili, and Zachary Lashkarashvili!"

How could they have one of us share a cell with such a man? We would've been a bad influence on him.

Sometime later, and with great pleasure, the warden showed me Major Sureykin's report. It was such a marvel that even those purveyors of Soviet absurdism Zoshchenko and Kharms would have envied it. I don't remember everything, but the episode with me and Zhora went approximately like this: "While fulfilling my duties, specifically while escorting Georgy Pavlovich Khomizuri (a Georgian, born in 1942 in the city of Baku, convicted of anti-Soviet agitation and propaganda) to the solitary confinement wing, I was approached by Levan Valeriyanovich Berdzenishvili, a Georgian, born in 1953 in the city of Batumi, convicted of anti-Soviet agitation and propaganda, who rudely addressed me, specifically using the following words: 'Sureykin, you're a motherf—.' I concluded that he did this for the purpose of insulting me—considering the fact that Georgians swear for that purpose only. Because of that incident, we sentenced Levan Valeriyanovich Berdzenishvili, born in 1953 in the city of Batumi, Georgia, to the isolation unit for fifteen days in accordance with the rights bestowed upon me by the law." Thanks to Zhora, the whole prison knew Sureykin's report by heart.

After his release, Zhora visited Tbilisi several times to see us. We met his family—his wife Nina, daughter Masha, and son Pavlik. Our families were quickly infected by our friendship.

The Khomizuris planned to move to Tbilisi, and their son Pavlik was especially eager—he loved the city and loved calling himself a Georgian. Unfortunately, his plan was not meant to be. Fate struck Zhora again in the cruelest way—at the age of thirteen, Pavlik passed away, and his daughter Masha became a nun.

A die-hard atheist (in the words of his beloved Rustaveli, "a wise man," that is, one who doesn't accept divine love of the heavenly sort), a materialist body and soul, a man of numbers and formulas, a professor of geology and mineralogy, Georgy Pavlovich Khomizuri, at the ripe age of two Khomizuris plus two, in order to support his struggle for Georgian identity, was baptized as an Orthodox Christian at the small Church of the Trinity in Tbilisi. Those in attendance—a godfather (yours truly) and a priest—were almost a half-Khomizuri younger than him. And this happened, of course, on August 26, i.e, on the Khomizuri of August, in the eighth, i.e., in the twenty-sixth (2+6=8) month of the year.

JOHNNY

T hough busy trying to quash the revolutionary movement, the great Russian reformer Pyotr Stolypin didn't
deprive the penal system of his care and attention. In
fact, he devoted much of his time to this system, which, I
believe, is even now a vital, if not the most important, part of
this state. He laid down his own rules for transporting state
prisoners to their places of incarceration, and the people "on
the other side of the barricades" instantly came up with a term
for that—Stolypin prisoner transport. In designated prisons,
special collecting stations were set up for prisoners sentenced
to the same destination. After several months, when their
numbers became sufficient to fill (or in Soviet times, to over-
fill) a certain number of train cars, the transport would start
moving. That's how my brother and I traveled through the
Rostov, Ryazan, and Potma prisons and, after a month-and-a-
half-long journey, finally reached the village of Barashevo in
Mordovia.

A few trees and a small garden with blossoming rosebushes
were the first things I saw in the yard of the Barashevo prison
camp. It was so contrary to my expectations that I thought it
wasn't a real prison camp at all, but just another stop on the
Stolypin prisoner transport. In my mind, roses didn't belong in
a political prisoner camp, or in any camp for that matter, unless
it's a Young Pioneer camp. Near the rose garden, I saw several
prisoners—a welcoming committee. One blond-haired young
man stood out among the others—he appeared to be ethnically

Slavic, but an experienced eye could unmistakably detect his Georgian origins.

Zachary Konstantinovich Lashkarashvili, or Johnny—born on August 12, 1954, in the village of Doeci in the Kaspi District, a member of the Communist Party of the Soviet Union—was an educated taxi driver from Tbilisi. Cabbie-dissidents were such a rare occurrence—not only in Georgia and the Soviet Union but throughout the world—that, with the exception of the French Resistance, there was no information about taxi drivers as political activists in any national liberation movement. On the contrary, most (if not all) Soviet cabbies were known to collaborate with the authorities. Zachary Lashkarashvili, on the other hand, while in the deep underground, created the Georgian National Liberation movement SEGO and embarked on a difficult and dangerous path, recruiting members by engaging his passengers in patriotic conversations.

In 1983, the leader of Georgia, Eduard Shevarnadze, had to demonstrate Georgian loyalty and obedience to Russia. Using the two-hundred-year anniversary of the Treaty of Georgievsk as a pretext, he began a massive campaign of pro-Russian sychophancy. Movies were made; plays were staged; verses, poems, stories, and novels were written; pictures were made in charcoal, oil, and pastels—in short, out of a hundred possible displays of colonial obedience, one hundred twenty were sent to Moscow. At that time, the Soviet State was descending into a deep economic crisis. In addition to vouchers for meat and butter, the population was now receiving exotic new vouchers—for beans. Inspired by one of Zachary's ideas, the SEGO members covered the statue of Mother Georgia, Kartlis Deda, in Tbilisi with bean vouchers as their protest against the anniversary celebrations.

The SEGO organization was uncovered on July 13, 1983, and its members were arrested and severely punished. The leader, Zakhary Lashkarashvili, was sentenced to five years in maximum-security prison and two years of exile, and his accomplices Gviniashvili and Obganidze, to four years in prison.

As it happened, Johnny was one of the best taxi drivers in the history of Tbilisi. Even though I've never had a chance to use his services, I can testify with complete confidence that during my long life as a passenger (I bought my own car late in life, and for twenty years taxis were my only means of transportation), I've never met any driver so well versed in the geography and toponymics of Tbilisi. For example, Johnny knew not only that there was a lane from my "native" (I put the word native in quotation marks for fear of being accused of claiming Tbilisi as my birthplace—I was born in Batumi and don't want to pretend that I'm a native Tbilisian) Vedzini Street to Kote Meckhi Street, but also that those two streets were connected by a narrow pedestrian path, or more precisely, two narrow paths—one a bit to the right of my house and the other about sixty-five feet down the street from me. In far-off Mordovia, Johnny, being a true taxi driver, described my address in the following way: "17 Vedzini Street. It's a house in the Mtatsminda district, near Arsen Street, at the intersection of Vedzini Street and 4th Vedzini Way. You know, the asphalt road ends right next to your house and then both Vedzini Street and 4th Vedzini Way turn into poorly-laid cobblestone streets." This is how I learned that the asphalt ended near my house—I'd never noticed it before.

Johnny was a natural-born geographer and Tbilisi wasn't the only object of his geographical explorations. He knew the physical as well as the economic geography of every country by heart. As a practicing taxi driver, he knew the major cities of the world and could give you a lecture lasting many hours about one-way streets, car routes, and traffic restrictions in Paris, London, or New York.

Such prominent authorities as Vadim Yankov, the omniscient mathematician, and the polymath Georgy Khomizuri often asked Johnny about religious denominations in Zaire or about the Zulu population in the South African Republic. Once, he easily explained to the members of the Petersburg Delegation (who would not utter the word "Leningrad" if their lives depended on it) how to get to Vasilyevsky Island from different points in the city and how much it would cost at different times of the day. Exactly at that time, Mikhail Polyakov, the recognized leader of the Petersburg group, said: "With a taxi driver like you, I'd go all the way to Finland, not just to Vasilyevsky Island!"

Zachary Lashkarashvili's love of geography also turned into a love of books—especially books containing maps or even technical drawings. If a book didn't have any maps, he would label it a work of futurist-democracy—his harshest critique. We were paid pennies for our hard labor and the money we did have wasn't real, but existed only virtually, on paper. But with our virtual money we could order real books, and Zachary ordered atlases. He ended up ordering *The Complete Atlas of the Soviet Union*, which cost twenty-seven rubles and twenty kopeks—an unprecedented amount of money for that time. Back then, there was a wonderful company, Books by Mail, that operated throughout the vast territory of our country, delivering books even to establishments such as ours. And so, Johnny's atlas was duly delivered, but the administration refused to pass it on to the addressee, claiming that the book could be used for escape purposes as it contained a map of Mordovia. Johnny wasn't too happy about that and suggested that the administration tear the map out of the book, but in his heavily accented Russian, it sounded like: "Let's tear down Mordovia!" The administration interpreted this as inciting a terror attack and was about to bring charges. After figuring out what Lashkarashvili really meant, the administration became even more horrified: "How can you tear out pages from a book? We're Soviets, not barbarians!" At this point, the head librarian, Professor Anderson, proposed a solution—to donate the atlas to the library so that the librarians, while keeping the book intact, could thwart any attempts to look at the map of Mordovia. The proposal was ridiculous, which is probably why it was accepted. They signed the book: "To the ZhKh 385/3-5 library from the administration," and the problem was solved. As it happened, the map of Mordovia was eventually torn out anyway. Many years later, when I was the head of the Georgian National Library, I came across many similar instances of vandalism.

Zachary Lashkarashvili wasn't married, but he used to tell us about his girlfriend in Tblisi. He was in love with a university student, Ketevan, and even their names seemed symbolic to him—Zakro and Keto were characters from a popular cartoon. He also told us how one professor offered Ketevan a passing grade in return for certain favors and how, right near the University on Varaziskhevi Street, the future political prisoner defended the honor of his beloved. I hope this professor reads my book and instantly recognizes himself because he was the exception in our country.

Eventually, Ketevan broke Zachary's heart, but despite all his passion, he gave up the relationship rather easily and embarked on his search for a new love that very day. I also witnessed his two prison loves. The first one was Tamara, the prison doctor. The rest of us rarely saw her, but Johnny had bad lungs and was often in the hospital, especially in winter, and so he had some contact with her. Of course, this love turned out to be one-sided and short-lived, and there were no serious complications, such as poems, epics, or attempts to escape this meaningless life. His last love (well, his last love in prison) was, however, entirely different. Johnny fell in love with the categorical enemy of all the prisoners, Mrs. Ganichenko, the censor.

Mrs. Ganichenko was a woman of truly remarkable, rare beauty, and in her case, there was no need to make any adjustments for lower prison standards. Her Ukrainian last name came from her husband, who, it turns out, was at some point a warden in our prison but, for his leniency toward the Stalinist Razlatsky (or more precisely, toward the Stalinist Razlatsky's mustache), was dismissed from his position and transferred to the neighboring maximum-security prison camp. His wife was a Moldavian. Johnny came up with the simplest way to describe this prison beauty: she was Nestan-Darejan (a character from Rustaveli's classic *The Lord of the Panther-Skin*)—her body was like a poplar, her face was white, her hair and eyes were black, and her lips were red.

When Censor Ganichenko entered the prison camp, the emotional temperature would rise by several degrees. Johnny wasn't familiar with the verses of the contemporary Georgian poet Tariel Chanturia: "Ah, guys, what a girl! What a woman! She raises the radiation level by a hundred percent!" and yet, he would say: "The radiation is rising." After such exclamations, most of us would be overcome with rage. In a political prison, the activities of the in-house censor didn't allow for any warm feelings, especially when Mrs. Censor conducted her dirty business with an attitude that is best described as *Schadenfreude*. Georgian linguistic equivalents are incapable of describing the feeling expressed in the beautiful censor's smile—a charming smile with a tinge of subtle intimacy—when on the last day of the mailing period she would return a letter to a prisoner saying that, unfortunately, from the censor's point of view, the letter was unacceptable. The imprisoned psychiatrist and psychologist Doctor Boris Isaakovich Manilovich, who was a follower of Freud, Jung, Adler, and Fromm, was convinced that our evil censor was actually a good person: returning a letter written by a prisoner to his family produced sensations akin to an orgasm, i.e., she loved that prisoner. Mikhail Polyakov used to repeat Oscar Wilde's axiom that "beauty is a form of genius, as it needs no explanation." And then, deep in thought, he would drift away to his faraway Petersburg and quote Pushkin: "Genius and evil are not compatible," or as another famous Petersburg writer said: "Beauty will save the world." However, neither the poetic support of those famous Petersburg residents nor the love of some Georgians could save Censor Ganichenko when the prisoners saw a pile of returned letters in her hands. At that moment, no one wanted to see her beauty!

Once, the censor's beauty even captivated me to such an extent that I burst out: "I would give myself to her!" which created a great deal of commotion among the majority of the camp's democrats. To redeem myself, I had to quote, with the consent of the omniscient Vadim Yankov, the passage in *The Iliad* where Homer skillfully describes the beauty of Helen, without saying a word about her body, face, or eyes. The wise men of Troy scold Helen, but when her divine beauty passes by, they gradually change their tune, ultimately concluding: "Yes, for such a woman, even wars can be started!" Even though Yankov acknowledged the exactness of my quotation and confirmed that, overall, Homer's words were fitting for my "situation," the socialist Fred Anadenko didn't approve of my outburst, reminding me instead of the wise saying by Mao: "Do not drink, for when you're drunk, you could hug even an enemy of the revolution."

In the beginning, Zachary Lashkarashvili was hostile to Ganichenko, which was understandable. There were three Georgians in our prison—as they used to say, three "-shvilis"—and at my brother David Berdzenishvili's suggestion, we, the three Georgians, began writing letters in Georgian from our first day in prison. Before that, all letters were written in Russian so that the censor could read the letters and return them. For three months, Ganichenko fought with us and, for three months, the Tbilisi KGB sent us warnings: "Stop this stupid prank!" For three months, our loved ones had no contact with us. However, the information about the incident—that prisoners were prohibited from writing letters in their native language—made it into the international press, and Ganichenko lost this war. Now our Georgian letters bypassed Ganichenko to be censored by the Tbilisi KGB. After our little victory, prisoners not only in our camp, but across the political prisons of the entire Perm region, began writing letters in their native languages. Naturally, that didn't add to Ganichenko's love for the Georgians and she began going after our incoming correspondence. She initiated strict new rules and wouldn't give me my wife's letters or Johnny his mother's, claiming that those were people with different last names and, therefore, couldn't be our mother or wife. That claim was taken seriously. I received a letter with the following return address: Inga Shirava, 17 Vedzini Street, Tbilisi. The censor wouldn't give me the letter and kept questioning who that Shirava was. I said that Inga Shirava was my wife, that in Georgia most women kept their maiden names after getting married, and this is why the last names of my wife and of Johnny's mother were different from ours. "You, Georgians, are all from the same tribe," Ganichenko proclaimed. "We can't trust you to testify on each other's behalf!" And so, she called Rafael Papayan, an expert in Caucasian affairs, as a witness. Papayan categorically stated: "In Armenia, my home country, the wives take their husbands' last names, and I think the same happens in Georgia." (It reminded me of a story I heard from one of my professors about the renowned Russian academic Sobolevsky who couldn't believe that, in a Georgian sentence, a subject could be in any one of three different cases. This infuriated him: "A subject can only be in the nominative case!") Obviously, after such a statement, the tension between the Georgians and the Armenians escalated to a height unknown since 1919. Each side brought up the thorniest issues, such as the Georgian alphabet, Jvari Cathedral near Mtskheta, Rustaveli, cognac, the Tbilisi "Dinamo" and the Yerevan "Ararat" soccer teams. At this point, Vadim Yankov, our Nestor, a truly wise man and the chronicler of our prison camp, intervened with his undeniable authority on the subject. (It was Boris Manilovich's idea to use the names Nestor, Achilles, Helen of Troy, and so on, as our avatars.) Not only had his Armenian wife kept her maiden name in both her marriages, but he also knew that Georgian women kept their maiden names and was familiar with the very difficult Lithuanian system of female last names, where an unmarried girl has one last name, a married woman, another, and a widow, a third, but all three forms keep the original root of the woman's maiden name. Vitautas Skuodis came out in support of Yankov, and Ganichenko reluctantly had to hand over my wife's letter, but she tortured Lashkarashvili for two more days.

So that was the monster our Johnny had fallen in love with. As soon as he saw her tall silhouette and slim figure, like a model on a catwalk, he'd exclaim: "Here he comes!" And off he went to greet her. Regarding grammatical gender, Johnny had his own system—after thousands of corrections, he would use a masculine pronoun even when talking about his own mother. I don't know what Ganichenko felt when, against the backdrop of hundreds of disgusted glares, she saw one gaze that was full of love and adoration. But the other prisoners started to worry—they couldn't believe that love was triumphing over class hatred. Johnny's and my slapdash translation of Galaktion Tabidze's "Once in the Evening" didn't help, either:

> . . . And the classes fought against each other!
> A shoot-out began, my side was White.
> But the grey masses of the Revolution's dragon
> Burned consciousness to death with the fire of being.

Everyone who considers himself a real Batumian, or associates himself with the city of Batumi, knows this poem, if not by heart then very close to it, because the poem is set there: "In Batumi, the sun was shining as it set, and a calm wind was playing upon the sea." It's a story about the tragic love between Veronica and a dandy.

The postrevolutionary ending of the poem, however, in which the angelic Veronica is transformed into a Bolshevik guerilla, the bloodthirsty murderess Verka of Kaluga, plays against the idyllic opening. At least to our eyes, Galaktion, who had a year before paid tribute to Veronica and, by analogy, Madame Ganichenko, was now arriving at conclusions of a very different kind. Fred Anadenko and Dmitro Mazur, however, often had no respect for Fredrich Engels, let alone Tabidze. (I won't say anything about Marx—I don't want to get mixed up with the prison Socialists.)

The prisoners even created special committees to deal with Johnny's infatuation, though the Georgians were considered biased and weren't allowed to participate. Even Khomizuri, who loathed Ganichenko, was turned away. They summoned Johnny and tried to show him the evil of his ways, but, as they say, what is bred in the bone will come out in the flesh. Johnny would make some sort of promise, but the next day "Here he comes!" would ring out with new force. Meanwhile, "he" chose a provocative tactic: She began paying even more attention to her clothes and makeup, which drove the prisoners insane. Even Anadenko couldn't resist her charms and once exclaimed: "She's as beautiful as a hellcat!" Then, one day, Johnny was summoned. The administration asked whether he was aware of Ganichenko's marital status, and whether he'd heard anything about Colonel Ganichenko, to which Lashkarashvili, brought up in the city of Kaspi, answered with a question: "Do you know who Giorgi Saakadze was?" And then he would add that they should know, as they must have read Anna Antonovskaya's novel *The Great Mouravi*, or at least seen the movie.[7] "But it's only a joke, I don't love him. I have a Georgian fiancé," Johnny added at the end, and, after that, they left him alone.

Russian wasn't easy for Johnny. He spoke with confidence, but proper grammar was beyond his grasp. When his mother arrived for a visit, Johnny had not yet earned the right to personal visits—in a maximum-security prison, a prisoner had the right once a year to a personal visit that could last from one to three days. We would usually get two days, while spies, traitors, terrorists, and war criminals got three, but Johnny was granted an exception. He was allowed a two-hour visit with a glass window, a telephone, and Trimazkin, who was one of the relatively decent administrative officers. When Johnny's mother said: "*Gamarjoba, shvilo!*" [Hello, son], Trimazkin yelled: "Russian only!" And with that, the torment of the Georgians began. Johnny later told us: "You know my Russian, okay? But compared to my mother's, I'm Pushkin! She doesn't know it at all." Whenever Johnny's mother switched to Georgian, Trimazkin would snarl at her and, in return, he'd get a "*Sikdvili da kubo!*" [Death and a coffin to you]. "In Russian!" Trimazkin ordered. And the mother would answer: "Death and a coffin!" But such colorful Russian was beyond the comprehension of Trimazkin, a man of Mordovian descent. Finally, if we're to believe Johnny, they started speaking a very specific Russian with a heavy admixture of Georgian words: "Natela got married. He was so beautiful, like *lamaz*, that *tvals ver vashoreb*, you know?" Trimazkin got anxious: "Who's beautiful?" "Natela, Natela is beautiful," Johnny answered.

---

[7] Giorgi Saakadze (1570–1629), known as "the great Mouravi," was an adventurer, Georgian politician and military hero. In Soviet times, he was turned into a national-patriotic symbol. The writer Anna Antonovskaya dedicated a six-volume novel to him, which won the Stalin Prize, and cowrote the screenplay that would became the basis for Miheil Chiaureli's 1942 film *Georgi Saakadze*.

I think when he told us about his mother's visit, that is, when he gave a solo performance in front of twenty prisoners, Johnny, as a true Georgian storyteller, exaggerated a bit. It's hard to believe that his mother didn't know even the most basic Russian, but that a mother and son, who hadn't seen each other in years, were not allowed to speak in their native language is an undisputed fact, or in the working language of one of the sons of that inhuman system who today have been promoted to positions of power: "Wie bekannt, es ist eine unbestrittene Tatsache" [As everyone knows, that is an undisputed fact].[8] And so, today, when people declare, "The collapse of the Soviet Union was a terrible mistake," and "Those who weren't upset by this collapse don't have a heart," Johnny, his mother, and I are utterly unmoved.

Like many a popular character from a Khazanov comedy routine, Johnny graduated from a culinary arts college. Because of his weak lungs, he had to spend a lot of time at the hospital and was entitled to a special diet. In the free world, a diet may be considered a bad thing, but in prison, that noble Greek word was charged with the most positive meaning. In prison "a diet" meant 1 boiled egg, 100 grams of white bread, 1 cup of milk, 20 grams of butter, 60 grams of cheese, and 120 grams of boiled beef a day. During the entire time of our incarceration, none of us had ever seen such fantastic cuisine with his own eyes. Johnny deprived his lungs of the butter, but collected it in a jar filled with water to treat his heart at the New Year's celebration: In 1986, Johnny Lashkarashvili baked a New Year's cake. As a substitute for flour, he used a special prison technique. Johnny cut the white bread we'd received on

[8] This is a reference to Russian President Vladimir Putin, who worked as a KGB agent in Germany before entering politics in Russia. In a 2005 speech, he declared the fall of the Soviet Union to be "the greatest geopolitical tragedy of the twentieth century."

May 9, 1985, into little pieces and air-dried them for eight months. Then, he beat them into a powder and sifted it using Rafael Papayan's personal micro-sieve. He saved the sediment to decorate the cake with—writing "1986" on the top. Using milk powder, cream, our prison "flour," and water, Johnny mixed biscuit dough, which was then baked in Grisha Feldman's famous oven. To make cream, he used butter, boiled condensed milk (carefully saved from a package I'd received back in September), and vanilla from his October package. (It was always like that: I'd get a package with nuts, garlic, dried red pepper, dried cilantro, and *khmeli-suneli* spice, while Johnny would get cinnamon, allspice, bay leaves, and vanilla.) The presentation of the cake took place on January 1, 1986, at zero hours and one minute, after toasting the New Year with our special homebrew.

Theatergoers know how it feels to experience an opening night success. Imitating Homer, I will try to describe the culinary shock we experienced in the first minutes of 1986: Khomizuri uttered only one syllable, "Vakh!" Rafik uttered the two-syllable "Pakh-pakh!" Henrikh uttered the three syllables, "Karabakh!" And I said, "It's better than Ganichenko!" (In Russian, "Luchshe Ganichenki!" We used to decline her last name in the Ukrainian manner. Chekhov, by the way, used to do the same. Since there were no other books in the Tbilisi isolation unit, I knew the last few volumes of Chekhov's collected works, including his correspondence, almost by heart.) Johnny was happy: "I told you I'm a master chef!"

Once, there was a "Georgitation," or a deeply Georgian incident. This means that only the ethnic Georgians were in any way involved. As it happened, Zhora Khomizuri adored Rabelais. I think this was due to his Georgian blood because I don't know of a more Georgian writer in all of world literature than François Rabelais, a Frenchman to the bone. Although, I must admit, Rabelais was no stranger in Mordovia—the remarkable literary scholar Mikhail Bakhtin, who studied Rabelais, spent many years of his imprisonment in Dubravlag and in Saransk—so, Rabelais was like a brother in our prison camp. One day, Zhora and I happened to be in the washroom, in the smoke shack, discussing Rabelais. Zhora wondered whether Rabelais had been translated into Georgian. I said that, of course, he'd been translated. There were even two versions: an abridged translation by Madame Bagrationi and a full translation by Gadmoaena Gogiashvili. The latter used an interesting literary approach, translating some passages into the Kakhetian dialect. At this point, another Georgian prisoner, Arsen Lolashvili, joined the conversation, and upon hearing "Kakhetian," got upset: "What are you saying about Kakhetians?" And he started to move aggressively toward me. There wasn't enough space in the smoke shack, so we moved to the prison yard. Johnny was holding Arsen back, and Zhora was holding me back. This unusual event, an inter-Georgian conflict, accompanied by lexical expressions not found in the most comprehensive dictionaries of the Georgian language, stunned ZhKh 385/3-5. No one dared approach us.

Arsen Lolashvili was a Georgian peasant from the Kakheti region. He'd never been especially law-abiding, and, after three run-ins with the authorities, he graduated to political crime. He was planning to cross the Turkish border with some sort of anti-Soviet writings. Reading his verdict, I couldn't figure out how and on what account he'd betrayed the Motherland. He was very angry and wanted to escape Georgia. He was so angry and was running away so fast that he didn't even pause to consider whether it was Turkey or Armenia that lay ahead of him. He didn't know much about politics and often confused human rights and democracy with sodomy. In my first days in prison, Arsen, Johnny, and I grew close, establishing a warm, friendly relationship. Only after we became friends with Zhora Khomizuri and Rafael Papayan did Arsen begin to fall out with us. He even gave us an ultimatum: "It's me or Zhora," offering some not-so-liberal reasons for his hatred of Khomizuri. We'd parted amicably, but it seemed he was still nursing a grudge against us.

It was a rather interesting scene: Georgians going after each other while other Georgians tried to pull them apart. Suddenly, Arsen pulled out a knife and stabbed Johnny, who was holding him back, in the stomach. It was a small knife—we all used those knives in the workshop, but we usually left them there or in the barracks. No one would ever think of carrying a knife around. After Johnny fell to the ground, Arsen, pushing Zhora aside, started moving toward me. I knocked the knife out of Arsen's hand with a kick. (The prison's official poet and chronicler Manilovich later devoted a short poem to the episode.) Half the prison leapt toward the newly unarmed Arsen, while Zhora and I ran to check on Johnny. His wound wasn't deep, but it was gushing blood. Arnold Arturovich Anderson, our father of herb therapy and the occult, cleaned the wound, covered it with plantain leaves and chamomile flowers, and then made a bandage out of an undershirt so skillfully that even the patient applauded him. After that, he wrapped Johnny in the bandage, which made him look like a silkworm. All this time, no one from the administration showed up.

Despite his wound, Johnny secretly approached Arsen and told him not to mention the knife. If asked, he said, just tell the story as if there were no knife at all. It was a well-known fact that the prison was full of spies and snitches, and soon the administration knew every detail of the fight except for the reason behind it. No one but Arsen was questioned. When asked if he'd had a knife, it seems that Arsen answered, "Yes," and was sent to the hole. Later, he tried to redeem himself by saying that he simply couldn't lie. If Zhora or I had committed a similar act, we would have definitely gotten an additional eight years and been transferred to the Chistopol prison (a euphemism for hell). But Arsen easily extricated himself from the ordeal. If he hadn't confessed about the knife, he probably wouldn't even have gone to solitary.

Several years later, when my brother David Berdzenishvili was elected to the first independent parliament of Georgia as a representative of Batumi and joined the opposition, a few people, with the help of what they considered to be a reliable source, were tempted to play the Arsen Lolashvili card and blame us for all the atrocities that happened in the political prison. President Zviad Gamsakhurdia found out about this act of vigilante justice, planned by a group of women, and about the fact that they'd already brought Lolashvili to parliament as a witness. The president then ordered Temur Koridze to send the women away, along with Lolashvili, saying that former political prisoners should be rewarded, not slandered. After that, he was outraged when the three-time convicted felon Lolashvili entered the Supreme Soviet—the same Lolashvili who used to insult Gamsakhurdia ten years ago before he was president.

There are no words in the Georgian language to describe Johnny's political views. You might call them extreme ultraradical, but that doesn't totally do them justice. His ideal was the Irish Republican Army because he believed nothing could be done without terror. Johnny would get angry if someone so much as mentioned liberal democracy. Terror, only terror, weapons, and fighting! And this from a man who never harmed a flea.

By February of 1987, all but two people had been released from the political prisons of the Soviet Union—Vakhtang Dzabiradze and Zachary Lashkarashvili. When, after some discussion, all the other political prisoners had come to an agreement that, in the new political climate, it was acceptable to submit a moderate petition (first signed by Andrey Sakharov and Yuri Orlov) and return home, the two Georgians refused to do so and spent several more months in the Gulag. On June 3, 1987, Zachary Lashkarashvili had to be practically kicked out of the prison.

After his release, Johnny couldn't find his place in the national movement. Proclaiming himself a radical and a revolutionary, he didn't attract many followers. Always strapped for cash and unable to make ends meet, he decided to emigrate. With the help of some local Georgians, he settled in Paris and worked for Radio Liberty, earning pennies for his reports. Then, a Judas put some poison drops in the ear of a local leader, who, being from Tbilisi, passed these tales on to the well-known dissident Alexander Ginzburg: "Don't trust Lashkarashvili. He's a KGB agent." In my life, I have come across many injustices, but this insult to someone who was almost a political saint is one of the most shameless and dirtiest tricks I've ever heard of. This plot was based on the premise that the word of the son of an educated and established family, of a future leader of the nation, would be worth much more than the word of an obscure taxi driver with some technical training. Ginzburg believed the Georgian leader, and Lashkarashvili lost the job that had taken him so long to find. After that, he could barely make ends meet and had to take any odd jobs he could find.

The best way to get to know Paris is to climb onto the upper deck of a special tour bus, put on the headphones, set them to your language of choice (a Western European language, Japanese, Chinese, or Russian), and open your eyes wide. If you're lucky, you might hear a strong Georgian accent in the driver's "*Entrez, s'il vous plaît.*" Then you'll know it's Zachary Lashkarashvili. He wanted to become a taxi driver, passed all the tests—driving, topography, routes—ten out of ten, but couldn't do anything about his French. So, his aspiration of being a Parisian cabbie remained an unattainable dream. Johnny married a girl from the West Georgian city of

Zestafoni—who else would he find in the capital of France? Now, these parents speak Georgian to their children, and the children answer them in French.

"They teach me French!" Johnny tells us on occasion.

RAFIK

I can talk and argue with Rafik more than anyone else on this entire planet. I can't think of another person with a command of as many topics for conversation and debate. Our incarceration, as well as our relationship, ended almost a quarter of a century ago, but there remain enough topics for conversations, arguments, and intellectual battles for centuries to come.

Rafik—Rafael Ashotovich Papayan, born in 1942, married, with two children—was arrested on November 10, 1982. He was sentenced to four years in maximum-security prison and two years of exile. In 1975, Rafik, along with Eduard Arutunyan, was one of the founders of the Armenian Chapter of the Helsinki Human Rights Union. When Arutunyan and two members of his group were arrested, the KGB searched Rafik's home, as well as the home of Edmon Avetikyan. Rafik wasn't arrested that time—he received only a stern warning. But that warning didn't do much to stop Rafik's activities. And so, he was arrested later on, along with Zhora Khomizuri, and sent to the Gulag.

In Armenia, Rafik's father, Ashot (Aramashot) Papayan, was best known as an actor, but he was also the author of several plays (mostly comedies) and screenplays. Incidentally, Ashot Papayan was born in Batumi, like Dato and I, so Rafik was not only our compatriot—he was almost a true Batumian.

There were several reasons why I considered Rafael Papayan to be such a special person. For the first time in the history of the Barashevo political prison, he, along with yours truly, proposed organizing an international collective, or kibbutz, "the Christian Federation of South Caucasian Nations." Before that, all the prison groups had been organized on a strictly national basis. Another reason Papayan was so special to me was that, among all the prisoners, he was my only true colleague, a philologist. Rafael had graduated from the Bruysov Institute of Russian and Foreign Languages in Yerevan. For his graduate studies, he went to the University of Tartu and there, at that excellent Estonian research center, he completed his Ph.D. in philology under the guidance of the renowned Yuri Lotman.

It didn't take long for me to realize that Rafik was a truly amazing person. And precisely because he was so amazing, I observed him constantly. For me, Papayan was a phenomenon worthy of study. He was a man of many talents—a brilliant historian who specialized in the history of Armenia and Georgia, an expert in Russian language and literature, a refined prose stylist, a talented poet, and a truly erudite individual. He was a man of rare tact and thoughtfulness, a person with his own unique sense of melancholy humor, and a man of indefatigable industry and patience.

Apart from being a polymath, Papayan's greatest talent was, in my opinion, his craftmanship. Anytime I try to describe Rafik succinctly, the life of Mesrop Mashtots invariably comes to mind. The preeminent medieval Armenian scholar and statesman, who is best known as the creator of the Armenian alphabet, was an educator, a missionary, and a saint of both Armenian churches—the Apostolic and the Catholic. But among all his merits, his grateful countrymen decided that Mesrop's most important achievement was his translation of the Bible, and so they referred to him as "the translator." In the same way, Rafik could be described by the word "craftsman." Armenian craftmanship is well known, and Rafik is one of its most talented representatives. One of his masterpieces (or "master-crafts," as Boris Manilovich would say) was a device that could make twelve *makhorka* cigarettes at a time. This unique device was my birthday gift the year I reached thirty-three, the age of Jesus Christ at his crucifixion. Unfortunately, the patience necessary for such a device was not included, so I mostly rolled my *makhorka* by hand.

In the prison workshop, he attached a handmade double fan propeller to his sewing machine. There was nothing better than sitting next to that sewing machine during the hot summers. He made so many improvements to his sewing machine that he was able to complete the daily quota of ninety-two pairs of mitts by 11 A.M. During the remaining hours, he worked for a rainy day—rumor had it that he'd stashed away several thousand pairs of mitts. I still wonder what kind of disaster he thought could make our days rainier than they already were.

Over the years, in his free time, Rafik created many marvels of engineering, such as an automatic garlic press (which was never used because where were we going to find that much garlic?) and an automatic nut chopper, which was mostly just a prototype, since nuts were such a rarity that only a few of the Georgians ever had any. He also designed a device for drawing lines on writing paper, a machine for waste-free fish bone extraction that left the flesh intact, a mechanical meat grinder made of wood (though, in my three years in the camp, I never saw any meat), an extremely precise scale that could measure weight to a milligram, and so on and so forth . . . He invented so many things it's hard to remember them all.

Over the course of my life, I've heard many arguments attempting to prove that geniuses of different times and nations had Armenian roots—although not from Rafik, I must say. On several occasions, I've heard there is "undeniable proof" that Rustaveli, Shakespeare, Byron, Mozart, Julius Cesar, Jesus

Christ, Buddha, Mohammed, Yuri Dolgoruky, Leo Tolstoy, and Leonardo da Vinci were of Armenian descent. If asked, I could offer some support based on Rafik's ingenious technical inventions alone.

Rafik was also a devoted hoarder, always saving, storing, hiding, conserving, and slicing thin. He saw no issue with stashing a jar of *kaurma* (prepared by his beloved wife Anait) for so many months that the delicious lamb stew went bad, only to be consumed by Grisha Feldman. Compared to other incidents, that wasn't even the worst. One New Year's Eve, he opened some cured sturgeon of an even older vintage (three years), thinking that he might not be here to share it with us in the future and, of course, he didn't want to eat it alone in exile!

After making a New Year's cake from the butter he'd saved in the hospital, Johnny Lashkarashvili earned a scolding from Rafik, who declared that there was plenty of food (this, in my opinion, was a slight exaggeration), and that he should have saved the butter because, "Who knows what will happen next year!"

There were high-demand and low-demand products in the prison store. For example, sunflower oil was in high demand (with the bottle, it cost 1 ruble and 2 kopeks, but the bottle could be returned for 20 kopeks the following month), as was black tea (90 kopeks), *makhorka* (15 kopeks a pack—I, for example, went through 20 packs a month), matches (1 kopek a box—you had to have them because no one would share), round candies that could function as sugar (3 rubles per kilo, but you weren't allowed to buy more than 200 grams a month), a composition notebook (a classic twelve-page Soviet one cost 2 kopeks), and a pen (30 kopeks, which was expensive). Products in lower demand included all kinds of jam (a jar cost 1 ruble, but an empty jar could be returned for 10 kopeks), fish pâté (76 kopeks), the unforgettable Soviet preserves called "Tourist's Breakfast"—a unique combination of fish, tomato paste, and rice (80 kopeks)—and luxurious tobacco products (for example, unfiltered Prima cigarettes for 15 kopeks). And there were some products that came from mythic worlds that were considered a direct insult to the inmates. For example, Marlboro cigarettes, made in a Kishenev tobacco factory, cost one and a half rubles a pack. There was no demand at all for such products and so they stayed on the shelves month after month. This is how the popular prison expression "There's butter in the store" was born. Butter wasn't a part of the prison store's meager stock, so this expression referred to an impossible situation and was often used as "Oh, c'mon!"

Rafik was born on December 22. During our first year of our prison life, Dato and I, being inexperienced, decided to surprise the birthday boy. From our combined monthly allowance of ten rubles, we sacrificed three and bought him an unparalleled gift—two packs of Marlboro cigarettes. We were sure that our friend would be overjoyed by such a financial sacrifice and, hearts pounding, we looked forward to giving him our precious gift. That evening Rafik invited us to a rather modestly laid table, and we gave him our elaborately wrapped present. The birthday boy began unfolding the newspaper and, as soon as he saw the cigarettes, he forgot the ancient wisdom about not looking a gift horse in the mouth, and reacted just like Ronald Reagan did when Mexican president Portillo gave him a real live horse. Rafik, the only son of the artist and playwright Ashot Papayan, appealed to his father in a tragic voice, denouncing us, his neighboring countrymen, to the heavens: "What have you miserable Georgians done? For three rubles, you could've bought three whole jars of jam!"

In one of the toasts during our celebratory tea, I called Rafik a knight of the hidden banners, and he loved it. He hid everything for a rainy day, and this is why Johnny called him the warehouse manager (he called me the museum director). In our prison camp, no one could compete with him in the realm of business. Once, an inmate desperately needed a stamp and, after searching the entire camp, he finally came to us. "I'm dead meat," he said, "If I don't mail this letter, I'll lose my letter rights this month. Help!" It's a terrible feeling when you can't send a thirty-two-page letter you've been writing for two weeks just because you don't have a measly three-kopek stamp. In prison, you can only reach your family by writing them a letter. If you miss out on the opportunity, you begin to descend into a vortex of emptiness and treachery, and after that, you don't want to live anymore. When my Ukrainian prison mate was explaining all this to me, his voice was trembling, and I could see that he was falling into a deep depression. "Don't worry, I'll find you a stamp," I said, trying to calm him down. I then set off on a search, like Vosh, the hero of Georgian folklore, or like Avtandil from *The Lord of the Panther-Skin*. Obviously, I went to see Rafik:

"Listen, Rafik, *ahper-jan, tsavatanem* [dear brother, I'll take away your pain]. I need a stamp. A good man is in trouble."

"A postage stamp is a rare thing," said Rafik. "Its price changes with the market. Is your client ready to pay?"

"Why does he have to pay? The man needs a three-kopek stamp!" I had no skills in market affairs.

"*Ahper-jan*, Levan-*jan*, I don't want to start on the subject of Georgian extravagance. You've wasted your own assets and now you're lecturing me about the price of a three-kopek stamp, as you call it?"

"So how much does a three-kopek stamp cost? Ten kopeks?" I asked, trying to sound as business like as possible.

"Ten is a good number, but I wouldn't treat this number as nonchalantly as you do. See, you're stressing the fact that in the store, one postage stamp costs three kopeks. Here, I'll multiply it by the emergency need coefficient of 10, and thereby set its emergency price at 30 kopeks, or two packs of *makhorka*."

"Why so much? Two packs of *makhorka*?!" I said, unable to hide my disapproval.

"Are we going to bargain?" Rafik asked with an expression

on his face that instantly made me lose any desire to negotiate. He then quoted Ilf and Petrov's *The Twelve Chairs*: "This is no place for bargaining!" Rafik said it in a stern voice, just like the character Kisa Vorobyaninov from this almost sacred book of our generation. Then he began naming other products that cost thirty kopeks—two packs of Prima, one matchbox of black tea, and so on. I went back to my anxious Ukrainian brother, explained the situation to him, and asked for a pack of *makhorka*. He happily agreed to the price and delivered the *makhorka* right then and there.

"You know that if I had a stamp, I'd give it to you for free, right?" I said.

"Yes, I do," he answered. "I would've done the same—if you needed a stamp and I had one. But now I need it so much that even a pack of *makhorka* can't stop me. It's good that he didn't ask for two packs—or more!" Being a tactful person, he didn't ask me who the owner of the stamp was, but I think he knew who in the prison traded in such rare goods. So, I added a pack from my own supply and went back to Rafik.

"You see," Rafik said, "how easily the client agreed to two packs? I should've asked for three!"

I didn't tell him that one pack was mine, especially after he divided the "profit" in two and handed my pack of *makhorka* back to me. I must confess that I added my own pack to my Ukrainian friend's payment not because I was such a nice person, not at all. I just felt ashamed asking for two packs for one little stamp. Meanwhile, Rafik decided to increase the emergency coefficient to fifteen for future deals.

Rafik was a man of principle and took part in all protests, and our protests usually took the form of a strike. When we started a strike, we wouldn't go to the workshop—we'd stop working completely. Some inmates would support the strike by writing a letter to Alexander Rekunkov, Prosecutor General of the USSR. A typical letter would say: To the Prosecutor

General of the USSR, in protest against such and such, from this to that date, I declare a strike, to which I testify with my signature—inmate so-and-so. Then the letter would go into an envelope and the envelope into the mailbox. We Georgians didn't miss a single demonstration, but we didn't acknowledge the Prosecutor General of the USSR and so didn't write him any letters. Either way, the powers that be knew who was on strike and who wasn't. Everyone else would write letters, though, and put them in the mailbox. Johnny Lashkarashvili constantly said: Rafik's from the Caucasus, there's no way he's writing letters to the Prosecutor General. When Rafik was dropping his letter in the mailbox one time, Johnny snatched it out of his hands, opened it, and beamed with joy at the blank sheet of paper in the envelope.

As I mentioned before, Rafik had been a student of Lotman for many years and, as it happened, Manilovich, Vadim Yankov, and I had also met this amazing scholar. Once we were playing the very intellectual and artistic game of charades. We formed several teams of two and began: One member of the group, using only pantomime, would try to relate a word or a phrase to the other member. In the end, Rafik and I (with the help of our coaches Khomizuri and Altunyan) beat the strongest team from Petersburg, Polyakov and Manilovich, coached by Donskoy and Tolstykh. Rafik was able to tell me with only gestures that the other team's phrase was the Bible of all political prisoners: *The Universal Declaration of Human Rights*. When the defeated team served us, the winners, tea, Rafik recalled how once, in a similar game, Lotman managed to explain to his partner a very difficult term—*Salazar's dictatorship*. (During Rafik's graduate school years, Salazar was still the dictator of Portugal.) First, he presented with gestures a classic dictator and then used wordplay in a rather untraditional way. In Russian, the word *salo* means "lard," and the name of Lotman's wife was Zara. So he invited her into the room and, with an invisible knife, pretended to cut off some of her *salo* . . . Then, using only mimicry, he suggested that we put the two parts together: *salo*-Zara. And that's how they won the game.

And, of course, we talked about the Georgian alphabet. Rafik was irritated by the fact that Zhora had studied the Mrglovani script, trying to find some cosmic order in its graphics. Evoking the authority of the prominent fifth-century Armenian historian Movses Khorenatsi, Rafik insisted that Mesrop Mashots, with the help of the translator Dzhaga, created the Georgian alphabet, and that Tzar Bakur, along with the Georgian Archbishop Moses, assisted him.

"Is it true that Mesrop didn't know Georgian?" I asked.

"According to Koryun, it is," Rafik answered, refraining from lying.

"You're a philologist, aren't you? And you believe that it's possible to separate phonemes without knowing the language?" I asked, preparing myself for a long discussion. My point was that you not only need to know the language—you need to have the deepest understanding of the language. You need to feel it in order to isolate the elements that carry meaning.

"Of course, it's impossible, but the Georgian phonemes were likely isolated by the translator Dzhaga," Rafik declared, suddenly discovering an unknown genius in fifth-century Georgia.

"You know the Georgians pretty well, don't you? Tell me, is ingratitude a Georgian national characteristic?" I asked him directly.

"I haven't noticed any particular ingratitude in the Georgians," Rafik answered cautiously.

"So how could it be that Mesrop didn't receive any acknowledgment after making such an enormous contribution?" I asked the question in a way that made it difficult for Rafik to continue a polite conversation.

"Maybe you Georgians acknowledged him before the

schism between our churches," Rafik answered, still trying to stay within the boundaries of politeness.

"Okay, let's assume that after the schism, we forgot our benefactor Mesrop. But then what did Dzhaga do wrong?" I asked on behalf of my newly discovered genius compatriot.

"Let me ask you now. You know your Leonti Mroveli said in the eleventh century that Parnavaz created the alphabet. Do you believe that?" Rafik asked.

"Our Mrglovani alphabet was created based on the Greek model and is a product of Christianity. Perhaps Leonti Mroveli meant another alphabet or another principle (because he was taking about writing in general, not about any concrete alphabet), for example, alloglottography."[9]

"If Parnavaz created another alphabet or laid the foundation for the alloglottographic principle, then can you tell me who created the Mrglovani alphabet?" Rafik asked, deciding to put me and all of Georgia up against a wall.

"We don't have sufficient information," I answered carefully.

"You Georgians never fail to surprise me," Rafik declared happily. "You say that ingratitude is not a dominant feature of your people, but then what did the creator of your alphabet do to you? How could you forget his name? Doesn't it seem a little strange that you Georgians don't know the name of the creator of your alphabet, or Rustaveli's biography, and that you've forgotten where Tsarina Tamar is buried? Is it normal that your finest poets—Rustaveli, Guramishvili, Besiki, and Baratashvili—died in an alien land?" my Armenian neighbor said, launching a full-scale attack.

"Is it normal that Vardapet Komitas spent twenty years in Paris and died in destitution in a psychiatric clinic in Villejuif?

---

[9] Alloglottography refers to the phenomenon of writing a text in a language different from the one in which it is intended to be read.

Is it normal that your real capital was in a foreign land and that our Tbilisi was your cultural center? Is it normal that, without a state of your own, you had your capital abroad?" I asked, refusing to yield.

At the mention of Komitas's mental illness, a complete change came over Rafik's face—apparently, he didn't think I knew about that. I restrained myself from reminding him that it wasn't the mental shock provoked by genocide that tormented Komitas, but schizophrenia and STDs, and who knew which of these would kill a man first.

"Who said that Tbilisi was the Armenian capital?" Rafik asked, as if he'd truly never heard this.

"Well, how about the Armenian Aghasi Ayvazyan, the author of the great short story 'The Gospel of Avlabari?' He was from Tbilisi."

"So, you won't acknowledge that your alphabet was created by Mesrop?" Rafik asked, returning to square one now that the conversation had started down a path he didn't like.

"Of course, not," I answered, feeling the breath of all Georgians born after the fifth century, and of all those yet to be born, on my neck.

"Then I'll give you the last piece of evidence," Rafik said, warning me of what was to come.

"I know you always have something saved," I said, unable to resist alluding to the postage stamp incident.

"When the Greek alphabet was developing, did the capital and lowercase letters form at the same time?"

"No, of course not. Only one Greek alphabet was created, and it had only capital letters. The same happened with Latin and Cyrillic, as well as with the Georgian and Armenian alphabets. Only centuries later were lowercase letters formed as a result of rapid writing," I retorted. With scholarly authority and confidence, I laid out the generally accepted theory of the development of phonetic alphabets.

"The Greeks, Romans, Slavs, and Armenians stopped at small and big letters, i.e., capital Mtavruli and lowercase Nuskhuri letters, but why didn't you Georgians stop? Why did you create the new Mkhedruli alphabet?" Rafik asked, finally presenting his main argument.

"Because we're such an unruly nation!" I answered, not very convincingly.

"No, Levan-*jan*, it's not that, *ahper-jan*. To me, the fact that you created a new alphabet is sufficient evidence to prove the hypothesis that Mesrop created the Georgian Mtavruli alphabet. I believe our historians!"

"And I believe *our* historians!" I declared, standing my ground.

"Oh, what historians do you have? You're a nation of poets!" Rafik said, trying to be cool by using my grandma Ivlita's line.

"I'm surprised to hear a poet treat other poets with such sarcasm. If you don't like Georgians poets, then why are you so attached to Rustaveli? Get your hands off Rustaveli!" I said, ending up with the slogan of the day.

"I never said that Rustaveli was Armenian. That's a provocation invented by Georgians and stupidly continued by Armenians. Anyway, you can see the influence of the linguist Nicholas Marr here, who was a Georgian on his mother's side. But, as Victor Astafyev rightfully pointed out, you're far from a Rustaveli."[10]

"Oh, no, no, no! Don't mention Astafyev and the Russians," Misha Polyakov interjected angrily. "Please, don't make me remind you of what Astafyev used to say about the Russians and the Armenians—nothing good will come of it."

---

[10] Nikolai Marr (1865–1934) was a controversial Georgian linguist whose work reached the height of its influence under Stalin. Victor Astafyev (1924–2001) was a popular Soviet and Russian writer. In the 1980s he was criticized for the chauvinism and xenophobia of his work. In the novel *Catching Gudgeons in Georgia* (1987), he repeatedly mocks the cult of Rustaveli.

"So, they performed the funeral rites of Hector, tamer of horses," Vadim Yankov declared, reciting the final line of *The Iliad* to end the first round of our Caucasian debate.[11]

In November of 1986, Rafik finished his prison sentence and was sent into exile. According to prison rules, in the last two months before a convict's release, he was allowed to let his hair grow long. Grow long, in this case, is something of an overstatement—hair can't grow much in only two months when it's been shaved down to the scalp. At least, that would be true for anyone but Rafik. In one month, Rafik's hair grew so long that it caused a scene that would make even Arkady Raikin, the famous stand-up comedian, envious. It happened during dinner when we were talking about Rafik's hair and about Armenian hair, in general. Suddenly, a tipsy Trifonov, one of the guards, stormed into the dining room and screamed at the top of his lungs: "Hats off!"

It was November, so a lot of us were wearing hats. Everyone took them off, including Rafik—all inmates become especially cautious before their release, even before their exile—and Rafik had never been a risk-taker to begin with.

"Take that sheepskin hat off, Papayan!" Trifonov yelled, approaching our table, but after everyone burst out laughing, he realized the origin of the sheepskin and joined in the fun:

"F . . . you all! Even hair grows differently for those Armenian democrats!"

"That will be the topic of my doctoral dissertation: *The Role of Democracy in Hair Growth Acceleration*," Rafik declared. (*Acceleration*, alongside *glasnost* and *perestroika*, was one of the most popular words of the Gorbachev era.)

"The Role of Democracy in Hair Growth Acceleration on the

---

[11] Homer. *The Iliad*. Translated by Robert Fitzgerald, Anchor Press/Doubleday, 1974, p. 594.

Armenian Head," Johnny Lashkarashvili corrected him, pointing in my direction: "As you can see, even democracy can't help a Georgian head." And he added a saying that only a Georgian can fully appreciate: "Even our ants are no use to us."[12]

Rafael Papayan later became the chair of the human rights committee in the Armenian parliament. Now he serves as a judge on the Constitutional Court of Armenia. Adding a mustache and a beard to his famously thick hair gave him a very distinguished look. He wrote an equally thick book, *The Christian Roots of Modern Justice*, and published an article in Lotman's journal. The Moscow publishing house UniPress SK printed a collection of his translations, *Armenian Poetry of the 20th Century: Selected Pages*, which includes his translations of sixteen Armenian poets, beginning with Hovhannes Tumanyan and ending with Hakob Movses. In the book's foreword, Papayan wrote that he'd decided to translate these poets purely out of love for their poetry. I remember how he'd talk for hours about Tumanyan, Isahakyan, Charents, Shiraz, Paruyr Sevak, and Misak Metsarents, so I can testify to that. Rafael also belongs to a rather small group of translators capable of doing translations in two directions—from Russian into Armenian and from Armenian into Russian.

Some years ago, a serious conflict ended the friendship between Rafik and Zhora. Rafik even published a few newspaper articles against him. It seems that rising to power requires serious sacrifices, and that the three-kopek-stamp approach was still a valid one in Rafik's life. But that stamp sent Rafik's letters to the wrong address.

---

[12] This is a reference to a passage in Nodar Dumbadze's novel *The Sunny Night*, in which one character mentions hearing on Voice of America about the discovery of a secretion from Spanish ants that makes hair grow. Another character responds: "Dammit, that's our luck! Even our ants are no use to us!" (See Dumbadze, Nodar. *The Sunny Night*. Translated by George Nakashidse, Washington Square Press, p. 172.)

After reading one of Rafik's latest newspaper triumphs, written in the most perfect Russian, of course, I recalled how he'd said that the Georgians forgot Mesrop's merits after the religious schism. Rafik and his friends very quickly forgot the merits of Georgy Khomizuri, who for many years fought for the preservation of Armenian history and for Armenian rights. But even after this decisive ideological divide, I can't forget the old Rafik, without his mustache and beard, a true craftsman who had yet to grow his hair back, sitting next to his night-stand creating, with his infinite patience, a device for making twelve *makhorka* cigarettes at a time.

HENRIKH

It's early morning on Friday, June 20, 1969. Even though Kharkiv is an industrial city and it's a work day, it's early enough that the streets are still empty. On Cosmonauts Street, three cars stop near an apartment building. Serious-looking men emerge from the cars and head purposefully for the first entryway. There are eleven of them: two investigators, seven officers, and two witnesses—two random passersby who spent the night in the Kharkiv Regional KGB along with the other nine. The two officers stay outside while the rest of them go up to the third floor. They proceed calmly and quietly, without hurry or fuss—it's obvious they know what they're doing. The officers take their positions at the top and bottom of the staircase. As soon as their positions are secured, the chief investigator rings the doorbell. You can hear the bell ringing behind the door, but no one answers. They ring again. The investigator smiles and knocks on the door, unhurried and unconcerned.

"Altunyan, open the door!" the chief investigator says without any threat in his voice. Thanks to the intelligence report, he's one hundred percent sure that Altunyan's at home. He knows when Altunyan arrived home the night before, where he was coming from, and why he returned. He also knows that the suspect hasn't gone out that morning. In general, he knows a lot of things. Not a single sound comes from behind the door.

"Open the door! We're from the Committee for State Security."

The door of the neighboring apartment opens, and a scared individual peeps out from behind the door. The chief investigator gives a sign and one of the officers sends the individual back into his apartment, goes inside with him, and firmly closes the door behind them.

"Altunyan, we know you're home!" the chief investigator says now in a loud voice, not doubting his information for a minute. He's sure that Altunyan is home, even more so, he knows that the suspect woke up half an hour ago, got up, had coffee, and started doing something. Meanwhile, there's not a sound coming from the apartment.

"Altunyan, it's better for you to open the door, or we'll break it down!" Now the chief investigator is almost shouting, but without any anger in his voice. He's a man who knows the worth of his own command. Nevertheless, it produces no result. With only a look, he gives a sign to his officers and they prepare to break down the door.

Suddenly, the door opens, black smoke pours out, and, surrounded by the smoke, a short, good-looking man in a military uniform appears, wearing glasses, a mustache, and a kind smile:

"I saw you from the window, my dear guests. So sorry I kept you waiting. I had a few extra papers at home, so it took me some time to burn them. My sincere apologies. But now, please, come in, good people, search as much as you like!"

"That's not a good sign," the chief investigator thought, paying special attention to that unnatural phrase, "good people." His hearing had been trained to detect the slightest anti-Soviet idiom—and this was a phrase from Bulgakov's *Master and Margarita*.

They entered the apartment and conducted a very scrupulous search. Not finding anything, they grabbed two books published in the Khruschev era, just in case, and left. Before they left, the chief investigator said: "We'll be back again, Major. Let me assure you, your circus performance this morning changes nothing. I'm sorry to tell you, but your fate has already been decided."

The chief investigator kept his word. On July 11, 1969, Major in the Soviet Air Force Henrikh Ovanesovich Altunyan, born in 1933 in the city of Tbilisi and now living in the city of Kharkiv on Cosmonauts Street, a member of the Communist Party of the Soviet Union until 1968, was arrested by the KGB. On November 26 of that same year, the Kharkiv regional court sentenced him to three years of incarceration. It was his first arrest.

He served his sentence in the Krasnodar region. Being an honest man, he didn't hide the fact that he still considered himself a Communist and a Leninist. During his first trial, he claimed that *he* was the true Leninist, not his KGB investigators. In prison, he read all of Lenin's works or, to be more precise, all of Lenin's works that were available in the prison library. If it happened that a multivolume collection wasn't complete, he'd raise a ruckus, demanding that the authorities restock the library. Interestingly, after he switched from Lenin to Marx, he began to have doubts and his belief system began to crack. This crack deepened, and after serving his first sentence, Henrikh left prison as a full-fledged anti-Soviet.

His metamorphosis wasn't lost on the Communist Party and the Soviet authorities. They also didn't forget that Altunyan was a member of a human rights activist group and that he'd protested Sakharov's exile. So his second sentence was for the maximum term stipulated in Article 70, the seven-plus-five term, i.e., seven years in a maximum-security prison followed by five years of exile.

Henrikh Ovanesovich Altunyan, or Genchik to his friends, was the kindest person I'd ever met in my life. He was transferred to our camp from the Chistopol prison. He was known to most of Barashevo's political inmates for his association with

Andrey Sakharov and General Pyotr Grigorenko, and as a legendary hero of the dissident movement. He began serving his sentence in Perm but managed to get into trouble even there, and his sentence was increased. From the eighth circle of hell, he was transferred to the ninth—to the isolation unit of a maximum-security prison.

When Henrikh was escorted to the camp, several of us were smoking *makhorka* outside the shack. As soon as the new inmate was spotted, the traditional intellectual game of political prisoners began: "Guess who I am and what my sentence is."

"Six months in solitary confinement," proposed Boris Manilovich, who was a real expert on the subject after doing solitary at the Petersburg Kresty and Moscow Lefortovo prisons.

"Too short," Misha Polyakov said, doubtfully. After spending that amount of time in the Kresty prison for having avoided arrest for one year and eight months, he'd become no less an expert on the subject. "It can't be fewer than nine months—look at the color of his face and the way he walks."

"Yes, but these days they don't keep anyone in solitary for nine months!" I said, surprised. During the Chernenko period newly-arrived inmates told us that the investigation process had been shortened to three months.

"Roman Jakobson compared a mountaineer walking on a flat surface to a poet talking about prose," said the omniscient Vadim Yankov, making an erudite allusion to Pasternak's famous novel: "Maybe, he's a doctor?"

"He's not a doctor. He's definitely a professional military man," Zhora Khomizuri said with confidence. "He's at least a captain or a major."

"His bearing and gait are very military," I agreed, recalling Major Kutsenko from our prison, who always walked with his back completely straight as if he were about to dance the *kartuli*.

"Maybe he's Georgian?" suggested Polyakov, who was well versed in the subject. "He's rather reserved."

"He looks more like an Armenian," I said.

"I don't think so, he's a bit too short," Rafik Papayan interjected.

"Unless my eyes deceive me, he's no shorter than Charles Aznavour," added Manilovich, who never missed a chance to say something witty.

"Even though he has a rather modest air about him, his bearing shows that he's someone important. If he's an officer, and we know that they don't keep anyone in solitary confinement for that long, then he might be coming from a maximum-security prison. Maybe, he was in the dungeon the whole time?" Misha Polyakov said, further developing our theory.

"He must've definitely been in the hole—you can only get a face that color in the hole," Manilovich said with confidence.

"If he's coming from the hole, and he's an officer, then we know him," Khomizuri said and called to the new inmate:

"Major Altunyan, we're waiting for you by the smoke shack!"

The convict approached us, nodded his head in lieu of a greeting, and reported with a smile:

"Major Henrikh Ovanesovich Altunyan, born in Tbilisi, Article 70, seven-plus-five, last location—Chistopol Prison, solitary confinement, nine months. Did you guess everything?"

"Yes, we did, everything but the place of birth," Zhora said.

We brought some food from our stockpile in the barracks, made our special "emergency" thermos tea, and soon had an official welcoming party for our new friend.

That evening, the Christian Federation of South Caucasian Nations once again had five members—after Dato's release, there were only four of us remaining. When it was time to vote on whether to admit him, the nominee requested the floor.

"Among so many Georgians, I'm the only one here who was born in Tbilisi. But you managed to create the South Caucasus Federation without any Tbilisians, which means that you're basically con artists! What would've happened to you if our dear KGB hadn't arrested me?"

In general, the dissidents and democrats were good people, and the scope of their interests was quite vast, but prior to Henrikh's arrival, soccer fans were rather underrepresented in our group. As it happened, Yankov had never been to a game, Misha, as a true Northerner, preferred hockey, and Zhora Khomizuri couldn't tell Neftchi from Pakhtakor. Henrikh changed all that—this Tbilisian was a Dinamo fan, and, at the same time, he was a big-time "Brazilian." Our "Brazilian dialogues" gradually became a spectacle and attracted dozens of people at any given time.

"My dear Levan, do you remember the year 1970?" Henrikh used to ask me, and then the show would begin:

"How can I not remember 1970? That year, Mao Zedong accused the USSR of neocolonialism, a Boeing 747 flew for the first time, Paul McCartney announced the breakup of the Beatles, the events in Cambodia began, there was a terrible earthquake in Peru, the Brazinskas, father and son, hijacked the Sukhumi-Batumi airplane, killing the flight attendant Nadezhda Kurchenko in the course of the operation, Salvador Allende became the President of Chile, Sakharov, along with Chalidze and Tverdokhlebov, founded the Committee on Human Rights in the USSR, the Americans invented the 'mouse,' I graduated from high school and enrolled in the State Polytechnic Institute, and for the third time, the Brazilian national team won the world championship at the Azteca stadium in Mexico City and took the Jules Rimet Cup home forever."

"I think they played the Italians in the finals," Henrikh said, deftly skipping over all the other events and explaining to our audience: "At that time, the Italian national team had won the World Championship twice, but that all happened before the war, in 1934 and 1938, with a lot of help from Mussolini."

"The Brazilian national team also won the World

Championship twice, in 1958 and in 1962, but after an unlucky performance at the 1966 World Championship in England, they had to fight their way back to the top."

"Do you remember the date of that game?"

"June 21, 1970. There were one hundred eight thousand spectators in the Azteca stadium, even though it could accommodate only one hundred thousand."

"Well said! Let's begin with the rosters. I'm a bit older than you, so I remember things better. So, for the Italian national team, the goalkeeper was Albertosi, the defenders, Facchetti and Burgnich, the midfielders, Rivera and Mazzola, and the forwards, Riva and Boninsegna."

"What, they played soccer with only seven players?"

"I can't remember any of the others—so that's that."

"Let's go through the Brazilians: Their goalkeeper was Félix, their defenders, Brito, Everaldo, Clodualdo, and Alberto, their midfielders, Gérson, Jairzinho, and Rivellino, and the forwards, Tostão and Pelé."

"There's one player missing," Henrikh said, trying to get even.

And with such conversations, we tried to raise the level of soccer literacy in our camp. For the first time, our fellow-inmates heard about Jules Rimet and the existence of the Cup named after him, about Kurt Hamrin, Tofiq Bahramov, Beckenbauer, Cruyff, Mário Zagallo, Telê Santana, the Italian vendetta of 1982, and about many other soccer myths and legends.

Henrikh also came up with many interesting ideas, for example, an evening of storytelling. In this competition, each participant had to present an impromptu story on a given topic in front of a distinguished panel of judges. To lighten the judges' burden, all the participants had to submit one topic to the common pool. The jury's job was to make sure that a contestant didn't get his own topic. The winner of the competition would get a matchbox full of tea as the prize.

The generally acknowledged wise man Vadim Yankov was

unanimously elected to chair the panel. As his assistants, Vadim chose two friends of literature (as he called them)—the well-known pharmacist Arnold Anderson and Professor Vitautas Skuodis of the Lithuanian State University. After that, the competition was officially opened. Boris Manilovich drew the first number, so Anderson fished out one of the neatly cut pieces of paper from the little bag and announced the topic for Boris's story. Boris presented a lyrical vignette about a cat named Gipsy, which was favorably received by the audience. It should be noted that the cat Gipsy was sitting right there, nodding his head in a rather distinguished manner, as if to say: "Of course, I understood everything."

After that, it was Zhora's turn, then mine, and after me— Johnny's. Zhora's story was based on a well-known anecdote about a Soviet dissident who, after emigrating to America, would see the Russian newscast *Vremya* in his dreams. My vignette was about a forbidden zone, and Johnny got the topic of our doctor Tamara, which he turned into a very funny Russian-Georgian sketch. When he had problems with his Russian, he would insolently, without warning, switch to Georgian, to the complete admiration of his audience. Everyone was laughing.

Henrikh told the last story. Anderson plunged his hand into the little bag, pulled a piece of paper out, and read the topic aloud with an air of utmost importance: Jailkeeper. Henrikh requested a thirty-second pause and then began his story:

> The title of my story is "The Best People." Once upon a time, our favorite jailkeeper took his yearly vacation—after all, he was a person, too. He was so much of a person, he even had a mother! When she saw her long-lost son, that very mother started asking him about everything—about this and about that—in the greatest detail. Mother and son talked for a long time. They drank two quarts of vodka, ate half a pound of cured pork fat, and finished half a loaf of black bread. Even though our jailkeeper had gotten pretty drunk, he was not a simpleton—he was after all *our* jailkeeper. He didn't

say anything of importance to his mother and didn't betray any state secrets. He didn't even tell her which prison he worked in. After their long and fruitful discussion, the mother finally came to the classic question posed in all Soviet kitchens: "What's happening? Where is it all leading to? Where are the people who can save our country?" And here, our jailkeeper threw caution to the wind and, with a deep sigh, calmly told his dear mother: "I know where those people are, I see them every day. I'm their jailkeeper."

Henrikh won first prize. The winner then put his trophy tea into the thermos, added another matchbox from his own stash, poured in some boiling water, and began the process of "marrying the tea" until it reached the desired strength. With our first and only glass, we toasted, of course, to the talented author and his story about good people. I was the toastmaster of this unplanned feast, and my toast, which was longer than the winning story, was favorably received.

Henrikh was born in Tbilisi, near Zemel Square. He used to say: "I'm Tbilisian, and I'm Armenian, but I'm definitely not a Tbilisian Armenian—that's a different phenomenon. For that you have to be born in the Avlabari neighborhood." His family lived on what was formerly Moscow Street. Now it's Brothers Kakabaze Street. As a child, he'd begun to attend the famous School No. 51, but then his father got transferred to another military division, and the family left Tbilisi. Henrikh knew the area around Zemel Square very well and liked to talk about it with Johnny and me. His knowledge of Tbilisi's streets was astounding, and he'd often amaze us by telling us something new about our own neighborhoods. For example, I learned for the first time, from Henrikh, that it was possible to get from Zemel Square to my street, Vedzini, without taking Rustaveli Avenue and the upper road. After being released from prison, I checked out his shortcut and called him in Kharkiv to say: "You know, following your directions, I made it from your place to my house without even thinking of going to Rustaveli Avenue and the high road."

I told Henrikh about the remarkable Tbilisian writer Aghasi Ayvazyan and gave him a book with the wonderful short story "The Gospel of Avlabari." Two days later, he returned the book to me saying that he didn't need it anymore because he'd learned the story by heart. It's not a long story, granted, but after teaching for some time, I believed that when Henrikh said "by heart," he actually meant "more or less"— that is, until I heard him recite it:

> You can see everything from Avlabari. All of Tbilisi with its narrow streets—Shaytan-bazar, Erivani Square, Mylnaya Street, Narikala, St. Sarkis Church, Sioni Cathedral, a Greek church . . . From Avlabari, you can see the rich mansions of Khatisov and Melick-Kazarov, Tamamshev's caravanserai, the theaters of Ter-Osipov and Zubalov, the sulfur baths . . .

Henrikh especially fell in love with Sarkisov's tavern, which sells "intoxication for the price of two *abazis*" [an *abazi* is a small Georgian coin]. As Ayvazyan explained it, this meant that "it's not that the wine costs two *abazis*, but for two *abazis*, you can drown yourself in wine. No matter how much you drink, the price stays the same." Henrikh would often read aloud this story about the unlucky love of Mirza Asaturyan as proof that love is a very serious business, and that the women we love are as capable of filling us with delight as they are of dragging us through the mud in front of the entire world. Meanwhile, as the story goes, before Asaturyan met his love, he was famous throughout the city as the wisest and the most educated of men. He was, quite simply, a walking library. In the Sololaki neighborhood, he would speak Armenian, in the Vakhi neighborhood—Georgian, in the churchyard, he would speak the Old Armenian language of Grabar, he would speak Ashkhabar to the wine-growers, on the Palace Square, he would use Russian, on the Turkish *maidan*—Persian, on the Brick Square—German, and with the people of Avlabari, of course, he would speak their own Avlabari dialect.

At this point Johnny Lashkarashvili would interrupt and say:

"You have so many languages, you know—there's Armenian, then there's Grabar, and then Ashkhabar and even Avlabarian—and you cry endlessly in all of them."

"Well, you can't accuse me of that, Johnny-*jan*. I'm a cheerful man. In solitary confinement, I would read Nodar Dumbaze in Georgian and die laughing."

"How come? You understood everything?" Johnny asked, suspiciously.

"What's not to understand? That the pig Serapiona had a litter or that Illarion shot Murad?"

"If you love Nodar Dumbadze so much, then perhaps you know what he wrote about our war criminals?" I asked. "If a Georgian soldier who'd been captured by the Germans was later interrogated by the Soviet secret police, he'd simply say: 'I don't know how I ended up being captured. Commissar Kutubidze put me on a train in Sadzhavakho, and the next thing I knew, the door was being opened by a German soldier.'"

Henrikh was drinking tea when he heard that. He choked, then started gasping for air. We had to resuscitate him—he was literally about to die from laughter. Later he tried to tell this story to the war criminals, but none of them found it funny. It seems that only a soldier sent by Major Kutubize or Georgians who remained at home could laugh about "finding yourself in captivity," and, of course, our jovial fellow-inmate Henrikh.

During his prison-free years, Henrikh happened to see the movie *Mimino*, and, of course, he knew all the popular dialogues by heart. And so Henrikh and I would use this movie as our special language.

"Levan-*jan*, 'Now, I'll tell you one very wise thing, but please, don't get upset,'" Henrikh would begin, imitating Frunzik, a character from *Mimino*, and then continue telling some sentimental or cautionary tale. I wonder how the person who wrote these dialogues managed to not die laughing. When I told Henrikh that the scriptwriter was Rezo Gabriadze, he was pleased—he knew Gabriadze back in Moscow, but he wouldn't say how and under what circumstances he'd made his acquaintance. That was the kind of man Henrikh was—he would never say more than was necessary. But it was obvious that he had only positive things to say about Gabriadze.

Henrikh had done time in many prison camps and transit stations along the Stolypin line, where he met an enormous number of inmates and learned amazing things. And if Yankov knew the information in every book and Johnny knew how many men, women, and children were in every country, Henrikh knew what was on people's minds in every city and village, on every street, in every district, region, and continent. As a true man of the Caucasus, he collected many stories in the hopes that, one day, he could slip them into his toasts. In one prison, he happened to meet a former district attorney for the city of Kiev who had a lot of stories to share. Once this prosecutor demanded that the court deliver a guilty verdict in a case that shocked even our hard-bitten Henrikh. A man was sentenced to five years in prison for "undermining the authority of the collective-farming system," which in reality meant that the unfortunate man had dared to wear his old boots when he had a new pair. Henrikh was laughing as he told us the story—the prosecutor ended up in prison too! And this rather unexpected conclusion made its way into a toast: "Let's drink, my friends, to Levan Berdzenishvili's old leather boots and his most enviable felt *valenki*!" (My release time was approaching, and many friends were eyeing my *valenki* and my old boots, hoping to buy them from me.)

I'm sure Henrikh was a brilliant teacher. His explanations were fantastic and he could present any material vividly and imaginatively, never complicating a subject and always avoiding intellectual abstractions. I'm sure that the lectures of Air Force Major Altunyan, a professor at the Kharkiv Military Engineering School of Aviation, covered a very broad range of topics. Being an open-minded person, he could see and appreciate context. Once, he asked me if I'd ever thought about the fact that Rustaveli and Richard the Lionheart lived at the same time and so, possibly, knew one other or at least had mutual acquaintances—just as I had mutual acquaintances with Andrey Sakharov.

He had seen a lot and gone through so much, but he never lost his sense of humor. Once he told me: "I spent an entire month in the hole at Chistopol, and you'd think that nothing worse could happen in life. But when Zico messed up the penalty shot in the game with France, that poisoned my soul, and at that moment the hole seemed like heaven to me."

In political prisons, everyone was technically equal, but, in reality, there was a hidden internal hierarchy. A prisoner's place in this hierarchy was determined by his inner life and outward dignity, as well as other factors—sentence length being first among them. Naturally, an inmate sentenced to the maximum term under Article 70, the infamous seven-plus-five, would be held in the highest esteem. If someone had already served a part of this sentence, then his authority would grow even higher. Based on all these rules, Henrikh should've been at the top of the ladder, but he didn't care for hierarchies. He never considered himself better than anyone else and never took advantage of his authority—he was both dignified and modest. In a word, Henrich had class—and as the Russians say, class is not something you can drink away.

After the collapse of the Soviet Union, during the first round of elections to the Ukrainian Rada, the people of the city of Kharkiv elected Henrikh Altunyan, an Armenian born in Tbilisi, as their representative from the People's Movement of Ukraine. His memoir, *The Price of Freedom*, is one of the best memoirs ever written by a Soviet dissident, and it is a very kind book, too. As one of his friends said: "It's impossible to read this book—it makes everyone seem like such a good person!" His recipe was simple: Henrikh wrote only about the people he loved, without ever mentioning anyone he found unworthy.

Henrikh had done a lot for the Crimean Tatars, even though they had nothing in common—not blood, culture, religion, or homeland. He simply knew that truth was on the side of this people who had been herded into train cars like cattle and exiled. And Henrikh fought for this truth—this is why in Crimea he is still remembered with high regard.

During the Ukrainian Orange Revolution, Henrikh Altunyan addressed the crowd on Independence Square: "The events that are happening right now happen only once in a person's life. And at least once in our lives, we need to have a heart!" The people greeted his words with great enthusiasm.

At one point, a discussion took place about the lyrics of the Ukrainian national anthem. Apparently, the first version had made an unfavorable mention of some ethnic groups living in Ukraine. As we learned later, Henrikh expressed that it was unacceptable for a country that dreams of European democracy to have such an anthem, at which point, one "true Ukrainian" woman, who was also a dissident, asked him why he, an Armenian, was worried about their anthem in the first place. He endured many such slights.

In the spring of 2005, Henrikh suddenly became very ill and was immediately flown to Israel, probably with the help of Natan Sharansky, a friend from the Perm prison who later became a minister in the Israeli government. The surgery was successful, but Henrikh's body, exhausted from the time spent in Perm Prison #36, Barashevo Prison ZhKh 385/3-5, and Chistopol Prison, developed complications, and this man who felt equally at home in Tbilisi, Kharkiv, and many other Soviet cities left this world in a far-off country.

Mikhail Vasilievich Polyakov, or Misha to his friends, was a true Petersburger. He looked stereotypically Nordic, but with unusually dark skin. His face, with its sharp features, reminded me of Varlam Shalamov, the sublime author of *Kolyma Tales*. He also happened to be the first cousin of Marina Vlady (Marina Vladimirovna Poliakoff-Baïdaroff), a popular French actress and the wife of Vladimir Vysotsky, the legendary Russian singer-songwriter and actor.

In any Soviet prison, groups of prisoners from Leningrad always made up a significant part of the inmate population, although the names of those groups might differ from camp to camp. The fact is that throughout its history, the former Russian capital has been renamed several times: from Saint Petersburg to Petrograd, then from Petrograd to Leningrad, and finally back to Saint Petersburg. This city even has its own nickname—Piter (pronounced with the stress on the first syllable). The inmates from Tsar Peter's city preferred to be called by the city name they were using, depending on their political orientation, at the time of their arrest. In our political camp, the Petersburg group was represented by Mikhail Polyakov, Heliy Donskoy, Boris Manilovich, Nikolay Tolstykh, Eugene Solonchuk, and Mikhail Kazachkov. With the exception of the joker Eugene, who used to work as a road construction worker, all the members of our Petersburg group were college-educated. Donskoy and Manilovich even held Ph.D.

Donskoy and Polyakov were not only true representatives

SACRED DARKNESS · 101

of the Russian intelligentsia, but also descendants of old Russian aristocracy. Heliy Donskoy was a direct descendant of Prince Dmitry Donskoy, the hero of the Battle of Kulikovo, who defeated the powerful commander of the Golden Horde, Mamai. I don't know if Heliy's sense of humor can be traced back to the glorious Grand Prince of Vladimir, but it was certainly of a rather peculiar nature, especially when it came to sex. Once, for example, Heliy Donskoy told Polyakov in front of all of us:

"Misha, you're going to be released before me. After you leave, do try my wife—you'll be pleased. She's not so bad."

This proposal shocked the usually calm and levelheaded Polyakov: "C'mon, Heliy, think what you're saying. These people from the Caucasus don't understand your idiotic Russian humor!"

Johnny Lashkarashvili then got upset: "Can someone explain to me what's so funny about this?"

While Donskoy was roaring with laughter, Boris Manilovich began citing Freud. Later, Misha joined the fun, explaining to Johnny that it's Donskoy's third wife, that he loves her dearly, but that he's in prison dying of grief and jealousy, so he expresses his love with stupid jokes. "You don't have a wife, so you don't get it!"

Seeing the Russians dying of laughter, I began laughing too. Instantly, Johnny started scolding me:

"And why are you laughing? You're married!"

It wasn't an easy task to navigate the labyrinth of permissions and bans imposed by the Soviet Union. For example, in the political prisons, prohibited items included red ballpoint pens, any kind of fountain pen, toothpaste (we were only allowed tooth powder, which our relatives rushed all over to find), deodorant, eau de cologne, gloves, and many other items. There were also prohibited games, such as cards and soccer, while volleyball, Ping-Pong, checkers, chess, and

backgammon were allowed. However, the KGB didn't prohibit shooting dice, "a generator of random numbers," as the
omniscient Vadim Yankov referred to it. Up to this day, I can't
figure out the KGB's logic.

Misha Polyakov and Heliy Donskoy played backgammon.
There was something mysterious in their game. First of all,
when the pieces were scattered, it was strange to hear: "Five
and five, six and five, three and two" instead of the Persian and
Turkish terms I was used to: "*Du besh, shashi besh, and ce bai
du.*" Another strange thing was that Misha and Heliy moved
their pieces soundlessly, without any of the clatter so typical of
backgammon. The third and the strangest thing was their total
lack of emotion—the players didn't curse fate, didn't call the
pieces "dog bones" or comment sarcastically on the other
player's decisions. They didn't cast doubt on their opponent's
intellectual abilities in public, and most importantly, they didn't
swear, which is so natural for a Russian in everyday speech. But
our Petersburg friends very quickly figured things out after
they caught onto the "backgammon song" they heard when I
played with Johnny. We played short backgammon, and I tried
to follow the example of my backgammon idols—my father,
my father-in-law, and my mother-in-law—imitating their style
as closely as I could by commenting on my opponent's moves
in the most colorful language: "*Du yake* and may your dog
bone go to f . . . *du ce!*" Johnny would answer: "Here's *ce bay
du* for you!" Inspired by our example, Misha and Heliy finally
began making the obligatory backgammon commotion, and,
most importantly, they hit their pieces with such force that they
were sometimes even louder than the Georgians. It certainly
would've made the Persian shahs or Afghani caliphs proud.
Pleased with his heightened emotions, Misha told us
Georgians: "Yeah, I see now . . . It's obvious that you guys are
here on a cultural exchange."

In the end, the Russians referred to the pieces in Persian—

du desh, *du bara*, and so on. Rafael Papayan, who was the expert in long backgammon, even tried to convince them to switch to the long version, but the Russians stayed faithful to their one true love.

Before his arrest, Mikhail Polyakov was in charge of the IT department at the Mikhail Saltykov-Shchedrin Leningrad State Public Library, and over the course of many years he used his department's copy machines to print anti-Soviet literature. He set his own daily quota, five hundred pages a day, and with the zeal of Alexey Stakhanov, one of the first heroes of Socialist Labor, he surpassed his quota year after year. At a time when the mere possession of such a photocopied work would be enough to warrant an accusation of anti-Soviet agitation and propaganda, resulting in a prison sentence, Polyakov made copies of approximately two thousand books and distributed them throughout the Soviet Union. In the end, the KGB could find only six volumes out of that sea of photocopied books. For comparison, I can tell you that my wife and I produced only thirteen copies of the first issue of our Republican Party's newspaper *Samreklo*, or *Bell Tower*.

For one year and nine months prior to his arrest, Misha had been hiding from the world-renowned Soviet State Security Services—an organization that was the first of its kind in terms of the number of employees and agents, covert and non-covert, per capita and was vastly superior to any other organization that came before it. For eleven of the twenty-one months Misha was on the run, he was on the USSR's most wanted list—no other political prisoners had such impressive statistics, but Misha never boasted. I had to dig this information out of him piece by piece over the course of many years. While the KGB was conducting its futile search, Misha traveled throughout the entire Soviet Union, including Georgia, where he visited Tbilisi and, moving west, almost reached my hometown of Batumi—making it as far as

Samtredia. He kept his contacts from that time a deep secret. He wouldn't tell us who those people were, not only while we were in prison, but even several years after our release. Only when Misha came to congratulate us on Georgia's independence did he finally introduce us to the people who had hidden him before his arrest.

Polyakov was sentenced to five years in a maximum-security labor camp and three years of exile, but his case wasn't closed. Once a year, a delegation from the Leningrad KGB would visit him in the prison, hoping in vain to break Misha down and obtain some information about the distribution channels for anti-Soviet literature. On one occasion, a new generation Chekist arrived, someone named Koshelyov. When I say new generation, I mean that this young man was a cynical Chekist, one who supported the idea of a nationalist state and not only cared little for Communists, but also spoke of the Communist Party with open disdain. Unable to get anything out of Misha, he talked to all of us, explaining his vision of the Soviet Union's future—an empire without the Communist Party in the leading role. Here Khomizuri interrupted him: "By refusing the leading role to the Communist Party, your empire will quickly collapse, and the KGB will be buried under its ruins." (Unfortunately, as is usually the case with such forecasts, Zhora's prediction only partially came true.) After Koshelyov indulged us with a discussion of Russia's omnipotence, Polyakov pointed out that if we loved Russia, then we should want her to exit the Soviet Union. Annoyed, Koshelyov gave up and went back to Leningrad.

Once, our infamous censor Ganichenko summoned Misha and handed him a telegram from his wife with the classic text: "I'm sorry, darling, I'm in love with someone else." According to Soviet law, as soon as a person denounces his/her spouse-inmate, the marriage is annulled. So, Misha went to Censor Ganichenko's office as a married man and left it as single man or, to use Manilovich's language, a playboy. However, to tell you the truth, the usually stolid and serious Polyakov didn't just leave the administration building—he flew out of it on the wings of happiness, declaring in front of his friends from Moscow, Petersburg, and Tbilisi that the poor Chekists didn't realize what a favor they'd done him. Barely a week had passed when Misha demanded to be married to Nadezhda, the woman he was really in love with. The prison administration wouldn't hear of it and the Leningrad KGB in particular was determined not to let the marriage happen. However, the entire international dissident community stood up, the West raised its voice, and Polyakov prevailed. Mikhail and Nadezhda Polyakov spent their two-day honeymoon in the ZhKh 385/3-5 room for conjugal visits. Polyakov came to his wedding carrying a bouquet of red roses, which grew in our prison camp.

To play Ping-Pong, we used a prison-made table that was rather far from professional standards, but the ball and paddles were authentic enough. For some reason, there were only a few Ping-Pong fans among us. Actually, not many of us played any games at all—there were only four chess players (with Manilovich as their leader), some backgammon players (where the Georgians held the leading position), and two volleyball teams: the Democrats (inmates convicted for anti-Soviet agitation and propaganda, along with two spies and one war criminal) and the Academics (professors, lecturers, and scientists). In political prisons, your indictment was a matter of public knowledge as it had to be presented upon request. And since my indictment stated that I was arrested while carrying my dissertation to a typist, the prison camp, in order to strengthen the Academics' team, gave me a "pass" on my undefended dissertation, bestowing an honorary Ph.D. upon yours truly.

As it turned out, Ping-Pong had the fewest fans, and most of the time it was just Polyakov and I playing against each other. Strangely enough, at some point the score would inevitably become zero-seven. Not a stranger to drinking, Polyakov was always amused by this combination, zero-seven—which was a slang term for the standard volume of Soviet alcohol bottles, 0.7 ml. As soon as the score would become zero-seven, we players would pour, right on the spot, some tea from our thermos, and Polyakov would come up with an impromptu toast, thus improving his mastery of Georgian traditions with every game. When my brother Dato and his wife visited Leningrad after our release, Polyakov invited them to his place. When the old friends gathered around the table, Dato was appointed toastmaster, but very soon the host took over and, just like Boris Pasternak, presented a beautiful example of how to conduct a dinner party in the best tradition of the sophisticated Georgian art of hosting.

In Barashevo, Ping-Pong had one exotic feature—there was a third energetic player-fan, who would join in. This wonderful creature's name was Gipsy because his fur was as black as pitch. There were only three cats in our prison camp—the very old cat Vasika, the fine young cat Gipsy, and the sweet gentle Ada, her full name being Adelaida Grigorievna Mazur-Donskoy as her guardians were Grisha Feldman, Dmitro Mazur, and Heliy Donskoy. Gipsy took part in our Ping-Pong games, trying to intercept the ball and jumping from one side of the net to the other. He would achieve his goal only at the score of zero-seven, when he could finally grab the ball as we listened to Polyakov's colorful toasts.

Being a rationalist to the bone, Misha was an adamant opponent of conspiracy theories. First of all, he didn't believe the myth of the Soviet State Security as omnipotent, ubiquitous, and invincible. When we would talk about violent intrigues and highly sophisticated operations conducted by the KGB during our secret suppers, Polyakov would politely interrupt us and say with a smile: "No, guys, it's a total mess over there!" Once we were discussing the KGB's secret operations abroad and began talking about Andrey Amalrik's death in Spain; there was talk that the author of *Will the Soviet Union Survive Until 1984?* couldn't possibly have died in a car crash without KGB involvement, to which Misha responded with a quotation from a masterpiece of dissident folklore:

> A car is following me—it's a Volga,
> But I am sure that it's the CIA!

He didn't believe that the KGB was capable of conducting such a serious operation in Spain. He used to say that all those myths were created by one of the KGB departments, and then they would use their numerous agents to spread those rumors among the masses. For the Soviet KGB, sophisticated methods were foreign: The weapon of a Russian man was, is, and always will be an axe. But if a secret operation were conducted with an axe, the mystery would easily be solved. (When, many years later, the Russian Secret Service, descendants of the Soviet KGB, eliminated their former agent Alexander Litvinenko, the English quickly detected their new axe in the form of Polonium-210.)

In Misha's indictment, it was stated that he had copied, stored, and distributed anti-Soviet books by Alexander Solzhenitsyn, Andrey Platonov, Varlam Shalamov, and others, as well as articles and letters to the government by Andrey Sakharov. Time passed, and at the beginning of perestroika and glasnost, the Soviet literary magazines began publishing formerly prohibited books. Misha declared that until they published Bulgakov's *Heart of a Dog* and Platonov's *The Foundation Pit*, he wouldn't believe in their perestroika. Collectively, we subscribed to almost all the major national and republican newspapers and literary magazines (after the prison store, it was the only way to use the money we'd earned through our hard labor). And so, it began: In 1986, the journal *Znamya* published Bulgakov's masterpiece *Heart of a Dog*, then the journal *Novy Mir* published Platonov's *The Foundation Pit*, and the journal *Neva*—Akhmatova's *Requiem*. Armed with these publications, Misha went to see the prison's warden, Major Shalin, and asked him a question:

"I was sentenced to five years of maximum-security prison and three years of exile for nonprofit distribution of these books, and now our Soviet government publishes the very same books in millions of copies and makes big money from it. So, what are we being punished for?"

Shalin answered him: "Get out of here, Polyakov! My heart is almost broken as it is. I'm afraid to even open *Pravda* or *Izvestiya*—afraid of seeing what anti-Soviet thing they've published now! As for your sentence, I can't help you with that, but here, if you want, you can have the latest issue of *Ogonyok*. It has Polikarpov's article about Fedor Raskolnikov and Raskolnikov's "Open Letter to Stalin"—a real bombshell. Only last year it would have gotten you a sentence of seven-plus-five, but now it's published in all the leading magazines!"

Polyakov left, waving the issue of *Ogonyok* and repeating the well-known lines from dissident folklore:

> Who is knocking at my door?
> Just the man I'm waiting for.
> He's going to give me a ride:
> Seven-plus-five, seven-plus-five![13]

As I've mentioned before, seven-plus-five—seven years of maximum-security labor camp plus five years of exile—was the maximum punishment stipulated in Part 1 Article 70 of the

[13] This is a variation of a nursery rhyme, "Postman" by Samuil Marshak. In *Verses for Children*. Translated by Margaret Wettlin, Foreign Languages Publishing House, 1959, p. 23.

Criminal Code of Russian SFSR (Article 71 of the Criminal Code of Georgia) for anti-Soviet agitation and propaganda.

Misha loved our singer-songwriters and knew the lyrics of Alexander Galich, Vladimir Vysotsky, Bulat Okudzhava, and Eugene Klyachkin by heart. When Heliy Donskoy sang their songs, Misha always corrected the words. Heliy would take the only guitar in our prison and begin singing the famous hit by Klyachkin:

> If you draw a circle with a cigarette,
> you'll put a dot on the snow
> with your burning match.
> We should try to save the precious things,
> but we never save them—that's for sure.
> It could be a goldfish
> I could capture with my hat, if I wished.
> It seemed so malleable at first
> but it turned out to be unstable.

And Misha used to correct him all the time: "It's not 'that's for sure' but 'for sure,' my dear Heliy." But Heliy would be adamant, responding: "Klyachkin played it at my house, and I remember what he sang very well." Then, squinting his eyes, Misha would ask: "By the way, how many bottles of vodka would Klyachkin drink?" "Usually, three," Heliy would answer. "Well, after three bottles, how can you trust him? And especially yourself?"

During one feast, where tea took the place of wine, the members of the South Caucasian Christian Federation started a light, somewhat entertaining, discussion about the nationality of Bulat Okudzhava.

"He's a Georgian, the son of Shalva Okudzhava," I declared.

"His mother was Armenian, hence, he's Armenian," Rafik insisted.

Instantly, Vadim Yankov provided us with an encyclopedia entry:

His father, Shalva Stepanovich Okudzhava, was, of course, Georgian, and his mother, Askhen Stepanovna Naldabyan, was a Tbilisi Armenian. It was a family of Communists who came to Moscow to study at the Communist Party School, and Bulat Shalovich was born and grew up there, in Moscow, on Arbat Street, in a communal apartment on the fourth floor of building # 43. And while I don't know whether he's Georgian or Armenian, I know for sure he's a Muscovite. His father was executed by firing squad on August 4, 1937, and his mother was arrested and sent to the city of Karaganda. She returned from exile only in 1955.

Misha, who was in charge of "the feast," offered a compromise: "From a Georgian father and an Armenian mother, we have a Russian poet who hates Stalin because of his love for his father and who loves Sergey Kirov because of his love for his mother (she worked with Kirov). You Georgians don't need Okudzhava—you have enough poets of your own. To pacify the Armenians, I'd offer them this: Leave Okudzhava to us, and we Petersburgers will admit the Armenian roots and the very long arms of Yuri Dolgoruky, the founder of Moscow."[14] (We were lucky there were no Muscovites at the feast.)

Cinematography was Misha's passion. He could easily navigate his way through the ocean of the world's best motion pictures, but there was one director whom he always mentioned with particular affection—the great Georgian director Otar Iosseliani. Misha knew all the maestro's movies down to the smallest detail, beginning with his first student film *Aquarelle*, which Iosseliani made in 1957 during his junior year, and ending with his masterpieces, *Once Upon a Time There Was a Singing Blackbird* (1970) and *Pastoral* (1975).

The movie *Aquarelle* was based on the story of the same name by Alexander Grin. The husband is a drunk and the wife

[14] The Russian name *Dolgoruky* means "long-armed."

(played by Sofiko Chiaureli) washes clothes for a living. To buy a drink, the husband steals the last money his wife earned and leaps out the window. His wife runs after him and the chase ends in an art gallery, where, suddenly, they're facing a watercolor drawing of their old house. In the picture, the house is warm and cozy, not as they remember it. And sadness descends. In the final shots, we see the whole family—husband, wife, and their four children—sitting in front of the house while the artist paints their portrait. Polyakov loved *Aquarelle*. He was especially pleased by Iosseliani's appearance in the movie in the role of an art expert, who, with his noticeable Georgian accent, says: "Look at this great picture. Warmth pours from this drawing. The inhabitants must be beautiful, honest, noble, and pure people."

I had a chance to see *Aquarelle* many years later and was amazed that Polyakov hadn't missed a single detail, not a single nuance from this old movie, in which you can already see the future master.

When Misha gave us his famous first lecture on Otar Iosseliani, the psychiatrist and poet Boris Manilovich, who was the chief psychologist of our prison, noticed that the romantic realism of Alexander Grin was perfectly aligned with the Georgian temperament. Then he added that Grin's real name was Grinevsky, that he was a Polish aristocrat, and that he was almost related to Polyakov by nationality and class. But Misha refused to acknowledge this "class theory," saying that the movie's success had nothing to do with Grin, whose story was just raw material for Otar, and that Iosseliani didn't need Grin's story to make a great movie—he could make one from cast iron. He was referring to Iosseliani's 1964 documentary that he'd made at the Rustavi Steelworks, where the blast furnaces and the people worked in unison to create the final product. Iosseliani showed the beauty and resourcefulness of people who know and love their job.

Many years would pass, the century and the millennium would change, and Misha would give me a gift of the nineteen-DVD collection of Iosseliani's movies, beginning with his famous *Pastoral* and ending with *Gardens in Autumn* (2006).

Misha supported the independence struggle of the Baltic Republics and Georgia with all his heart. In April of 1989, he and his wife came to Tbilisi to pay homage to the April 9th victims and, on his own behalf, to ask the Georgian people for forgiveness. He visited Lithuania as well to offer his condolences to the victims of the January events in Vilnius. In the end, Misha declared that it became impossible for him to live any longer in Russia.

"My Russia is dead," he said and left for the United States.

Misha's wife, Nadezhda, died tragically, and he had to raise his children alone in a strange land. The people of St. Petersburg named Misha citizen of note of their city and entered his name in the city's encyclopedia. Often when I hear talk about conquerors and their cultures, and when people who are mad at Putin and the Russian Federation begin attacking Dostoevsky (one of our ministers of education even called him a bad writer), I recall one of the greatest people I had the good fortune to meet—Mikhail Polyakov, who was born in the very building where Dostoevsky lived.

BORYA

A vision often appears before me from Mordovia, the village of Barashevo in the Tengushevsky District, and the political prison ZhKh 385/3-5. It's as clear as a shot by Antonioni or some other talented director: The two of us are standing next to the forbidden zone, we're dressed in striped prisoner jackets, and we're almost touching the wire fence. From the watchtower in the corner a vigilant prison guard stands watch, pointing his Kalashnikov rifle straight at us. It's cold and dark. Snow is falling. The poet recites his poem, then asks me in a trembling voice: "Did you feel it?"

I don't remember the poem—I've forgotten the rhymes, rhythms, length, and words—but I remember how it made me feel. I remember how excited he was, my fellow-inmate, the poet from Petersburg. And I remember feeling so special and grateful for having had the privilege of being the first to hear those verses.

The poet's name was Borya—Boris Isaakovich Manilovich—born in 1940. He was a psychologist and, as a true Soviet dissident and intellectual, he had a second, more practical, occupation—as an electrician. He was arrested on November 11, 1982, in Leningrad. The Leningrad regional court found him guilty of a socially dangerous act as stipulated in Part 1 Article 70 of the Criminal Code of the RSFSR. He was sentenced to four years in a maximum-security prison followed by two years of internal exile. It was a high-profile case. Before Manilovich, two leaders of this group had been arrested—first, Vyacheslav Dolinin, and then Rostislav Yevdokimov. We knew about this group arrest because the information had found its way into an issue of the underground publication *The Chronicles of Current Events*, the Bible of *samizdat*. (Incidentally, there was a report about Vadim Yankov's arrest in the same issue.)

Boris was a man of puns. He loved plays on words so much that occasionally he would be imprisoned by his own wit—after making his way into the linguistic depths, he often had a hard time getting back out. His work as a psychiatrist also gave the inmates reason to say that Boris himself was a little cuckoo.

All his life Boris had been a victim of anti-Semitism, and he couldn't escape that misfortune even in a political prison full of democrats and liberals. There was an older inmate, Pavelsons, who would talk only to his fellow Lithuanians, and to Latvians and Georgians. He considered all others unworthy of his attention. Pavelsons was a military man, an officer in the Lithuanian Army. He'd fought against the Germans when Lithuania was at war with Germany, then he fought alongside the Germans against the Russians when Lithuania was at war with Russia, then, minus the Germans, he fought against the Russians when Lithuania fought Russia again. Officer Pavelsons followed his country's orders and fought against everyone who fought against his Motherland. The Soviet Union didn't appreciate his patriotism, and after Lithuania was conquered, these patriots were denounced as traitors. Pavelsons was upset that, having been faithful to his country his entire life, he was convicted as a traitor to the Motherland. And this was the old man who constantly accused Manilovich of stealing.

During work hours, all the inmates sewed work mitts. The ninety-two pairs, our daily quota, were put together, tied in a stack, then delivered to the guard. (The mitts were delivered inside out, but would later be turned right-side out and shaped on special equipment.) Once Pavelsons lost his stack and, without a moment's hesitation, accused Borya: "You stole my mitts, now give them back!" Manilovich kept telling the old man that he hadn't stolen the mitts, and that, after stealing a pastry from his Aunt Marusya when he was a kid, he'd never taken anything from anybody ever again. Pavelsons, however, continued his attack with decidedly military determination. When we tried to figure out why he'd singled out Manilovich and decided that he was the one who'd stolen his stack, Pavelsons answered us with sincere surprise: "Well, he's a kike!" He stood fast: "There's only one Jew in our workshop, who else would steal the mitts?"

Pavelsons's stack was soon found. It turned out the Ukrainian Strilitsiv had taken the mitts to turn them inside out, but the former officer of the Lithuanian Army wasn't going to apologize, having probably come to the conclusion that the Ukrainian and the Jew were in on it together, but then got scared and returned the stolen stack.

Boris's sense of humor worked in unpredictable ways. In the camp administration, there was a guard named Kiselyov. We inmates called them guards, but they preferred the term "controllers." Anyway, the controller-guard Kiselyov wasn't known for his high level of intellect. He was a simple man who farmed in addition to his work at the prison.

Around the barracks, Kiselyov was a guard of moderate cruelty, and at home, a farmer of moderate laziness. He was moderate in all ways but one: he drank immoderately. He drank so immoderately that over the years, no one had seen him even close to being sober. It's possible this had an effect on his mind, but the opposite is also possible, that his mind ordered him to drink this much. His face always had a ruddy glow. Sometimes his hands would start trembling and he would suddenly disappear. Soon after, he would return wearing a satisfied look, his hands no longer shaking, and he'd be in the mood for talking.

And so, one fine spring, Kiselyov approached Boris and me with his moderately unstable gait, and began complaining: "It's haying time, but I can't handle it all by myself and it's hard to find any help. No one knows how to use a scythe, and the guys who can handle one are busy with their own hay fields. And it's the same today, after my shift I'll have to do the harvesting all night long by myself. What's the point in trying?"

Cunningly squinting his eyes, Manilovich began: "Do you know, Kiselyov, where the country Georgia got his name from?"

"What's there to know? All the Georges from Russia moved over there, and that's how you get the name."

"You surprise me, Kiselyov! Georgia is a country of peasants. Georgians are people of the land. You must've heard that Georgia is a peasant country before. This very convict Buttzenishvili (this is how the Barashevo controller-guards pronounced my difficult last name), whom you see here in front of you, is a true peasant, born with a scythe in his hand. He's spent his whole life harvesting hay. As for me, my entire extended family used to work on kibbutzim, which are essentially agricultural communes, and I can handle a seven-foot scythe as if it were a toy. Take Levan and me to your plot of land, and each of us will cut down enough grass for three harvests."

"That's great—six haystacks is no joke," he said with noticeable enthusiasm in his voice. "But how can I get you out of here?" Kiselyov asked, clearly betraying his business interest.

"Simple! Trimazkin took us out last year (everyone knew that Trimazkin and Kiselyov were irreconcilable enemies—they didn't even speak to each other), so you could ask him how he did it. You're colleagues, aren't you?"

"The Tambov wolf[15] is his only colleague!" Kiselyov said, now angry. "We'd have to come up with something smarter than that."

[15] This is a reference to a popular Russian proverb "Tambovskii volk tebe tovarishch" [The Tambov wolf is your only friend].

"It's not that easy," Manilovich said.

"Nothing comes to mind," I said, sharing his concern.

"I've got it!" Borya finally exclaimed. "I've got it! You have to go to Shalin, the prison warden, and tell him: 'I need people for haymaking, give me Berdzenishvili and Manilovich. They can help me with the harvest as I have two extra scythes. I'll check them in tomorrow morning.' Most importantly, tell him you won't give us any vodka, because, as you know, inmates and vodka is a touchy issue."

"Of course, I'll tell him all that, but I'd give you a little anyway. But only if you make six . . . or even five haystacks!" said the good-hearted Kiselyov, who then began walking toward the administrative building.

Borya rushed into the barracks and brought half of the camp outside to enjoy the fun. Five minutes hadn't passed before Kiselyov flew out of the warden's office, screaming tragically: "You walrus kike, what the f—are you doing telling me those phony things!"

"It's a pity Aeschylus is not alive!" Borya said, regretting the passing of the Ancient Greek tragedian twenty-five centuries ago. "Don't you think that when Kiselyov's angry, he looks just like Agamemnon when he was being destroyed by the cunning of Clytemnestra and Aegisthus and exclaimed: 'O-oh! I have been struck deep, a fatal blow!'?"

That day Kiselyov drank more than usual, and over the next two weeks he wouldn't come anywhere near Manilovich and me. But then the offense must've worn itself out or the haymaking must have ended because Kiselyov renewed his intellectual conversations with his tormentor Borya.

The incident with Kiselyov wasn't the only episode of that kind. Incidentally, Manilovich was our representative and, basically, our only contact with the administration. The majority of the inmates avoided the administration, considering any contact to be undesireable. But as an experienced convict, Borya wasn't of that mind. It seemed as if he'd developed some kind of immunity, and so his contacts with the administration didn't affect his standing. This is why, when talking to the administration was necessary, he was willing to step forward and help. He would begin with a long speech, invariably opening with "Citizen Warden" (in a political prison, no one convicted for anti-Soviet agitation and propaganda used this form of official address—no one but Manilovich). Once Vitautas Skuodis, the author of the book *Intellectual Genocide in Lithuania*, dropped a bottle of sunflower oil, which he'd purchased with virtual money saved with great effort. The bottle broke, and the spilled oil damaged a major prison asset—a package of black tea. Borya went to see the warden, greeted him with the traditional "Citizen Warden," and wheedled two additional rubles out of him on the pretense of buying stationery for the famous Lithuanian intellectual. (Previously, such an honor had been bestowed only upon spies and war criminals.)

Borya loved chess, and this love was a special source of pride. At that time, many countries had Jewish grandmasters on their national teams. There was a popular Soviet joke that one Jew is a businessman, two Jews are a world championship in chess, and many Jews are the USSR Academy of Sciences. Borya loved chess and played it very well, but for some reason the democrats in our political prison didn't worship Caïssa, the goddess of chess, so Manilovich had to look for partners among the spies and traitors. He found a worthy partner, from a chess-playing point of view, in Akhper Radzhabov, a spy who, for a certain compensation, had passed on the technical drawings for the intermediate-range ballistic missile SS-20 to Americans in Yugoslavia.

Borya and Radzhabov had been playing chess for some time, but this didn't bring them closer. In fact, the opposite happened—their frequent matches only highlighted their ideological, ethnic, and religious differences. Being a man of

SACRED DARKNESS · 119

vision, Mikhail Polyakov predicted that a conflict was unavoidable. How right he was. Once, toward the end of a match, fortune began to favor Borya and the balance shifted to his side, which stirred the pot. First came check, then came checkmate, followed by a quarrel, which brought an unexpected development: Radzhabov brought a feces-covered stick from the bathroom and smashed it in Borya's face. Deeply upset, Borya came to us and announced that he wouldn't answer this disgusting insult since it was obviously a provocation by the authorities, and he prohibited us from doing anything about it either. I don't remember how he managed to stop Dato and me, as we strongly believed that certain provocations deserved a response, especially if that was the only way to maintain your dignity. The Petersburgers led the post-conflict negotiations and managed to restore peace between the two men. Our position, however, didn't change then and it remains the same now—Radzhbov never received an adequate comeuppance for trashing Borya's honor.

In the end, after I'd had many chances to observe how tolerant Borya was of anti-Semitic jokes, I realized that he was blessed with immense patience, especially when compared to Dato and me. One of these "jokes" came from the prison's movie projectionist, Lismanis, who, out of love for Gogol's *Dead Souls*, started calling Manilovich Sobakevich. (The landowners Manilov and Sobakevich were two of the main "souls" in Gogol's masterpiece.) But Borya wasn't offended—or at least he pretended not to be—despite the fact that calling someone a *sobaka*, or "dog," was the worst possible insult, even worse than arrest itself.

As a true Petersburger or, as he liked to call himself, "a rotten intellectual of Semitic descent," Borya knew Russian literature intimately. He was especially fond of, again using his own term, the Hamito-Semitic branch of Russian literature. (I'm sure by using the term "Hamito," Borya meant it only in the linguistic sense, stressing the contribution of his people to Russian literature and culture.)

Once I told Borya that the term "Hamito-Semitic" was not used anymore and that, beginning in the 70s, it had been replaced by "Afroasiatic," a term introduced by the American scholar Greenberg. Now the term "Afroasiatic language family" was used instead. This really bothered Borya:

"What's that Greenberg's first name? Is it Yoska, by any chance? Is he from New York?"

"Yes, Joseph Greenberg, born in Brooklyn in 1915. He works in two linguistic fields—linguistic typology and genetic classification of languages, and he's known for the identification of linguistic universals."

"Yoska is related to me! Just like you Georgians, we Jews are all related to one other, but we're rather distant relations. How do you say it—a raven is the aunt of a jay?"

"Yes, that's right! An aunt, but on your father's side, is the sister of the father of the jay."

"There's the same idiom in Yiddish, too."

In front of his Russian friends, he liked to list the stars of Russian literature (typically in alphabetical order)—Isaac Emmanuilovich Babel (born as Bobel), Eduard Georgievich Bagritsky (Dzyubin), Ilya Arnoldovich Ilf (an acronym for Iechiel-Leyb Faynzilberg), Osip (Joseph) Emilyevich Mandelstam, Boris Leonidovich (before 1920, Boris Isaakevich) Pasternak, Mikhail Arkadyevich Svetlov (Scheinkman), and Korney Ivanovich Chukovsky (illegitimate son of Emmanuil Solomonovich Levenson).

When Borya added painters, doctors, chess players, cosmonauts (here, he would include American astronauts for "species enrichment," as he explained), and scientists to that list (each category would have its own alphabetized list), the final tally would be almost infinite.

Another term Borya coined was "the sixth column," which

was the same as "the fifth column," but this column actually loves the country as much as the first four columns, even though the country sees the sixth column as its enemy, like the fifth column. From this sixth column of Russian-Soviet literature came Borya's passion, his literary love—Isaac Babel, the author of *The Odessa Tales* and *Red Cavalry*, a remarkable writer and a brilliant stylist, who, by a decree personally signed by Stalin, was executed by firing squad in 1940.

In *The Odessa Tales*, Babel provides a romantic description of Odessa at the beginning of the twentieth century through the lives of Jewish criminals and simple people. He constructed a monument to the exotic and strong personalities of tradesmen and thieves, petty merchants and robbers. In these short stories, the most memorable character was the well-known burglar Benya Krik, whose prototype was Odessa's legendary gangster Mikey the Jap. In real life, Mikey the Jap, aka Moisei Wolfovich Vinnitsky, who died in 1919, was an extremely vibrant "noble" burglar, who supported actors and other creative individuals. He was called the Jap because of the unusual shape of his eyes. It's interesting that there was another kingpin known as the Jap, aka Vyacheslav Ivankov, who died just recently and also got his famous nickname for the Japanese shape of his eyes and his love of theater. They say that in the character of Benya Krik, Babel expressed his long-held dream of a Jew who could stand up for himself. This idea was deeply rooted in the author's past, when the ten-year-old Isaac, born and raised in Odessa's Moldovanka neighborhood, escaped the terrible Jewish pogrom of 1905 by a miracle—he was sheltered by a Christian family—but among the three hundred Jews slaughtered in Odessa at that time was his grandfather Shoil Bobel.

When we were sentenced to our political prison, the popular singer Alexander Rosenbaum was writing and performing *blatnye*, or criminal songs set in prerevolutionary Odessa with Babel's Benya Krik as the main character.

Not everyone shared Borya's passion, however. Zhora presented several nonliterary counterarguments: In December of 1917, Babel worked in the *Cheka* (the future KGB), he was sent to the First Cavalry as a reporter under the name of Kirill Vasilievich Lutov, and he was later promoted to political supervisor. Borya answered these attacks with enviable patience: "You know that the harshest attacks on *Red Cavalry* came from the legendary Red army commander Budyonny, who claimed that these stories slandered the First Cavalry. Then in 1924, another Red army commander, Kliment Voroshilov, complained to the Central Committee member Dmitry Manuilsky, who later became the secretary of the Comintern, that the style of *Red Cavalry* was unacceptable and the father and leader of all nations, Stalin, believed that Babel 'writes about things he doesn't understand.' And so, Zhora, do you really want to stay in such splendidly Red company with Comrades Budyonny, Voroshilov, and Stalin?" Manolovich asked cunningly, squinting his eyes like Mikey the Jap.

"And why exactly was Babel hanging around with Dzerzhinsky, Menzhinsky, and Medved if he was such a good person?" Khomizuri responded, unwilling to let up. "Besides, what kind of a writer is he, anyway? Definitely no Dostoevsky!"

"What does all this have to do with Dostoevsky and Pushkin? Please, leave my countrymen out of it!" said Misha Polyakov, now getting involved. "Marc Zakharovich Chagall was a Red commissar, too! Of course, it was in the arts, but nevertheless he served as a commissar in the Vitebsk region!"

As usual, Polyakov hit the nail on the head. Zhora worshiped Chagall almost as much as Borya worshipped Babel, or maybe even more, and many of us, including me, shared his passion. Years later, my best friend would invite my wife and me to the enormous, almost complete, Chagall exhibition at the Grand Palais in Paris, where I would have one of the most breathtaking and unforgettable experiences of my life. After this argument, Khomizuri stopped saying anything bad about Babel, and Borya was free to continue promoting his favorite writer.

I'd liked Babel even before all of this happened, though I was only familiar with *Red Cavalry* in Georgian translation. After meeting Borya, however, my respect for Babel turned into love, and after his endless lectures, this love became a hundred times stronger. Borya quoted his favorite writer on every occasion. I even noticed a certain pattern—if, when inserting a quotation, which he very often did, Manilovich didn't name the author, then it had to be Babel. It wasn't always easy to recognize the quotation if you weren't familiar with Babel's *oeuvre*, especially *The Odessa Tales*. For example, when introducing an academic theory, let's say some complicated concept in psychoanalysis, Borya would suddenly ask: "Do you see what I'm saying, Muginshtein?" Borya expected the audience to know that he was referring to an episode from *The Odessa Tales*, or more precisely, to the short story "How Things Were Done in Odessa." The story is about Benya Krik's first criminal operation before he becomes known as the King. While robbing the millionaire Tarkovsky's store with three other bandits, Benya Krik takes time to explain to the store manager, poor Muginshtein, that it's his boss's obnoxious behavior that provoked the bandits, and a few minutes before a random bullet tragically injures Muginshtein, Benya offers him a philosophical observation on their meeting: "Pigs never greet, but men may always meet. Do you see what I'm saying, Muginshtein?"

Boris always finished his talks about Babel with the following epigram by an unknown author, which was preserved by Valentin Kataev:

With the cannons' thunder and the clanking of swords,
From Zoshchenko was Babel born.

Being a psychoanalyst, Manilovich knew all the scientific literature on the subject, beginning with Freud, Jung, Adler, Fromm and finishing with Lacan, Melman, and Le Goff. I had rarely come across a person who had so much respect for different, sometimes even mutually exclusive, theoretical positions. Borya would talk for hours about fundamental or slight differences between Freudian psychoanalysis and Jungian psychology. When the conversation became overly saturated with scientific terminology, Borya would switch to colloquial language, or the "people's" language:

"I can see some similarities between Freud and our Zhora Khomizuri, or, more lovingly, Zigmund Pavlovich Khomizuri, our Khomizigmund. He would also strictly and uncompromisingly think for everybody and, just like Stalin, he would not stand for 'to each his own,' but 'to each—mine.' For him, all people were identical Oedipuses. He thought that every doctor, even a doctor of philosophy, has no more than six feet of earth (of course, here he was quoting Babel). Jung is more like Grisha Feldman ('Gregory Jung—it even sounds good!'). Grisha Jung is religious, and he cares more about the salvation of his soul than other people do."

"But it's well known that his soul is located in the most sacred part of the body—his stomach," Grisha would add with a kind smile.

"And Adler?" I would ask.

"Adler is like you. He's an individualist, filled with a student's love, and a universal teacher. Levan Adler—sounds good too! If there were any order in this world, Sigmund Freud would've been born a German aristocrat instead of an Austrian Jew. Carl Gustav Jung, the follower of Ulrich Zwingli, wouldn't have been a German-speaking Swiss, but a French Calvinist, Charles Gustave Jengle, and the Austrian Alfred Adler would have been a Georgian, Fridon Adlerashvili."

After this conversation, Borya called me Levan

Adlerianovich instead of Levan Valerianovich (especially if he needed a favor).

Borya was a real treasure trove of anecdotes, most of which were about politics or Jews. One I remember particularly well because Manilovich didn't tell it like a story, he performed it like a stand-up comedian:

> Morduhai and Sarah had three unmarried daughters—Anna, Deborah, and Leah. Once, Moshe came and married Anna. Time passed, and Moshe comes back to Morduhai and Sarah saying, "There was a terrible disaster, Anna passed away." The parents mourned Anna and married her sister, Deborah, to Moshe. Time passed, and again Moshe comes: "You wouldn't believe it, but Deborah died too." The parents mourned Deborah, and married Leah to Moshe. A little time passed, and Moshe again comes to Morduhai and Sarah saying, 'You'll laugh, but Leah died too.'

Borya liked joking about his life: "I've had two wives—both of them are alive, both of them are Jewish, and both of them are intellectuals. Now, they both take turns visiting me in prison. I loved them both and still love them, but neither could convince me to leave for Israel. Also, my second, highly intellectual wife would torture me with the most sophisticated cruelty. Like reading a book during sex, for example. Now I've found myself a Russian woman, but I'm afraid she's the one who'll make me return to my historical motherland. You know the modern Russian folktale: From Ryazan to Kazan, knives are dangling. / Darling, do the circumcision, / And to Israel we'll be traveling."

Borya was right. His Russian spouse was the one who got him to move to Israel. And Borya Manilovich was lost to us. Polyakov, Khomizuri, and I have looked for him everywhere. We didn't even know if he was still alive when, by chance on the Internet, I came across an interview with the head of psychological services at the Israeli Ministry of Health, Boris

Manilovich, in which the gray-haired professor, introduced as one of the leading specialists on "the psychology of dependence," talked about addiction to alcohol and narcotics (see how consistent and true to himself he is!), placing special emphasis on the differences between an alcoholic and a drug addict. The entire interview was devoted to discussing this difference: An alcoholic suffers from anosognosia, he denies his addiction and is incapable of critically evaluating his condition, while a drug addict understands rather quickly that he is sick.

Even after discovering this interview, I couldn't reach Borya through the Internet, but I was happy to find out that he was alive and had remained true to himself.

Borya said that before his arrest he'd read Solzhenitsyn, and that the great writer thanked his lucky stars for the chance to be imprisoned. Dostoevsky and Mahatma Gandhi wrote the same. Manilovich used to say that only after his own arrest did he start to believe these great writers.

VADIM

Vadim, aka Vadim Anatolievich Yankov, was a mathematician by education, but in real life he was a topologist, philologist, philosopher, polyglot, mathematician, physicist, chemist, brainiac, or, to put it more succinctly and affectionately—an *–ist* and an *–ian*. He was also one of the most talented and erudite people I'd ever known. My brother Dato named him Cos, and this is what we Georgians called him. Dato loved him deeply, I believed he was a post-Nietzschian *Übermensch*, Zhora argued with him constantly, and Johnny chuckled softly at his expense.

Arrested in 1982, Vadim Yankov was sentenced to four years in a maximum-security prison and three years of internal exile. After finishing his prison sentence, he was exiled to Buryat ASSR.

Even though he was born in Taganrog, in prison Vadim was the star of the Moscow group, which included other intellectuals, such as Sasha Chernov, Zhora Khomizuri, Misha Ryvkin, and Yasha Nefediev, and was an integral part of our political prison. (ThoughVadim was the true star of the Moscow group, he wasn't its leader. Moscow political prisoners never had a leader in any of the political prisons. The same was true of the Georgian prisoners.)

Vadim knew English, French, German, Spanish, Italian, Ancient Greek, Latin, and Sanskrit. He was fully versed in questions of general and Indo-European linguistics, especially the Romance languages. He was familiar with old and new

Georgian linguistics, often quoting works by the Georgian linguists Tamaz Gamkrelidze, Givi Machavariani, and Bakar Gigineishvili. He could talk for hours about the systems of sonants and the ablaut in Old Georgian. He knew Ancient Greek so well that during our joint seminars, which we gave in turn for anyone who was interested, Vadim read excerpts from Homer in impeccable hexameter, and I don't remember him ever making a single mistake. (Specialists in classical philology would understand the level of knowledge this requires.)

Vadim was a friend of Merab Mamardashvili and also a "Socratesian," in the broadest meaning of this word. Like Socrates, he put writing above speaking, however, he used to joke that the Latin idiom "*Nulla dies sine linea*" (no day without a line) sounded different for him—"*Nulla dies cum linea*" (no day *with* a line, meaning that there shouldn't be a day for writing even a single line, or never write anything). Vadim's wife suffered the most from this principle when, in response to her long letters, she'd receive the shortest possible letter filled with enigmas—her husband would spare no time in creating these laconically expressed paradoxes.

After many elaborate tests, I finally concluded that Vadim knew practically everything we would ever need to know. The entire prison population addressed their most controversial questions to him. Arnold Anderson, the father of Soviet multivitamins, consulted Vadim on vitamins and bio-supplements; Yuri Badzyo, the leader of the Ukrainian Social-Democrats, wanted him to clarify the meaning of History; Zhora Khomizuri, our chief geologist, passionately argued with him about geosynclines; Dmitro Mazur, one of the leading theoreticians of Ukrainian nationalism, talked to Vadim about positivism, which Dmitro himself considered to be totally unacceptable; Borya Manilovich, the psychologist, psychiatrist, poet, and underground Zionist, asked him to reveal secret arms information about the Israeli Army; Kan-Chan-Kho, the

Japanese spy and Korean Communist, conversed with him on the subject of yellow dog as an ideal dish; and the Balkarian Ruslan Ketenchiyev asked him for a futurological analysis of the situation in the North Caucasus. I can say with certainty that in our political prison, Vadim Yankov, omnipotent and always ready to help, embodied in the pre-Internet era the combined capabilities of Google, Yahoo, and Wikipedia.

His wife was Armenian, and he had a lot of respect for the Armenian people, but, as he used to say, he loved Georgians and had many Georgian friends in Moscow as well as in Tbilisi. I once asked him: "You know so many languages, but why, out of respect for your wife, wouldn't you learn Armenian?" And he answered me: "If I learn Armenian, I'll have to learn Georgian, as well as Mingrelian and Svan, and then Abkhaz, Ossetian, and the North Caucasian languages. How can I handle so many?" I don't know if this was what he said to his wife, but the fact remains: Only in prison did he show any interest in the Armenian and Georgian alphabets and asked Rafik and me to teach him. He quickly learned all three Georgian alphabets and could read better than Khomizuri.

Vadim was in charge of the special committee that planned cultural and educational activities. (In the end, I volunteered for this committee too, becoming its youngest member.) The committee gave me the assignment of preparing a lecture series about the poet Vazha-Pshavela. I was pleased. "It's great that you know who Vazha-Pshavela is!" I said. Cos then responded, trying to shame me: "How could we not know Vazha-Pshavela when he was a poet of cosmic scale and a philosopher of skepticism? And his Aluda Ketelauri was the first dissident! How could someone with any knowledge of Russian literature not know the works of Vazha when Pasternak, Zabolotsky, and Spassky translated him?!"

As is always the case with talented people, there were many strange things about Vadim. One such feature was his relationship to his own ethnicity. The child of a Russian father and a Jewish mother, he identified himself as Russian one moment and as Jewish the next. Most importantly, there was no logic in the choice of his ethnicity *du jour*, and no one could predict when he would become Russian, and when Jewish. Vicious tongues joked that when Jews were being harassed, he'd become Russian, and when it was beneficial to be Jewish, he would deny his Russian origins and become a Jew. Well-wishers, on the other hand, admired the fact that Yankov would declare himself a Jew as soon as harassment of Jews began. The prison administration was composed entirely of aggressive anti-Semites, and among the inmates, the anti-Semites were in the majority, with the Ukrainian Banderovtsy and the Baltic war criminals heading the list. In such an environment, proclaiming yourself a Jew, even from time to time, was an act of heroism.

I liked to invite Cos to share my meager table, but there was one unexpected difficulty I had to face. At times, with a deep sigh, Cos would refuse half a piece of *salo*, be it Russian, Ukrainian, or Lithuanian, that I'd managed to score, while on other occasions, with the same deep sigh, he would crave it. In the end, this problem was resolved through the active efforts of his namesake, the hijacker Vadim Arenberg, who openly preached Zionism but was secretly a KGB informant working for the administration. In return for his not-so-kosher actions, a few Jewish yarmulkes appeared in the prison, and so it became fairly easy to detect Vadim's ethnicity *du jour*: When he was Jewish, he'd wear his yarmulke, even inside, but when he was Russian, there was no yarmulke in sight.

During the time of Arenberg's affair with Zionism, Vadim, wearing his yarmulke, would always sit at the same table during dinner as Yasha Nefediev, Grisha Feldman, and, of course, Arenberg himself. Once, the administration, led by the controller Trifonov, burst into the dining room during dinner.

"Hats off!" Trifonov yelled. There were two Muslims wearing skullcaps, which they instantly removed. Yankov, Yasha, and Grisha removed their yarmulkes as well, but Arenberg and Ryvkin kept theirs on, ignoring Trifonov's second order. As a result, Misha Ryvkin was arrested for disobedience, sentenced to eight additional years in prison, and transferred from our camp to the hole. But the professional provocateur Arenberg was left in our camp until, unable to tolerate the atmosphere of total hatred any longer, he requested a transfer to the Perm political prison. From that time on, Vadim Yankov stopped wearing his yarmulke, and I stopped offering him any *salo* until he invited me to share a piece of black bread, a small piece of Lithuanian smoked *salo*, and a quarter of a garlic clove.

There was one question that caused serious disagreement between Vadim Yankov and the Georgians. Vadim couldn't grasp why we were so eager to leave the Soviet Union to form our own independent state. "Don't you think it's better to combine our efforts and defeat Communism, build a liberal democracy together, then go merrily our separate ways?" Vadim used to ask. And we would always answer: "Give us our country back, and we'll take care of the Georgian Reds ourselves."

Misha Polyakov proposed his own solution—take Russia out of the Soviet Union. But this didn't change anything for Yankov: "If you exit the Soviet Union, Russia would lose its chance for democratic development. The nationalists would take power and find that the only possible solution for Russia would be to go to war with you. Though, it wouldn't be a war with nuclear weapons, just tanks and jets," Yankov said.

I told him, by that time Georgia would be a member of the UN and NATO, and no one would dare start a war with us. "You have a big problem," Misha said. "Abkhazia!" Needless to say, our visions of the future didn't change.

Despite our different visions of the future, Yankov always tried to find positive and peaceful common ground, sometimes even by experimental means. It was his idea to begin the Socratic dialogues, where the presenter would appear in the role of Socrates, and the listeners would be his opponents or his students. I remember one of the lecture-dialogues especially well because I gave a talk to the hungry inmates about the highest achievement of Georgian cuisine—*satsivi*. To this very day, my former prisonmates tell me, or write to me, that never since have they had the chance to see a spectacle even remotely close to the one about *satsivi* that Vadim Yankov and I staged in our prison camp.

In that dialogue, I played the role of the ingenuous Socrates who asked the experienced Sophist Vadim Yankov, an expert in international cuisine, questions, and in the end Yankov admitted that there was nothing better than *satsivi*. I can't reproduce our entire dialogue, but this is approximately how it went:

Socrates (Me): What do you think, Anaxagoras, how many nations are there in the world?

Anaxagoras (Vadim Yankov): It depends on what you mean, my dear Socrates. If you only count nations with governments, then it's no more than two hundred, but if you mean ethno-linguistic groups, then it's about five thousand.

Socrates: Let's talk about nations with governments. So, you think there are two hundred of them?

Anaxogoras: There are fewer of them now, but when certain separatists win, there will be two hundred and, possibly, even more.

Socrates: What features distinguish nations from one another?

Anaxogoras: According to one short sadist with a mustache, nations differ in terms of language, religion, territory, and culture.

Socrates: I didn't think you'd quote that sadist, Anaxogoras.

Anaxogoras: He's from your clan, so why are you picking on me?

Socrates: What do you mean by culture?

Anaxogoras: Everything that is created and cultivated by human hands—*colo, colui, coltum, colere*—this is Latin for "to cultivate."

Socrates: Is cuisine a part of culture?

Anaxogoras: I don't think so, my dear Socrates—culture deals with higher matters.

Socrates: Do people prepare food?

Anaxogoras: Yes, they do, Socrates.

Socrates: Do they do it with their hands?

Anaxogoras: In general, yes, my dear Socrates.

Socrates: What do you mean by in general?

Anaxogoras: They make wine by smashing grapes with their feet, and some tribes use their feet to tenderize meat.

Socrates: But most of the time, they use their hands, do they not?

Anaxogoras: Precisely, my dear Socrates.

Socrates: That means that food is created and prepared by human hands, does it not?

Anaxogoras: Of course.

Socrates: But isn't that your definition of culture?

Anaxogoras: Therefore, it follows that cuisine is part of culture, my dear Socrates.

Socrates: How many nations did you say there were, my omniscient Anaxogoras?

Anaxogoras: Fewer than two hundred.

Socrates: How many cuisines do we know?

Anaxogoras: About twenty.

Socrates: Do you count Thai and Chinese cuisines as one?

Anaxogoras: Not at all, my dear Socrates!

Socrates: Do you include Iberian cuisine in that twenty?

Anaxogoras: Twice, my dear Socrates—Eastern and Western.

Socrates: How many Spanish restaurants do you have in Moscow?

Anaxogoras: None, my dear Socrates.

Socrates: Argentinian?

Anaxogoras: None.

Socrates: And Mexican ones?

Anaxogoras: Not even one, my dear Socrates.

Socrates: Eastern Iberian?

Anaxogoras: Too many to count, Socrates! And Aragvi is the only one worth going to.

Papayan: Aragvi's chef is Armenian.

Socrates: You see! Is Georgian cuisine included in the world's ten great cuisines?

Anaxogoras: Without a doubt, my dear Socrates!

Socrates: Now, Anaxogoras, please list these ten cuisines in alphabetical order so as not to offend anyone.

Anaxogoras: What could be easier? Afghan, Chinese, French, Georgian, Indian, Italian, Japanese, Mexican, Spanish, and Thai.

Socrates: Georgians say that their best dish is either *khachapuri* or *satsivi*. Let's assume it's *satsivi*. What can you say about other outstanding dishes, Anaxogoras?

Anaxogoras: For Afghanis, it would be *kebab koobideh*, for Spaniards—paella, for Indians—curry, for Japanese—sushi, for Italians—pizza, for Mexicans—tacos, for the Thai—tom yum with shrimp, for the French—escargot, and for the Chinese—tiger and dragon stir-fry.

Socrates: Let's start from the end. When you speak of the tiger-dragon dish, by dragon do you mean snake?

Anaxogoras: Precisely, my dear Socrates.

Socrates: Do you know many nations in the world that eat snake?

Kan-Chan-Kho: We Koreans eat everything below man on the food chain, including snakes and monkeys.

Anaxogoras: No, if we don't count the Far East and mythical wood spirits.

Socrates: Then it can't be an international dish.

Anaxogoras: It appears so, my dear Socrates.

Kan-Chan-Kho: It's because you've never tried it.

Socrates: Does everybody eat escargot?

Anaxogoras: No, and, therefore, it can't be an international dish either.

Socrates: What would you say about fans of raw fish, Anaxogoras?

Anaxogoras: I believe they are in the minority.

Socrates: What are the chances for sushi?

Japanese Spy Orlov: Sushi isn't raw, it's not a completely raw dish.

Anaxogoras: Sushi's chances are minimal, my dear Socrates.

Socrates: Are there any shrimp in the Volga River?

Anaxogoras: Half the world doesn't even know what shrimp are.

Socrates: Can you imagine, Anaxogoras, tom yum without shrimp and coconut milk?

Anaxogoras: No, I can't, my dear Socrates.

Socrates: Think hard, my dear Anaxogoras, and tell me which is better—Spanish paella or well-prepared Uzbek pilaf?

Anaxogoras: I can't lie in the presence of Rakhimov—Uzbek pilaf, obviously.

Socrates: That means paella is not suited to be an international dish. What do we have left?

Anaxogoras: The magnificent five: Afghani *kebab koobideh*, Indian curry, Italian pizza, Mexican tacos, and Georgian *satsivi*.

Socrates: Don't you think that there are similarities among Italian pizza, Georgian *khachapuri*, and Russian *vatrushka*?

Anaxogoras: You know, my dear Socrates, how I feel about *khachapuri*. Let's leave pizza out of it—I don't like it very much.

Socrates: But what is the nature of the Mexican taco? Isn't it like *solyanka*? I think it's almost the same but with more ingredients. But isn't *solyanka* better?

Donskoy: I agree, *solyanka* is better. The pickles alone make it worth it!

Socrates: Let's take a moment to discuss Afghan kebab and Georgian *shashlik*, Armenian *khorovats*, and the pan-Soviet *shashlik*. Have you ever made *shashlik*, my dear Anaxogoras?

Anaxogoras: Of course! Didn't we make *shashlik* all the time in Peredelkino?

Socrates: But then, *koodibeh* is what we Georgians call kebab, and Afghan kebab can't be better than the kind from Azerbaijan.

Anaxogoras: You're right, my dear Socrates. Anything I can cook well just can't be the best dish in the world. Not to mention the fact that Armenian *khorovats* is better than any *shashlik*.

Socrates: Now, let the competition begin for dishes with nuts. Curry or *satsivi*?

Anaxogoras: That's a tough choice. They're very similar.

Socrates: Tell me, Anaxogoras, what meat is used for curry?

Anaxogoras: Chicken.

Socrates: And for *satsivi*?

Anaxogoras: Turkey.

Socrates: Which bird is larger?

Anaxogoras: My dear Socrates, what point are you trying to make?

Socrates: Which one is thicker, *satsivi* or curry?

Anaxogoras: *Satsivi*.

Socrates: Which one has more nuts?

Anaxogoras: *Satsivi*.

Socrates: What will fill you up more: one bowl of *satsivi* or one bowl of curry?

Anaxogoras: *Satsivi*, my dear Socrates. I admit, *satsivi* is the best dish in the world. Now you have to tell us how to make it.

The recipe for *satsivi* then followed. Hungry people wept and congratulated us on the success of our first Socratic dialogue. Yankov and I, emotionally spent and artistically exhausted, drank two thermoses of strong black tea and swore that, after leaving the prison, we'd find the best curry and *satsivi* cooks and then, on the culinary field of battle, determine the winner. (This simple gastronomical dream of ours has yet to be fulfilled.)

As I mentioned before, Vadim was close to an expert on Ancient Greek, but in some ways he was more of an amateur than a professional. For example, he theoretically understood *accusativus cum infinitive*, but in a text, he might miss it. In the prison, he had a copy of the Ancient Greek textbook by Sobolevsky and had read all the texts a thousand times and knew them inside and out. This is why I decided to give him a real gift for his birthday. In the Books-by-Mail system, there was a famous books series, *Teubneriana*, from the German Democratic Republic, that had all the works of Ancient Greek literature in red covers, and all the works of Roman literature in blue. Despite my dubious return address, the Leningrad House of Books accepted my order and sent me a red volume of Euripides that included the Ancient Greek scholarly edition of *Alcestis*, one of the author's masterpieces. I can't even describe Yankov's emotions when he received this gift of the original, unabridged Greek text. In addition to having a reasonable dictionary in Sobolevsky's textbook, Yankov also had me (a certified specialist with almost a Ph.D.) as a bonus!

Before all that happened, Vadim had tested me on his own "life paradigm," as he called it. "Imagine that God gave you just enough water to cross a desert, not one drop more, not one drop less. You're crossing the desert when a thirsty man approaches and asks for some water. What do you do?" Vadim asked. I answered that I'd give the man some water and we'd continue the journey together. "In this case, both of you will die. There won't be enough water, and you won't be able to leave the desert," Vadim said. "No, God gave you life in the form of water, and you have to save it for yourself. You shouldn't let another man drink it!" I answered that I would share my water anyway, and the argument ended there.

Vadim dove into the book I gave him. The idea of Alcestis captivated him—making sacrifices for someone you love, dying in someone else's place. He was mad at Euripides, whose ideas didn't align with his "life paradigm," but Alcestis, the literary progenitor of Antigone, attracted him intensely and at the same time irritated him tremendously. He said that Admetus's elderly mother was right to not die in place of her son, and that his father was right as well when, following the paradigm, he, too, refused to die in place of his son. "But how could his wife, Alcestis, so young, not save her God-given life? I don't understand it! I don't want to understand it!" Yankov exclaimed.

This was probably the reason Aristotle called Euripides the most tragic poet. "How could he write something like that, how was it even possible?" Vadim kept asking himself. "If we assume that such a sacrifice is possible, then we shouldn't compare Alcestis with Antigone, who died for an idea." And here Vadim quoted the first line of the wonderful French song "Mourir pour des idées" by Georges Brassens: *Mourir pour des idées, l'idée est excellente* [To die for your ideas—is an excellent idea].

Once, Boris Manilovich suggested we organize an evening of poetry when every inmate would have five minutes to present his favorite poet. In those five minutes, a participant should be able to recite a verse or an excerpt from a poem and, in a few words, tell us about the poet's work or about the participant's own relationship with the poet. To keep track of the time, we used an hourglass that had been quickly made by the prison's chief handyman Rafael Papayan. Zhora and Misha presented a husband and wife: Khomizuri introduced Nikolay Gumilyov with a masterpiece about a worker who made a bullet that pierced the poet's chest, and Polyakov introduced Anna Akhmatova's poem "The Sentence," from *Requiem* ("Today I

SACRED DARKNESS · 139

have so much to do . . . ").[16] The evening's organizer chose his favorite poet, Osip Mandelstam ("For whom winter is arak and blue-eyed punch"), while I chose Galaktion Tabidze's "Mary" ("You were married that night, Mary! Mary, that night your eyes were dimmed . . . "),[17] Rafik—"Liturgy for Three Voices" by Paruyr Sevak, Heliy Donskoy—Alexander Blok (the appropriate, but sad, "A Young Girl Sang in a Church Choir"), Sasha Chernov—Boris Pasternak's "Sunrise" ("You were my life sometime ago . . . "), and Vadim—Marina Tsvetaeva.

That day, Vadim surprised us all. Usually composed and ironic, he recited with rare emotion several absolutely amazing excerpts from "The Poem of the End" by the great Marina Tsvetaeva. He finished his presentation by reminding us about the tragic events of the last year of her life. When pushed to the edge of despair and starving, Tsvetaeva was about to take a job as a cleaning lady in the House of Writers, which her few remaining friends were able to find for her, when the great poet learned that she wouldn't be getting even that job. It turned out the famous writer Ilya Ehrenburg thought there was a worthier candidate. And with that, her fate was sealed. Vadim mentioned the last place she lived, Yelabuga—a tragic little town in the middle of nowhere that no one had heard of before, but that Marina Tsvetaeva made immortal in the same way that Napoleon immortalized Waterloo as the site of his only defeat. Few remember Austerlitz, Marengo, Rivoli, and the pyramids, but no one can ever forget Waterloo. Her exuberant life in Moscow, Koktebel, Berlin, Prague, and Paris ended with her quiet death in Yelabuga as a reproach to all the living.

[16] Akhmatova, Anna. "The Sentence." In *Poems*. Translated by Judith Hemschemeyer, Zephyr Press, 1990, p. 105.
[17] Tabidze, Galaktion. *Discover Galaktion. Galaktion Tabidze: A Selection of His Poems in a New Parallel Translation.* Translated by Innes Mirabishvili, Critical, Cultural and Communications Press, 2017, p. 59.

This is the way the world ends,
This is the way the world ends,
This is the way the world ends,
Not with a bang but a whimper.

There were ten seconds left at the end of his presentation, during which Cos managed to say that these final words from T.S. Eliot's poem "The Hollow Men" resonate with the final lines of Tsvetateva's "The Poem of the End":

So, into the hollow waves,
Of darkness—hunched over—
Without a sound, without a trace,
As a ship sinks.[18]

At that moment, the last grain of sand in Papayan's hourglass fell.

Vadim had never shown any love for poetry before, let alone for the poetry of Tsvetaeva. After the performance, almost everyone changed their opinion of Vadim, who was definitely a science-driven man (our poet and psychologist Manilovich was fond of the term "science-driven." It had only been used in the technological and industrial spheres until perestroika, when it became more broadly applied). Most excited of all was Zhora, who made no effort to hide his feelings. Despite the centuries-long competition between the two capitals, the leading Petersburger Misha Polyakov had to admit: "Wow, Vadim surprised us all."

Johnny was the only person who wasn't moved by the tears welling up in Yankov's eyes during his talk about Tsvetaeva. "He's an actor," he tried to explain to me. "Why are you so surprised?

[18] Tsvetaeva, Marina. *The Poem of the End*. Translated by Nina Kossman, Ardis, 1998, p. 93.

You Gurians are very strange people. As soon as you see a tear, you're ready to forgive everything! This is the same man who, according to his idiotic 'life paradigm,' wouldn't give you any water in the desert and would leave you to die. Didn't Solzhenitsyn say that in prison true heroism is not finding some extra soup, but sharing that soup with someone else?" How could I explain to the skeptical Johnny that by quoting the final lines of "The Poem of the End," Vadim had shared a part of his soul?

In 1986, Vadim Yankov was released from prison and sent into exile. According to prison tradition, he gave away all his possessions before he left. I got his library, almost one hundred books, among them, the Ancient Greek textbook and *Alcestis* by Euripides, its pages covered with his notes and comments in Ancient Greek, documenting his sharp polemic with the writer.

Today, the seventy-four-year-old Vadim Yankov teaches at the State Humanitarian University of Russia, giving lectures on the history of philosophy and mathematics. He has forgotten his old principle, *Nulla dies cum linea*; however, he didn't go back to the classical *sine linea*—he wrote and published several articles. Experts most often cite his article "The Structure of Matter According to Anaxogoras." During the Yeltsin era, he attempted to go into politics but lost when he ran for the State Duma—he ended up behind a communist from Zuganov's party and a liberal-democrat from Zhirinovsky's party. In my opinion, the Russian Duma is not ready for such high standards. Just like in our conversation about the final year of Marina Tsvetaeva's life, Vadim said that in Russia (and in neighboring countries as well), there is always "a worthier candidate."

ANADENKO

In one of Vysotsky's popular songs, there's a line that says: "I've heard that Fischer's very bright!" And that's exactly how I'd describe Anadenko—bright, and unforgettable. Odd and nervous, just like Bobby Fischer, the "brightest" World Chess Champion, Anadenko was the unrivaled champion of political prison ZhKh 385/3-5. The other pretenders to the title, Arnold Anderson from Moscow, Akhper Padzhabov from Baku, and Boris Manilovich from Petersburg (from all the chess capitals!), had no chance of knocking Anadenko from his pedestal.

When we met, Friedrich, aka Fred Filippovich Anadenko, was about fifty years old. He was born in the Far East, on the shore of the De-Kastri Bay in the Amur Province of the Khabarovsk region, where his father served in the army. According to his passport, Fred was Russian, but he used to say that there was also Ukrainian, Belorussian, and a little bit of Gipsy blood in his veins. It wasn't hard to guess why his parents had given their Soviet child the foreign name Friedrich—it was out of respect for Friedrich Engels, of course. (Anadenko's older brother was named Karl, and if Fred had had any younger brothers, their names most likely would have been Vladimir and Joseph.) So that made our Anadenko a Marxist by birth. He was a Marxist with an Engelsian accent, in other words, a classic centrist with trace elements of liberalism.

In 1960, Fred graduated from the Sevastopol Higher Naval

Engineering School, a school that many Soviet youth dreamed about, but few would ever reach. Immediately following his graduation, the newly minted officer and missile engineer was sent to the cosmodrome, where, just one year later, Yuri Gagarin would be launched into space. The young Anadenko took part in the rocket testing, and he instantly became a part of world history.

Anadenko was nineteen years old when he became interested in the true nature of communism and began studying the classics of Marxist-Leninism on his own. In all fairness, his studies were truly self-guided because he studied the forbidden works of Karl Kautsky, Leon Trotsky, and Mao Zedong, along with the officially recognized works of Marx, Engels, Lenin, and Stalin. Sincerely believing in his chosen path, he became a member of the Communist Party in no time and was awarded the rank of major, and so the possibility of a successful military career seemed inevitable. This came to an end, however, in 1968 with the events in Czechoslovakia, when Warsaw Pact tanks watered the flowers of the famous Prague Spring with the blood of women and children. In addition to the Soviet army, armies of other Warsaw Pact member-states, except for Romania, took part in the invasion, but that didn't deceive the major. In October of that same year, Major Anadenko made a decision—as an act of protest, without hesitation, he withdrew from the Communist Party and, of his own free will, left his prestigious military career in the elite missile forces.

Fred started a new life. For twelve years, the former major and military missile tester worked as a simple laborer, first in the Kiev metro system and later at a Kiev paper factory. During that period, Fred didn't waste any time, as he put it, and worked intensely on his first political book, *Natural Course*, which eventually put him behind bars on April 2, 1982. Then, on October 29, 1982, at the request of the Head of the Kiev

KGB, the blood-sucking Stepan Mukha, the Kiev regional court sentenced Fred Anadenko to the maximum term, the notorious "seven plus five."

It's interesting that in his indictment, which Fred showed us Georgians the moment we asked to see it, the book's subtitle *From Lenin to Brezhnev* was altered with Chekist delicacy to the following: *From [leader's name] to [leader's name]*. It seems that in such "sacred scrolls," as we jokingly referred to our indictments—true masterpieces of KGB epistolary style—even a fleeting mention of the untarnished names of Lenin and Brezhnev was unacceptable to Ukrainian Chekists.

When Dato and I first arrived in the prison, "the locals" welcomed us novices in the finest tradition of political prisons. They even organized a special welcoming committee that included our fellow Georgians, Johnny Lashkarashvili and Zhora Khomizuri, and our fellow South Caucasian Rafael Papayan, as well as the Russians Vadim Yankov and Fred Anadenko. Fred thoroughly examined the principles of the Republican Party we had created and was pleased to note that our economic program (of course, we had our own economic program) aligned with his own economic theories. (Here, I must confess that, looking back, it's clear that our "program" would make specialists in the field of economics today laugh. Even college freshmen would scoff at our ideas.)

Anadenko considered himself a social democrat and a "bloodless" Marxist. He was definitely against the respective methods of Lenin, Stalin, and Mao, but it was impossible to say anything bad in his presence about Antonio Gramsci, Palmiro Togliatti, Maurice Thorez, Georges Marchais, Alexander Dubček, and especially the recently deceased leader of the Italian Communist Party Enrico Berlinguer, whose main achievement was, according to Fred, his ability to turn the traditionally strong and influential Italian Communist Party away from a Marxist-Leninist position to the platform of European

Communism and begin connecting with politicians of other worldviews. In 1980, after the Soviet Union sent troops into Afghanistan, Berlinguer voiced his strong objection, which caused a split between the Italian and the Soviet communist parties. As a result, the newspaper of the Italian Communists, *L'Unità*, disappeared forever from our newsstands, and Soviet soccer fans lost access to its last page—which was an illustrated Bible of soccer. Despite the fact that Berlinguer's popularity dramatically rose after he criticized the Soviet Union, members of the Italian Communist Party were never elected to the national government, either independently or as part of a coalition, even though the local governments were filled with Communists.

Almost every morning began with the short, but perpetual, argument between Anadenko and Khomizuri about whether "noble" communism was possible. The only reason their morning debates were short was the fact that they would begin during the first head count in the prison yard and continue in the dining room, but had to end before we entered the workshop. The noise from the electric sewing machines didn't permit political or scientific discussions—we could barely exchange a couple of words. In those morning debates, Anadenko would sing the old song about socialism "with a human face," while Zhora would declare that socialism couldn't have a face, let alone a human face, only a wolf's grin. Anadenko believed that communism had nothing to do with Lenin's sick ideas ("any cook should be able to run the country"), or with Trotsky's idea of permanent revolution, or with Stalin's cruelty and his Gulag, or with the dictatorship of the proletariat, an idea that was supported by many Communist parties (although the Marxist Anadenko didn't like the proletariat very much).

Sometimes, the Stalinist Razlatsky would join the debate, and then poor Anadenko had to fight a two-front war—on the right and the left. Nevertheless, all the debates would end in a civilized manner, without insults, and any unanswered questions were regarded as something for later discussions. And sure enough, Anadenko would come up with new arguments, and the debate would begin anew: Enrico Berlinguer, Antonio Gramsci, Pablo Picasso, or Paul Éluard.

The nature of the debates would change in the evenings after work, moving from the political sphere to the more academic— here Anadenko and Yankov would argue about Marx, Engels, Trotsky, Freud, Lacan, and Popper. The works of Karl Raimund Popper were the subject of an especially heated polemic because, for Yankov, Popper was as untouchable an authority as Marx was for Anadenko. I first learned about Popper from those debates, and about his concept of an "open society," which proved to be disastrous for the future of Georgia.

The debate between Anadenko and Yankov, the two luminaries of our political prison, often took the form of public Socratic dialogues, during which, as a rule, the prison's intellectual elite played the role of the Athenian people.

"People of Athens," Yankov (Socrates) said, addressing us. "So now the scholars—Karl Marx and Democritus from Abdera, the founder of atomic theory—have arrived to argue with me."

"Why not? I can be Democritus," Anadenko said, agreeing to be from Abdera. "As we know, Marx's doctoral dissertation was *The Difference Between Democritus's Natural Philosophy and the Natural Philosophy of Epicurus*. Hence, Democritus was one of *us*."

"I greet you, my dear Democritus. Since you were born in 460 BCE and died in 370 BCE, that makes me nine years older than you, though, with the help of your beloved Athenians, I died before you in 399. We truly could have met. Even so, I can't say for sure whether we did or not. Tell me, Athenian Levan, did we meet?"

"You did meet, and more than once, my dear Socrates. Democritus made a special trip to Athens to listen to you and the Sophist Philolaus," I answered, enthusiastically joining the debate of the famous Athenians.

"Look around, my dear Democritus," Socrates began. "Pay attention to the barbed wire . . . sorry, I mean the olive trees, the tall towers . . . sorry, the chapels, where the beloved guards of the Ministry of Internal Affairs . . . sorry, the priests of Ancient times . . . point at us the creation of the twice-named Hero of Socialist Labor Mikhail Kalashnikov—the automatic weapon, renowned throughout the world . . . sorry, I meant to say that they are blessing us with olive branches, just as in the prologue of Sophocles's famous tragedy *Oedipus Rex*, the people of Thebes, tortured by plague ('The new tribe of ancient Cadmus'), blessed their King Oedipus."

"Why, yes! Of course, my dear Socrates, I see the olive trees and the priests, the wire fence and the assault rifles, the best in the world. The only problem is, I can't see the connection between these olive trees and pagan priests and our discussion for today."

"It's very simple, my dear Democritus. According to the teachings of my beloved Pythagoras, in 1945, in accordance with the rules of metempsychosis (or reincarnation), my soul migrated into Karl Popper's body, and I wrote the sociological masterpiece *Open Society and Its Enemies*, in which I would appear as the most merciless enemy of totalitarianism. I would support democracy and an open society, and remove the elite classes from power without bloodshed or revolution. I would support this on the grounds that the process of knowledge accumulation is impossible to predict, and so, an ideal theory of state government simply doesn't exist. Political systems must be flexible in order to allow governments to gradually adjust their policies. Society must be open to all points of view and subcultures—this is, my dear Athenians, what we called pluralism and multiculturalism. And you, my dear Democritus, after your reincarnation as Karl Marx, would establish the only mechanism of development—the class struggle over the means of production, where political pluralism does not exist, and the chief weapons of mankind are revolution and murder. This is how you would lead us to the olive wire fence and the priests of Kalashnikov!"

"Let me disagree with you, my dear Socrates. My spiritual son, Karl Marx, never told Comrade Stalin to imprison half of the population in this pigsty we call the Gulag, planting olive trees along the perimeter and appointing priests with AKs. As is the case with all geniuses, Marx had both good and bad students. Kautsky was a good student, but Lenin was a bad one. The students of the good students were, for example, Antonio Gramsci and Enrico Berlinguer, and the students of the bad students were Leon Bronshtein (Judas Trotsky) and Joseph Stalin (Big Joe). And the worst of all the bad students was Mao Zedong."

"My dear Democritus, my fame was due to my favorite students, Plato and Xenophon, and even your Marx earned his dubious international reputation through his best students, Lenin and Stalin, not Bronshtein and Kautsky."

"My dear Socrates, your best student, Plato, was also a Marxist by nature because of his doubts about private property rights."

"Yes, I know these baseless accusations that Plato was a Communist, and Heraclitus was the founder of dialectical materialism or Marxism. You've only skimmed the works of Plato that are necessary to come to such a conclusion, without realizing that, after my death, I didn't have much of an influence on him. After my reincarnation as Karl Popper, however, I was able to tell mankind the main thing, that pluralistic ideas rule history, not rigid Marxist schemas and the class struggle for hegemony."

"Our conversation is not going well, my dear Socrates. You

don't believe in the mortal class struggle, and I don't believe in your spectacular pluralism. Let history judge. I give you my word, if I ever get free, I'll study Karl Popper and devote a good essay to him from a Marxist perspective."

Aging war criminals made up a significant part of our political prison. By number, they were second only to the "democrats," who had been convicted for anti-Soviet agitation and propaganda in accordance with Article 70 of the Criminal Code of the Russian Federation. Nevertheless, we democrats were in the minority, because the war criminals were a part of a larger group that included spies, terrorists, and the traitors to the Motherland, which was not only the majority in terms of number, but also the most privileged group in terms of favors from the administration. One of Barashevo Prison's war criminals was the Ukrainian Mikola Verkhovensky, who served in the German police force during the war. After the war, he changed his last name to Verkhovin, moved to Donbass, and began working in a coal mine, where he mined so much coal it earned him the title of Hero of Socialist Labor. The Secretary General of the CPSS, Comrade Leonid Brezhnev, himself heavily decorated with medals, solemnly bestowed the Hero of Socialist Labor medal upon Verkhovin, which was filmed. This episode made it into a newsreel program—the kind that used to be shown before movies in all Soviet movie theaters. And when this newsreel, along with a new movie, came to the village of Verkhovina, the birthplace of Mikola Verkhovensky, his old neighbors instantly recognized their fellow villager and one time German police officer, which led to his arrest twenty-five years after the war. The Supreme Court of Ukraine rescinded his honorific title and sentenced him to capital punishment, but after spending six months in solitary confinement awaiting execution, Verkhovin was pardoned by the Supreme Court of the USSR (being a Hero of Socialist Labor probably helped), and the sentence of capital punishment was replaced by the maximum prison term, which was at that time fifteen years. When those fifteen years were coming to an end, Verkhovin held the honorary position of cook in our political prison.

As soon as Verkhovin left the prison, Anadenko approached me with a rather strange proposal. Anadenko was Russian, but had lived in Kiev, where he adopted Ukrainian manners, one of which was his use of a patronymic even when talking to close friends. This is why he didn't call me Levan as all the other Russians did, but Levan Valerianovich, placing a very distinct stress on the first syllable of my first name (which, incidentally, should be placed on the second), and always with my patronymic. So, my friends and I were in the smoke shack watching Verkhovin leave. We followed him with the envious parting glance of inmates left behind. I was smoking a huge *makhorka* cigarette, which I'd rolled from a piece of the newspaper *Izvestia* (Johnny Lashkarashvili, in the spirit of future Georgian language purists, called such cigarettes *tvitkhveuli*), when Anadenko suggested we go for a walk to discuss an important issue.

It was getting cold. The temperature had dropped to minus 30 degrees Celsius, and so going for a walk in our prison meant going at a fast pace from the hole to the gates and back. When two people were treading this path, everyone knew that they were discussing an important issue. We spent the first half of our walk in silence, but as we were turning back, Fred asked me: "Levan Valerianovich, you know that after Verkhovin's release, there will be a vacancy in the kitchen. Would you like to take his place if all the democrats convicted under Article 70 support you?"

This offer was simultaneously unexpected and, to tell the truth, in a certain sense insulting as the kitchen wasn't *our* place—in other words, it was a place where only spies, traitors to the Motherland, terrorists, and war criminals, who were close to the administration, could work and stuff their bellies. On the other hand, it was clear that Anadenko was up to something and didn't mean to insult or test me.

"You know very well, Fred Filippovich (I decided to become a Ukrainian, too), that the kitchen is not a place for us. Even in Tbilisi, the head of the detention center, Colonel Tariel Dilibazashvili (excuse me, Fred Filippovich, but I don't know his patronymic) and his 'good people' didn't dare offer me work as part of the service staff. And do you really think I've taken such a long journey, ending up in the Mordovian ASSR, in the Tengushevsky District, in the village of Barashevo, only to sell myself for a full stomach?"

"You're getting worked up over nothing, Levan Valerianovich. No one is suggesting that you sell yourself. But why should it be impossible, despite many years of tradition, for honest people to work in the kitchen? People who wouldn't steal our rations or let them be stolen!"

"If you need an honest man in the kitchen, why not you? No one doubts your honesty, and if you already know how to make rocket ships, I'm sure you could straighten out the kitchen."

"This just shows how young and inexperienced you are, Levan Valerianovich! I've told you that every inmate convicted under Article 70 would support you! But who would support me, someone who's written complaints about half the inmates here and sent them to the Prosecutor General of the USSR, Comrade Alexander Mikhailovich Rekunkov? And then personally handed a copy to the person he complained about?"

"I only know your letter to the Prosecutor General about Feldman eating a pigeon, which you found unacceptable because a pigeon is related to a dove, the symbol of peace. And you asked the Prosecutor General to act upon this fact," I said, quoting him absentmindedly.

"I also wrote Alexander Mikhailovich Rekunkov a letter about the inmate Kan-Chan-Kho, a Japanese spy, eating a yellow dog that had accidentally wandered into our prison."

"And what exactly does a yellow dog symbolize?"

"How can one eat a dog, when a dog is a man's best friend?!" Anadenko exclaimed, becoming unusually agitated.

"I wouldn't argue with you, Fred Filippovich. I believe that a dog is man's best friend, and it's not seemly to eat one's friends, but first, Kan is Korean and grew up eating dog meat, and second, while I believe in canine friendship, I can't say anything about friendship with dogs like Rekunkov."

"You know perfectly well, Levan Valerianovich, that Rekunkov is not my friend—if I had friends like that, I wouldn't have been sentenced to 'seven plus five'—but Rekunkov must uphold the law," Anadenko said with deliberate coldness.

"And since when does the law prohibit eating dog meat?" I asked, defending the rather dubious, in my opinion, culinary choices of our Korean fellow-inmate.

"It's immoral to eat dogs! By the way, it's also immoral to crumble bread into your borsch, as your brother, David Valerianovich, does!"

"We Georgians don't know that! In our homeland, borsch is a rare dish and Dato had no idea that your national pride would be offended when he crumbled some bread into his bowl! Have you already written the Prosecutor General of the USSR, Comrade Alexander Mikhailovich Rekunkov, about that?" I asked, letting the true Gurian out from inside of me, and continued in a loftier tone. "By the way, Comrade Friedrich Filippovich Anadenko, as a sign of our friendship, I can get you the address of the Secretary General of the United Nations, the Peruvian non-Comrade Javier Pérez de Cuéllar. From 1969 to 1971, this man was the Peruvian ambassador to the USSR and Poland, and so he must've mastered the art of eating borsch!"

"Oh, please, Levan Valerianovich, I only wanted to hypothetically offer you the position of cook. There are reorganizations happening all over the country, and I thought you should take that position," Anadenko, said, in full retreat.

"In the future, Fred Filippovich, please think twice before suggesting that proud Georgians become prison cooks. You know, Jews love birds, Koreans—yellow dogs, Russians—prosecutors general, and Georgians are as proud as peacocks! In other words, they are a very proud people. Very."

"We also have our points of pride, Levan Valerianovich," Anadenko said with a sly smile on his lips. "As for your national character, we've already had the chance to study another historical specimen, on a larger scale. We don't need quarrels and misunderstandings. My proposal seems to be ridiculous—you're the fourth person to tell me this, so I'll have to believe it."

"Who refused before me?"

"Vadim Anatolievich Yankov, Mikhail Vasilievich Polyakov, and Pyotr Alekseevich Butov," Anadenko answered, naming his candidates without a pause.

"Why didn't you ask Boris Isaakovich Manilovich?" I asked, knowing perfectly well that Fred would never offer Borya such a position.

"I had my reasons," Anadenko said importantly.

"I can guess what those reasons might be, and I think you're wrong," I said, refusing to let Anadenko get away with his acts of anti-Semitism, however slight. "And what do you think will come from all this?"

"After all this, my dear Levan Valerianovich, in accordance with our long tradition, the corrupt administration will find a 'worthy' candidate from among the spies and the traitors to the Motherland. For example, they might pick Akhper Mekhtievich Radzhabov, who sold to the Americans, along with a Persian rug, the technical documentation of the SS-20 missile, the pride of our military, and he will hand over half of our rations to the prison warden while shamelessly stealing the other half for himself. Then, I'll have to write a new letter to the Prosecutor General," Fred said, ending our dialogue with a gloomy smile.

As I've mentioned, in the Barashevo prison all the inmates had to sew work mitts. They had only one digit, a thumb, but the rubber palm compensated for that shortcoming. I've seen our mitts many times at different building sites both before and after my imprisonment. These Gulag masterpieces were even used by the workers building the Moscow Metro. Our daily quota was ninety-two pairs. As a rule, everyone sewed ninety-three pairs, but suddenly, one beautiful day, Anadenko began sewing two hundred pairs.

At first, no one paid any attention, but when Anadenko turned in three hundred pairs of work mitts, a grumbling could be heard throughout the workshop, and the problem became public. The underground resistance committee, which at that time included me and was led by Anadenko himself, scheduled a meeting for 3 A.M. in the smoke shack. The committee members attending were, in alphabetical order: Altunyan, Anadenko, Berdzenishvili, Butov, Donskoy, Khomizuri, Manilovich, Polyakov, and Yankov. The meeting lasted fifteen minutes. As Anadenko explained to us, the prison warden had denied his right to a visit from his wife, and so the inmate conceived of a way to punish the warden. It turned out that Anadenko had sewed so many pairs in order to confuse Major Shalin and provoke him into doubling the daily quota. No one would be able to complete the double quota, and we'd have an eternal strike. Shalin would be dismissed, and we'd get back to our old quota. The committee did not approve of the plan, seeing it as extremely risky and dangerous. Chairman Anadenko quickly agreed, saying: "Thank God. I'm already exhausted from working so much."

After his release and rehabilitation, Anadenko wrote a huge manuscript about Marx and Popper. A Ukrainian journalist interviewed him and summarized his opinion about the interviewee as follows:

Internal depth and critical thinking,
Independence and responsibility,
Firmness and tactfulness,
Industriousness and generosity,
Modesty and chivalry.

You've got to give it to the journalist—he really "got at the root of it" if he was able to understand so much in just one interview. It took me three years of intense observation in a maximum-security prison camp and twenty-three years of delirious freedom to figure Anadenko out.

BADZYO

N ot so long ago during a long flight across the ocean, a few rather strange questions began occupying my mind: Who was the most cheerful person I'd ever met in my life? Or a more interesting question: Who was the most serious person? The answers turned out to be not so simple. In the running for the most cheerful, the winner was selected without much effort—after two or three hours on the plane, I awarded first place to Irakli Shengelia, my unforgettable professor, the best Latinist in the history of our country, and a great-grandson of the famous Georgian writer Iona Meunargia. Irakli Shengelia spent his childhood and youth in the Gulag and then in exile in Kazakhstan. He possessed a special *joie de vivre*—that unique brand of Georgian cheerfulness, a phenomenon so well described by the renowned philosopher Merab Mamardashvili, who came in second.

Choosing the most serious person proved to be more difficult. Among the many claimants to the title were the following: first, my only non-smiling professor, a specialist on Saint Grigol Khandzteli, and his spiritual clone (anyone associated with Tbilisi State University would easily recognize this professor); second, my speechless barber—no one in his family had laughed for a century; third, my gloomy neighbor who said hello to me for the last time twenty years ago; and fourth, my fellow-inmate Yuri Badzyo. During the tenth hour of my trans-Atlantic flight, the Grammy and Oscar in the category of "most serious" were justly awarded to Yuri Vasilievich Badzyo, a stouthearted political prisoner, an expert in hunger strikes, a Prometheus fighting for prisoner rights, and the founder and first leader of the Ukrainian Democratic Party.

Yuri Badzyo was born on April 25, 1936. In 1958, he graduated from the University of Uzhhorod with a degree in philology, and in 1964 he finished graduate school at the Literature Institute of the Ukrainian Academy of Sciences. He worked as a professor in several institutions in the Transcarpathia region, had an active social life, and was a member of the local youth club. During the Khrushchev Thaw, he became a member of the Communist Party, but in 1965 he was expelled for participating in various dissident actions, and, as a natural consequence, he was denied the right to teach.

After losing the right to work as a professor, he found a job at a bakery, doing heavy lifting. At the same time, he started his underground activities, distributing *samizdat* publications and so on. In 1972, he began working on the most important book of his life, *The Right to Live*. In 1977, when the book was almost ready, the KGB dispatched agent who managed to become Badzyo's girlfriend. She betrayed his trust and stole the manuscript. After a long bout of depression, deep disappointment, and frustration, Badzyo began writing the book again from scratch.

In 1979, he was arrested for his dissident activities. The court sentenced him to the maximum under Article 70—seven years in prison and five years of exile. He served his time in Dubravlag, in our beloved ZhKh 385/3-5 political prison.

When Dato and I were transferred to this prison, the first thing we saw was a very serious-looking man sitting near the rosebushes who didn't even look in our direction. He was sitting at a table with two open books and a watch in front of him, quickly writing something in his notebook and occasionally checking the books.

The welcoming committee began with the usual questions, but we had a question for them, too: Who was the man with his nose in his books? Khomizuri told us the man's name was Yuri Badzyo, that he was a social-democrat and a good man, but when he worked, it was impossible not only to talk to him, but even to come within three steps of him. Now he's working on his book, but in a few minutes, without a break, he'll switch to studying English, and exactly forty-five minutes after that, again without a break, he'll switch to German. And his alarm will announce the time change with a dull ring.

"Where did he get his clock? Are they even allowed in prisons?" I asked, regretting my lack of a clock or watch.

"No, they're not allowed. To get that clock, Badzyo had to go on a hunger strike for six hundred seventy-five hours, or four weeks and three hours. He achieved a great deal with his strike: He got an alarm clock, and now every forty-five minutes, the clock lets him know that it's time to change subjects—from political parties to philosophy, then English and German. If at some moment you need to know what time it is, you have three options: You can try, but only from a distance, to peek at Badzyo's clock, you can go to the barracks and listen to the radio (very soon, you'll learn their programming schedule), or you can go to the library and see Anderson, who will tell you the exact time by looking at his original 'herbal clock.' If there's a dire need, you can ask Arkady Dudkin, just don't ask him about the year. When it comes to hours, though, he's usually right."

This is how we met Yuri Badzyo on our first day in the prison. Even now, I can see his skinny, pale silhouette. He always comes to mind when I should start working, but am feeling too lazy to do anything important.

The Ukrainians, who were the second largest group in our prison after the Russians, were represented by Yuri Vasilyevich Badzyo, a social-democrat from Uzhhorod, Vasily Stepanovich Strilitsiv, a teacher and educational reformer from Ivano-Frankovsk, Vladimir Petrovich Deledivka, who was from Kiev and held a Ph.D. in Engineering, Gregory Fokich Nichiporenko, an engineer from Dnepropetrovsk, Dmitry Dmitrievich Mazur, a teacher from Zhitomir, Major Gregory Petrovich Kutsenko from the village of Ivanovka in the Kiev Region, and many others.

During that period, the head of the Ukrainian KGB was Stepan Nesterovich Mukha, who was notorious for his cruelty and his strange last name [*mukha* in Russian means "fly"]. This man would never spare his dissident compatriots, and almost all the above-mentioned Ukrainian inmates were sentenced to the maximum term specified under Article 70 (Article 62 in the Ukrainian Criminal Code): seven-plus-five.

Almost one hundred percent of the Ukrainian inmates were nationalists or were fighting for the independence of Ukraine. The only exception was the Ukrainian Russians—Fred Filippovich Anadenko from Kiev and Pyotr Aleksandrovich Butov from Odessa. The Ukrainians kept very close ties among themselves and took good care of one other, always ready to help and share their last piece of bread. The Ukrainians in Barashevo, unlike the Russians, had a clear and well-respected leader. All of them recognized the leadership of Yuri Badzyo, who earned his authority through his heroic struggles inside and outside of prison.

In prison, Badzyo was the first to begin writing letters in Ukrainian. Ganichenko, the censor, whose husband was Ukrainian, spent most of her life in Western Ukraine and knew Ukrainian perfectly well. Nevertheless, she'd return Badzyo's letters with the cynical verdict: "Unknown language." Badzyo continued writing in Ukrainian, unwilling to yield. The fact that Badzyo's family wasn't receiving any of his letters was of no concern to Ganichenko. After reading one of Badzyo's long letters, she would write "unknown language" and return it to the author. This lasted until perestroika, when the Georgians won the right to compose letters in their native language, opening the gate to a heroic flood of correspondence in Ukrainian, Lithuanian, Latvian, Estonian, and Armenian.

As soon as the right to compose letters in our native languages was announced, Yuri Badzyo came over to us with two pieces of Ukrainian *salo* and a rather large piece of real black bread, which he'd received from Kiev, and then, with a mug of strong tea, which was our drink of choice, he offered a toast to international friendship in Ukrainian. When it was our turn to toast, he asked us to do so in Georgian. The entire Ukrainian delegation came to listen to our toast and, of course, all the Georgians were present as well. I was brought up in a Georgian household—I was ten when my uncle appointed me *tamada*, or toastmaster, for the first time, and since then I have proposed a great many long toasts. Of course, not all of them were very good—a certain number were hackneyed, banal, and insincere. But never before or after have I given a toast to compare in terms of eloquence with the one I proposed in Georgian at the Barashevo prison. The toast was so long that our tea got cold, Strilitsev became ill from excitement, and Nichiporenko wiped away tears. From that day on, we all knew that Badzyo was our friend, even though his schedule never changed—political parties, philosophy, English, then German—leaving very little time for friendship.

As the leader of the Barashevo prison's science club, Vadim Yankov organized a weekly lecture series, which became so popular that others followed his example, and very soon we had weekly lectures on national cultures and political theories. During one such lecture, Badzyo gave a talk about how to create a political party based on his experience with the Ukrainian Democratic Party.

It's too bad that our know-it-all theoreticians, especially the young ones, don't have the opportunity to read that lecture—Badzyo never bothered to write it down. Although I call it a lecture, in reality, it was one of our typical dialogues, with Badzyo playing the role of Socrates, and I, the role of the naïve and self-assured Ion.

"Good evening, beloved Athenian people! Good evening, Ion! Good evening, guardians of our peace, in other words, our jailers, or, excuse me, controllers," Badzyo-Socrates calmly began.

"It's a good thing our jailers can't hear you, my dear Socrates," I, Ion-Levan, slyly interjected, addressing the thick-haired Badzyo, who in terms of the growth rate of his hair was second only to Rafik Papayan, and so had a long way to go to reach the baldness of Socrates. (As the future would show, he never achieved that status.)

"They *can't* hear me, or they can't *hear* me?" Socrates asked, artfully changing the stress of the question.

"They neither listen nor hear," Ion answered, keeping pace with his teacher's irony.

"The most important thing is that you hear me, my dear Ion. So, you're saying that you and your friends, young as you are, have established a political party?"

"Yes, my dear Socrates. The people and the 'sacred scroll,' or my indictment, are witnesses to the fact that the Georgian Republican Party was created by four people with an average age of twenty-two and a half," I said, quickly calculating the average age of the four founding fathers on May 21, 1978.

"That's a great age for playing soccer," Socrates said innocently, attacking with his first jab.

"I object! There was no soccer in the fifth century BCE," one of the Athenians, Zhora Khomizuri, interrupted in annoyance. The fact that, once, Tbilisi Dinamo, as the visiting team at Razdan Stadium, managed with only ten players to beat Yerevan Ararat with a score of 4–1 was probably the only thing Zhora knew about soccer.

"Quiet in the agora!" Socrates shouted, calling the public

to order. "Let me be more specific: It's a prime age to participate in the Olympic Games, not to establish a serious political party."

"One way or another, we established that party and the state officials paid us their respect by prosecuting the party," Ion declared with some immodesty.

"What are the goals of your party?" Socrates inquired.

"To put an end to the Communist order, make Georgia independent, and establish democracy," Ion answered, boldly presenting the modest program of his young political party.

"And why do you, a Greek, put yourself in danger for the sake of Georgia?" Socrates asked without smiling. [The surname Berdzenishvili means "son of a Greek" in Georgian.]

"If the great Socrates cares about Ukraine, then what's wrong with small Ion caring about small Georgia?" asked Ion, who at that time was at least twice as heavy as Socrates.

"So, you wanted to achieve all three goals, did you? Decommunization, independence, and democracy?" Socrates asked, stoically listing the goals.

"Precisely, the Holy Trinity," Ion boldly said.

"We Greeks have not three but three thousand gods. There are twelve Olympian gods alone," Socrates, the patriarch of pluralism, explained sternly. "The Holy Trinity was not yet born, or, more accurately, no one was talking about their birth."

"Let's not split hairs, my dear Socrates."

"After you've achieved your glorious objective, when Communist rule is overturned and Georgia has become an independent and democratic country, do you plan to disband your party?" Socrates asked.

"Please repeat the question, my dear Socrates!" Ion said.

"You understood perfectly well what I was asking."

"How could I not understand it! But my ears are ringing with those golden words 'independent' and 'democratic.'"

"Say there are no Communists, Georgia is a member of the

SACRED DARKNESS · 163

UN, and fair elections are held regularly," Socrates said, offering a straightforward description of the future. "What will the Georgian Republican Party be doing at that time? Will it announce its dissolution, or will it change its objectives? Answer me honestly, my dear Ion, without any diversions."

"Change its objectives," the inexperienced Ion answered, quickly agreeing with the idea that freedom and democracy would fall from the sky.

"And the party will pursue new goals?" Socrates asked benignly.

"Exactly, a new political situation requires new goals," Ion answered without hesitation.

"Wouldn't it be better if from the very beginning you'd specified those 'new' long-term goals, Ion?" Socrates asked.

"You got him! You got him!" Vadim Yankov, one of the Athenians, exclaimed, unable to hide his excitement. Vadim didn't like the idea of independence for the former Soviet republics. He'd always supported the idea of fighting Communism together and achieving the democratization of the entire Soviet Union. Otherwise, he didn't see the possibility of preventing Russia, which would find itself isolated, from becoming an aggressor.

"A political party is a public organization that proclaims certain goals, such as holding state power, retaining that power, and using state institutions to satisfy the interests of a particular social class. The party participates in elections, organizes campaign platforms, and voices political protests. Isn't that true, my dear Ion?" Socrates asked.

"That sounds like a complete definition, my dear Socrates. Even the editors of the famous *Britannica* would envy you. It seems to me, however, that your definition doesn't apply to all political systems," Ion answered, allowing himself a hint of criticism.

"I assume, my dear Ion, you'll now say that in a one-party

political system, a political party doesn't voice protest. Is that what you wanted to say?" the Ukrainian Socrates asked, squinting his eyes.

"You've read my mind, dearest Socrates," Ion exclaimed, unable to conceal his excitement.

"Let's agree, dearest Ion and the citizens of Athens, that a one-party system is not a political system but a political prison, in which all other parties are prohibited, arrested, or turned into cultural or pro-military organizations. A primitive political system is like a historical drama, beginning with a second political party having the same rights, and ending with a fully-developed political system—characterized by a multiparty, pluralistic political environment that includes the entire political spectrum."

"It's a good thing our guards can't hear you and can't understand you, dear Socrates. Your state and legal theory would get you at least eight more years," Ion said, generously delivering Socrates a new sentence.

"There are only five ideal parties," Socrates continued, returning to the traditional Greek mode of rhetoric: "An elite party, a party of the masses, an ethnic party, an association of voters, and a party representing a particular movement. Each of these has its own subdivisions. For example, an association of voters can be divided into an individual party, a majority party (the so-called catchall party), or an issues-based party. The US Democratic Party is the party of the majority, but the US Republican Party is a platform association. Now answer me, my dear Ion: To what type of party does your child, the Georgian Republican Party, belong?"

"I never thought about it, my dear Socrates, but at first glance, I can say that it's not a party of the masses, and it's not a party of a narrow ethnic orientation either. Our party is not an electoral association—it's a long way to Georgian elections. If there are no other parties (and how can I doubt your analysis?), then it follows that it's a party of the elite."

"This means you understand that there's a difficult road ahead of you before you achieve national support. It's good that you created a fundamentally pluralistic party. That means you'll achieve your first real success in about forty years."

"Oh, no, Socrates! That long?" Ion asked, gasping in the face of this prediction.

"If you don't behave well, years will be added, not taken away. I can see a more or less democratic situation emerging by 2017, the hundredth anniversary of the October coup. How old will you be then, Ion?"

"I'll be sixty-four, my dear Socrates. I don't like that number. The great John Lennon sang a song about being that old, but he was killed at forty."

"I must say that your ambitions are astonishing, my dear Ion," Socrates said, being the self-proclaimed number-one Beatlemaniac in the prison. "However, if truth be told, it should be pointed out that this was Paul's song, not John's—in fact, it was one of Paul's first five songs. And speaking of Paul McCartney, he is, thank God, alive and well, and may live not only to sixty-four but to a hundred and four. Your fans—if you have any fans—may disappoint you, but they won't kill you. When you're retired, you'll have time to enjoy your country's beauty, freedom, and democracy."

"But that time is so far away, my dear Socrates."

"I'd like to talk to you about your party's finances, dear Ion. You must've thought about this question, too, when creating your party."

"The party is to be financed by membership dues and supporter donations," Ion declared and recalled how difficult it was to discuss membership dues every time he'd brought the subject up.

"How many members are in your party?" Socrates asked, demanding the revelation of confidential information.

"Let's say, three hundred."

166 · LEVAN BERDZENISHVILI

"How much are the dues?"

"Let's say, one ruble."

"Three hundred years will have to pass before you manage to collect one ruble in dues from three hundred people. Please, believe my bitter experience, young Ion. What donations are you hoping for?"

"Some businessmen will donate, my dear Socrates."

"Don't count too much on this either, young man."

"What can we do then? Rob a bank, like Stalin?" Ion asked, upset at the loss of his party's finances. Besides, he knew all too well that Stalin hadn't only robbed banks but also, while in political exile, had used criminal support in his political battles with his opponents, which was mentioned on several occasions by his party comrades.

"And why do you free the state from this responsibility, dear Ion? Why shouldn't the state give money from a special budget line to a more or less serious political party, if during past elections, the number of votes collected by the party exceeded the lawfully established minimum? Shouldn't the state have funds to promote pluralism?" Socrates asked, igniting serious disapproval among the Athenian citizens.

"What a utopia!" Vadim Yankov exclaimed, now truly excited. "I won't live long enough to see that!"

"I don't know about Russia, but, truly, I'm sure it wouldn't burden Ukraine's budget, and Georgia's even less so. States like Georgia and Ukraine must provide support from their own budgets to protect the stability and independence of their parties from foreign governments, for example, Russia."

The subsequent development of this dialogue was rather dramatic. For some reason, the drunk and outraged guards Trimazkin, Trifonov, and Kiselyov stormed the room and sentenced the dialogue participants, Socrates and Ion, as well as the judges, Yankov and Khomizuri, to fifteen days in solitary confinement. (It looked like the provocateurs from the

Council of Interal Order had worked hard on this operation.) And so, our renowned Greeks had to finish their state, or rather anti-state, dialogue in the hole.

Not so long ago, the memory of Yuri Badzyo's *The Principles of Political Hunger Strikes* overtook me. When an activist got sick during one of the political strikes in Tbilisi, I vividly relived the time when I'd read Yuri's original manuscript. I had some difficulty with the Ukrainian language and so was constantly running to Volodya Deledivka or Grisha Nechiporenko to ask the meaning of this or that word. This immortal work became a textbook on how to conduct a hunger strike as an effective weapon of political protest. And I must say that on numerous occasions, the grand master of long hunger strikes—"wet" as well as "dry"—was able to test the main principles of his book for himself.

According to Badzyo, a hunger strike—or as he called it, "the queen of nonviolent struggle"—comes in three types: regular, when you refuse any food; dry, or absolute, when you refuse food and water; and partial, when you refuse *almost* everything—for example, sticking only to "some bread and water," or when you refuse particular food, for example, "state-provided food," and restrict yourself to eating only from the packages sent from home. (Georgian political prisoners used this type of hunger strike for many years in Georgian prisons. Zviad Dzidzigury used to tell me that he didn't even know what prison food tasted like because neither he nor his followers ever touched it.)

Badzyo listed four reasons for hunger strikes—political, social, economic, and personal. And, finally, hunger strikes could be classified by whether they were individual or collective.

After three days of a dry (absolute) hunger strike, the process of ketosis begins in the human body. Followers of the popular Atkins diet know that when deprived of carbs, the body uses its own fat as energy instead of the glycogen stored in the liver. A dry hunger strike of three or four days is not dangerous because the body will produce up to one liter of metabolic water as a product of the fat burning reaction, but after five days of a dry hunger strike, irreversible processes begin to take place in the body, damaging the kidneys, liver, and heart.

According to Badzyo, in order to conduct a long-term and "fruitful" political hunger strike, it is necessary that the first three days be dry and that water intake begin on the fourth day.

To successfully accomplish a two-week hunger strike, one must go through a period of preparation that should include one-day, three-day, and seven-day hunger strikes. All inmates must undergo one month of preparation, beginning with a one-day hunger strike, for example, on a Monday. The next week, it's the same one-day hunger strike on Monday. The week after that, you can start a three-day (Monday–Wednesday) strike, and after a week, a seven-day strike (Monday–Sunday). Only after a month of such preparations is an inmate ready for a new test—a three-day dry hunger strike. If a person has undergone a seven-day hunger strike and a three-day dry hunger strike, he is ready, physically and emotionally, for a two-week hunger strike, the first three days of which should be dry. According to Yuri Badzyo, after such preparation, a person is even ready for a forty-seven-day hunger strike.

Badzyo's personal record was sixty-three days. He undertook this two-month-long hunger strike in secret, without announcing it publicly, because the Soviet penitentiary system didn't recognize political hunger strikes, and one week after announcing a hunger strike, the inmate would be subjected to force-feeding. They say that Anatoly Marchenko, the steadfast warrior for human rights sentenced to 15 years for anti-Soviet propoganda, died in the Chistopol prison on

December 8, 1986, when the KGB executioners decided to use force-feeding. Marchenko was the last Soviet political prisoner to die in prison, out of the millions convicted under Articles 58 and 70 of the Soviet Criminal Code.

On September 23, 1986, in front of the White House, the American astrophysicist Charles Hyder began a hunger strike, demanding that the Reagan administration engage in disarmament. If we are to believe Soviet TV, this hunger strike lasted for two hundred eighteen days. Later, it turned out that the whole episode was invented by Hyder and the Washington-based Chekist and TV reporter Vladimir Dunaev. Hyder was seen near the White House only on rare occasions, but to create the illusion that he was constantly there, Dunaev would wear a different suit every time he appeared next to Hyder on the screen. Sometime later, Dunaev's son told the world about his father's activities, but in the Soviet Union, Hyder's hunger strike was such a high-profile PR event (though completely unknown in the US) that even the Secretary General of the Communist Party of the Soviet Union, Mikhail Gorbachev, wrote a letter in support of the American dissident. (Regardless, the American professor made scathing anti-Soviet statements at a later date.) In reality, Hyder wasn't on a hunger strike, though his doctors had prescribed a strict diet due to his being overweight. As soon as Badzyo saw Dr. Hyder on the newscast *Vremya*, he instantly realized that this hunger strike was fake—the fact that the American was consuming juices and vitamins was written all over his face.

In 1988, Yuri Badzyo was released from exile and moved to Kiev, where he began organizing the Democratic Party in opposition to the Communists. By the spring of 1990, Badzyo completed *The Manifesto of the Ukrainian Democratic Party*. On May 14, 1990, in Kiev, the party's inaugural conference took place, where after some revisions, *The Manifesto* by Badzyo was adopted as the central document of the Ukrainian

Democratic Party. Yuri Badzyo was elected party leader during the Democratic Party Convention on December 15–16, 1990.

In 1992, after establishing the Ukrainian Democratic Party, the second political party ever to exist in the history of Ukraine, Badzyo left politics. After Ukraine became independent, Badzyo's once stolen manuscript was returned, and he was able to complete his life's goal, and, in 1996, he published *The Right to Live*. I believe this is one of the most serious books of the twentieth century, and it has already been translated into twenty languages. In 2005, the president of Ukraine, Viktor Yushchenko, awarded Yuri a special Medal of Merit (but only of the third degree).

At present, Yuri Badzyo works at the Institute of Philosophy of the Ukrainian National Academy of Sciences. It is possible that most of his colleagues don't even realize how lucky they are to have the honor of living and working next to such a hero. We, mere mortals, can only imagine how much good a man capable of holding a secret hunger strike for sixty-three days will accomplish in this world, without self-promotion.

RAZLATSKY

As a rule, the warden of the Barashevo political prison, Major Alexey Shalin, came to work early in the morning, before the inmates were up, even before the solemn and exalted voice on the radio started to thunder the Soviet anthem—which would make all the inmates leap from their bunk beds. This tradition was seldom broken. If Shalin had to pass through a courtyard full of prisoners during the day, he would walk fast, straight to his office, always keeping his head down and trying not to look around him. All the older inmates knew exactly why he behaved this way.

The Ministry of Internal Affairs wrote in one of its instructions that the prisoners' visible hair must not exceed two millimeters, regardless of whether the hair was on their heads or on their faces, in the form of a beard or a mustache. The punishment for violating the two-millimeter rule was severe, ranging from losing the right to shop in the prison store to losing the right to see family or even spending time in the hole.

Despite the severity of the punishment, one inmate proudly wore a real Stalin-like mustache, several millimeters in lengths, imitating his beloved leader, father, and teacher. But Shalin looked past it, because if he chose to see this prisoner, he'd have to immediately punish him, and all punishments, whether light or severe, had been exhausted a long time ago; even solitary confinement had failed. It was also clear that the idol symbolized by the prisoner's mustache wasn't a mere mortal for Major Shalin either.

The mustachioed Stalinist inmate, Alexey Borisovich

Razlatsky, hailed from Russia's sixth-largest city, Samara (which was called Kuybyshev from 1935 to 1991), and represented a truly rare species in the postwar dissident movement. As a Stalinist and the founder of the Party of the Dictatorship of the Proletariat, he was convicted under Article 70, which had become almost mythic by that time.

From the far-left, this extremely dangerous man criticized the, in his words, "feudal" Communist Party of the Soviet Union in the Khruschev-Brezhnev era. To guarantee this Bolshevik's absence from the political scene, the KGB and its obedient servant, the Soviet courts, sentenced him to the maximum term of seven years in a maximum-security prison and five years of exile. Already in the seventies, Razlatsky was predicting the fall of "developed socialism" and the imminent collapse of the Soviet Union.

As with many inmates holding strict ideological positions, Razlatsky was incredibly persistent, unwavering, and inflexible, combining the qualities of a poet, a dissident, a mathematician, and a philosopher.

As I see it, out of the three characteristics—being honest, being intellectual, and being a communist—only two are compatible. In my opinion, an honest and intelligent man can't be a communist, an intelligent communist can't be honest, and an honest communist can't be intelligent. For me, this is an incontrovertible fact, but as it happens with all such artificial generalizations or intellectual jokes, if you will, life always provides an unpredictable response. And Alexey Razlatsky was just such a response. No one doubted his honesty, the number of political and scientific manuscripts he published in *samizdat* and *tamizdat*[19] testified to his

---

[19] Formed from the word *sam*, meaning 'oneself,' and *izdat*, meaning 'published,' *samizdat* refers to works that were self-published, that is, published and circulated outside official channels in order to avoid censorship. Tamizdat, formed from the word *tam*, meaning 'there' and *izdat*, meaning 'published,' refers to works that were first published abroad, another method for avoid Soviet censorship.

intelligence, and the fact that he was a devoted communist was confirmed by the KGB and the severity of his punishment.

As far as it is possible for someone to be sure about any-thing, Razlatsky was one hundred percent certain that his beliefs were correct. He called us incurable liberals and oppor-tunists and promised to execute us all as soon as he rose to power—although he used to say this with a benevolent smile. Razlatsky had a son, Alexey Alexeevich, whom he loved dearly. He talked about his son all the time, missed him intensely, and wrote him letters. Whenever he received a letter in return, he was over the moon. Once, Dato and Zhora asked him: "What would you do if your son became a liberal? You know, the twentieth century is almost over, the twenty-first century is approaching—anything can happen. Anyway, what if your son suddenly told you that Stalin was a tyrant who'd brought noth-ing but misery upon Russia, humankind, and you, personally?" Razlatsky began to think. He was so deep in thought that he didn't even notice that people were gathering around us. Manilovich tried to brief the newcomers on the matter at hand. In fact, Razlatsky was so deep in thought that he didn't hear Manilovich's ironic comments and paid no attention to Zhora's wager, nor did he react to the humanist Polyakov's plea: "Guys, leave him alone! Have a heart! It's true he's a Stalinist, but he's a human being, too!" Time passed, and finally Razlatsky reached a conclusion. As he pronounced his verdict, the face of this kind man turned to steel:

"In the event my son, Alexey Alexeevich Razlatsky, failed to understand Stalin and spread revisionist lies, I would condemn him to death and execute the verdict myself—I'd shoot him as a traitor."

Disappointed, Polyakov gave up, Khomizuri was happy to win his bet with Donskoy, Dato was shocked, Rafik Papayan wiped away tears, and a few minutes later, Johnny asked inno-cently, "What happened?"

Once upon a time, a guitar appeared in our prison. No one knew where it came from or how it got there, but it was there nonetheless. It was a classic six-string guitar, but depending on the user, it could be tuned in major thirds (e-b-g-d-a-e or *me-ti-so-re-la-mi*), or in a Russian key (d-b-g-b-g-d or *re-ti-so-ti-so-re*). Two groups formed, the Spaniards and the Russians, according to their choice of key. Manilovich and I sided with the Spaniards, but Donskoy and Papayan were with the Russians. When someone from the Spaniards' camp would get the guitar from the Russians, they would have to retune it. They wouldn't change the second, third, and fourth strings, but the first string would be tuned as the second, the sixth—as the first, and the fifth—as the sixth. It wasn't a complicated procedure, if you could carry a tune. But as the guitar changed hands so often, the strings lost their original tones, and even though they were major thirds with respect to each other, it was difficult to say if the first and the sixth strings were still real *mi* or had become *re* or even *do*. And so, it became almost impossible to restore the proper sound. Obviously, a tuning fork would have helped, but where could we find one of those in prison?

Once, Rafik and I were discussing our lack of a tuning fork while smoking in the shack. (Today, when I travel the world and see a smoking room in most modern airports, it always reminds me of the smoke shack in prison, except that these airport smoking rooms are clean and comfortable.) "I have an idea!" Papayan exclaimed. "We need to memorize the tonality of the Soviet anthem, which they sing every morning on the radio. Then we can find a way to get the anthem's score, and that should be enough for tuning our guitar."

"It's true that you dissidents are rotten people," Razlatsky said, suddenly entering the shack and interrupting our conversation. "But, unlike me, you're real prisoners under the law, so why do you torture yourselves so much?"

"Perhaps you could offer a better solution?" Rafik asked

politely, giving me a sly wink, as if to say: What does this Stalinist
dinosaur have to tell us, intellectuals from the Caucasus?

"First of all, you don't need the score of the Soviet anthem
because I'm a living version of that score. Revisionists and feudal pseudo-Communists have dared to change the words, but
the music and key are still the same. The first syllable of the
word you hate so much, "*So-yuz*" [the Union] is the note *so*,
which is the third guitar string in both keys. Then *do-so-la-ti-mi*:

> *Soyuz nerushimiy respublik svobodnykh*
> *(so) (do) (so) (la) (ti) (mi) (mi) (la) (so) (fa) (so) (do)*

Razlatsky sang the full version of the Soviet national anthem,
the one from 1943, in a state of bliss. When he reached the
verse about Stalin, his voice trembled and tears welled up in his
eyes. He took a long pause and then finished in a full voice:

> *Nas vyrastil Stalin—na vernost' narodu,*
> *Na trud i na podvigi nas vdokhnovil.*
> [We were raised by Stalin to be true to the people,
> To labor and heroic deeds, he inspired us!]

"But you don't even have to do that—don't waste the
anthem of the great Soviet Union on your stupid guitar. I'm a
living tuning fork, and I'll give you the correct *la* whenever you
like," Razlatsky continued, inspired by the solemn anthem.

When I asked where that perfect *la* came from, Razlatsky said
that every political prisoner had a second occupation. For many
years, while the Georgians drank, the Petersburg aristocrats
worked as street cleaners (he meant Polyakov and Donskoy), and
the petty bourgeois of the Bund party (Manilovich and Feldman)
worked as electricians, the proletarian from Kuybyshev was
working as a piano tuner and served as head judge at festivals for
independent singer-songwriters, or bards.

Razlatsky's musical history didn't end there. During the

"Music of the Caucasus" evening organized by the Christian Federation of South Caucasian Nations, Ruslan Ketenchiev sang a difficult Balkar song, Rafik performed the famous Armenian song "*Tsitsernak*" (The Swallow) in Komitas's interpretation, and I decided to sing "Suliko." When I reached the part "*gulam-oskvnili vtirodi*" (bitterly cried), Razlatsky began singing along in perfect Georgian and in harmony so beautiful that the audience gathered in the smoke shack burst into applause and I got first prize—a matchbox filled with black tea. Razlatsky refused to share the prize with me. Unfortunately, after that Khomizuri began to hate "Suliko" as a symbol of Stalinism. Even when I told him that the lyrics were written by Akaki Tsereteli in 1895 and that Varenka Tsreteli wrote the music in the same year, he didn't change his mind. He was furious: "During Stalin's time, 'Suliko' was all we heard on the radio! How could you, as chairman of the jury, award the prize to Berdzenishvili for the Cannibal's favorite song, especially when sung as a duet with Razlatsky?"

The jury chairman, Vadim Yankov, didn't take this outburst seriously; but he made an official statement: "The Father of All Nations and of All Times, Generalissimo Comrade Stalin, also loved wine, and if I'm ever released, I, without fearing you or Stalin, will drink wine and maybe even sing 'Suliko!'"

As a true Russian and a defender of the proletariat, Razlatsky, of course, was a drinking man. Once we were discussing salaries, and our Stalinist friend evaluated the growth of his monthly salary in relation to the price of one half-liter vodka bottle. To our surprise, his approach was better at describing the tax brackets than the old or new rubles.

"In the beginning, my monthly salary was very small, only five bottles. After defending my Ph.D., I got a raise, and my salary increased to twenty bottles. When I became a research associate, my salary reached the ideal level—fifty bottles. If you subtract the price of food and entertainment, that leaves thirty bottles. I say it's ideal because there was one bottle for every day, and if you missed a day . . . Then when I got my own lab, my salary increased significantly—to seventy-two bottles and a few shots."

When Razlatsky talked about vodka, it was almost like poetry. As he explained to us: "I respect Lenin a lot, but I can't forget the fact that he supported the law outlawing vodka, a silly thing started by Tsar Nicholas II. Alcohol was prohibited until 1924. But as soon as Lenin died, Stalin lifted the ban. How could a Georgian, who was also a good poet, prohibit drinking?"

Razlatsky knew several of Stalin's speeches by heart, including his address to the Fourteenth Party Congress, where he talked about vodka as a source of reserves. Apparently, this is literally what Comrade Stalin said:

> We cannot go into bondage to the West-European capitalists, not being able to accept the enslaving terms that they offer us and which we have rejected; only one alternative remains—to seek resources in other spheres. After all, that is better than bondage. Here we have to choose between bondage and vodka, and those people who think that it is possible to build socialism in white gloves are grievously mistaken.[20]

In 1951, being such a good student, Razlatsky was awarded a trip to various sites throughout the Soviet Union with ties to Stalin. Several children and three teachers went on the trip. One of the teachers, a workshop instructor, happened to be a war veteran. During that trip, they visited Tbilisi, Gori, and Batumi, among other places. I can't say the same for Tbilisi and Batumi, but I'm certain that Razlatsky knew Gori much better than I did. And better than Johnny Lashkarashvili, too, who grew up near Gori, in the village of Doeci. When it came to the Stalin museum, Razlatsky even knew all the employees

[20] Stalin, J.V. "Political Report of the Central Committee." *The Fourteenth Congress of the CPSU(B)*. Marxist Internet Archive.

by their full names. He visited that museum at least twenty times, every time he'd go to the city of Gori. (Of course, he didn't go there to see the seventh-century Ateni Sioni church, as some of us did.) He knew about the Stalin monument in amazing detail, but as it happened, he was also familiar with the famous Gori cutlets and knew all the local places where they served excellent *lobio*. Once, finding himself in the middle of a heated discussion between Rafik and me about the Ateni Sioni church, Razlatsky said: "I've never been in this church, only heard about it, but I know Ateni wine very well, and I have to tell you: This is Georgia's true heritage!"

Alexey Borisovich was an interesting person to talk to. He liked to listen and was very good at it, but most of all, he liked to ask questions. When he talked, you could detect a Georgian accent, which he loved very much. His accent was different from the one the Russian standup comedians used on stage—a general regional accent, which, in reality, was a mixture of Georgian, Armenian, Azerbaijani, and Chechen accents. No, his was a truly Georgian accent. Razlatsky must have not only read all of Stalin's writings, but also listened to all his speeches. Along with his co-conspirator, Razlatsky wrote the most important anti-Soviet manuscript of his life, which later earned him a prison sentence, and named it, in the best Russian revolutionary tradition, *To Whom Must We Answer?* The chapter titles followed the same tradition—"Who Must We Ask?," "Where Do the Questions Come from?," "Where Do We Look for Answers?," and "Who Should Ask the Questions?" According to his indictment, this book slandered the Soviet social order and the Soviet state, the Communist Party and Soviet government policy, and contained a program for fighting Soviet power. The Kuybyshev KGB officers were convinced that Razlatsky's manuscript was an adaptation of the program of the Polish Solidarity movement.

Alexey Razlatsky used to say that he had two teachers who were very different from each other—Socrates and Stalin.

Which made Manilovich joke: Pay attention, both their names start with an *S*, and neither of them ever wrote anything, the former—because of principle, and the latter—because he was illiterate. According to Borya's theory, Stalin's numerous volumes were written by thousands of associates at the Marxism-Leninism Institute during those nights when the leader didn't sleep (or did he?). I must admit, though, that Razlatsky loved asking questions, just like Socrates. I would even say that there was something of early communism in Razlatsky, or even high communism, as well as pre-Marxist, Platonic, and, in general, classical communism. I can't say anything about his relationship to the principles of communism, but Razlatsky, just like Plato, didn't believe in private property, and he was that rare man who, along with the Georgians, would let Arkady Dudkin smoke some of his *makhorka*.

Razlatsky and I also found a topic that interested both of us: the trial of Socrates. As is well known, Socrates was tried in 339 BCE. The trial followed all the democratic formalities: both sides were represented, the prosecution and the defense—there were two votes, no one doubted the vote count, and so on—and Socrates was sentenced to death. Razlatsky considered Socrates the first communist and blamed his prosecution on proto-revisionists (this was his own term).

"The trial of Socrates showed not only the weakness of Western democracy, but also its complete inability to see the advantages of the new doctrine of communism. By sentencing the first communist to death, ancient democracy buried itself alive," Razlatsky proclaimed and, giving his words a suddenly unexpected twist, added in Georgian: "*Tavi dai-SAMARA*[21], as Stalin would say."

"So, do you think that Socrates was a proto-communist and

[21] The phrase *Tavi dai-Samara* is Georgian for "Democracy buried itself," but the Russian city of Samara is also Razlatsky's hometown.

that the Georgian language was a proto-communist language?" I asked with feigned innocence.

"Socrates was a communist, not just a proto-communist. He denied private property, he supported the working class, the slaves, by giving them knowledge, and he loved music," Razlatsky stated without explaining the connection between music and the communists.

"Obviously, there has always been communist potential in the Georgian language as well," the poet and dissident from Samara continued. "Wasn't it Rustaveli who said: 'Give the workers the means of labor and free the proletariat?'"

"So you're saying that, according to your theory, Rustaveli was a Marxist too?" Zhora Khomizuri asked, taken aback. As an anti-Communist and a lover of Rustaveli, he felt like someone had just stolen his favorite toy.

"Not just a Marxist, but a true Stalinist," Borya Manilovich responded. "Don't you know that 'His own enemy is he who will not seek for a friend' was said about the First Communist International?"[22]

"'Give my treasures to the poor, let my slaves have their liberty.'[23] That's what Rustaveli said, and there weren't any workers or proletariat in *The Lord of the Panther-Skin*. It wouldn't make sense!" I exclaimed.

"Levan, you still seem like a decent man, even though you're a democrat," Razlatsky began.

"However, in reality, you have to understand that you're wrong, and if Razlatsky hasn't shot you yet, it's only because the Georgians aren't the first on his execution list," Manilovich said, finishing Razlatsky's thought.

[22] The saying is taken from Rustaveli's *The Lord of the Panther-Skin*. See Rustaveli, Shota. *The Lord of the Panther-Skin*. Translated by R.H. Stevenson, State University of New York Press, 1977, p. 102.
[23] Ibid, p. 96.

"For example, cosmopolitans of all stripes," Razlatsky said, making Boris, who had brightened up momentarily, fall silent. "Anyway, Levan, you haven't lost your chance to establish the truth of class."

"Well, let's just say that's the case," I answered, agreeing with him, despite the fact that I always reacted badly to the word "class."

"You have to at least agree that Rustaveli has a very low opinion of the petty and haute bourgeoisie alike. Like in *The Lord of the Panther-Skin* when Avtandil accuses the merchant class of a military crime."

"Avtandil just says, 'You merchants don't know how to fight,'" I said, trying to remove any taint of class theory from Rustaveli, who, I feared, might soon share the fate of "Suliko." Admired by both Stalin and Razlatsky, Rustaveli would be completely rejected by the others and would never make it to the level of St. Gregory of Narek, the author of *The Book of Lamentations*, who was adored by Vadim Yankov, Sergey Averintsev, and Rafik Papayan.

"But aren't Rustaveli's merchants bourgeois?" Razlatsky asked. "Aren't Georgians, to this very day, against the bourgeois, and isn't the majority of the Georgian population made up of workers and peasants? Isn't it true that Georgians see commerce as a shameful occupation and distance themselves from their fellow countrymen selling flowers in Moscow because they see them as members of the hated bourgeoisie?"

"Since when do communists have such a tender love of peasants?" Borya Manilovich asked, rousing himself after being accused of cosmopolitanism.

"It's misguided to represent true Communists as protectors of only the interests of workers. The peasants and the working class, sickle and hammer—together they make up the masses. Democrats, bourgeois, and intelligentsia are not the masses. They are waste products."

"And who made those subjects into waste products? Maybe it was God-the-Father?" I asked.

"Levan, aren't you an atheist? Or like your beloved Greeks, a pantheist, which is basically the same? What God are you talking about? There is no God!"

"How much does the opium of the masses cost?" Zhora Khomizuri, another dubious atheist, asked.

"I don't want to talk about priests today," Razlatsky said.

"It's probably because a certain child studied in a seminary, namely Stalin," Manilovich said, offering his own explanation of Razlatsky's religious tolerance.

"No, it's because, in reality, religion is not our enemy. Our real enemy is the bourgeoisie," Razlatsky said, resolutely.

"Is this why during the war Comrade Stalin asked the Church and all its saints for help?" Khomizuri asked.

"All the saints were communists deep down," Razlatsky said.

"And Hitler used to say that Jesus Christ was a Communist, and Peter and Paul were the first Bolsheviks," Manilovich said, suddenly lending support to Rosenberg's position, despite being a victim of those same ideas.

"You don't understand anything. I don't have anything else to say to you," Razlatsky said, beginning to get mad. "Let me talk to my Georgian. He understands me."

"Let's see if I understand. So, in your opinion, all good people beginning with Socrates, continuing with the saints, and finishing with Rustaveli were communists?" I said, summarizing Razlatsky's theory.

"That's an oversimplification," Razlatsky said. "But it will do as a working hypothesis."

"If there is no God, then it follows that the saints were communists. It's logical," Khomizuri concluded.

"That means the text written about the life of Francis of Assisi, *The Little Flowers*, is, in fact, a manifesto of the

Communist Party," Manilovich said, unable to hide his sarcasm. He had an old grudge against Catholicism and often talked about the secret collaboration between the Vatican and Hitler.

"Levan, did you know that Alexey Borisovich wrote a special manuscript entitled *The Second Communist Manifesto*?" Zhora asked.

"Of course, I know. I read Alexey Borisovich's indictment," I said. "As far as I understand, Razlatsky is Marx, and his accomplice, Isaev, is Engels."

"Alexey Borisovich Marx, Gregory Zinovievich Engels, Shota Vissarionovich Rustaveli, Francis Assisi Plekhanov, Petr Pavlovich Lenin, and Jesus Josephovich Stalin," Manilovich said, creating another of his signature lists.

"You're all monkeys! I'd line you all up against the wall and shoot!" Razlatsky yelled, getting very mad. In my humble opinion, he was hurt most of all by the senseless insertion of the revisionist Plekhanov's name in Manilovich's list of "good people."

Everyone burst into laughter.

"And the fact that you're Georgian won't save you," Razlatsky said to me, adding one more bullet to his list. "Your nation has already given the world more than enough, so there's no need for the rest of you . . . "

"So come, brothers and sisters, for your struggle carries on," Manilovich sang, trying to imitate the melody of "The Internationale."

* * *

Perestroika brought freedom for Alexey Razlatsky. When all the political prisons released their inmates in February of 1987, Razlatsky was pardoned, too. (This pardon is sometimes called Gorbachev's amnesty even though there wasn't any amnesty—technically speaking, each political prisoner asked to be pardoned in a single sentence, and the USSR

Supreme Court granted their requests.) Returning to Kuybyshev, he continued writing poetry and smoking four packs of cigarettes a day. He liked to joke: "You know, I'll only live as long as they make my favorite *Sever* cigarettes." For six months, he couldn't find a job. Then, finally, the economist Razlatsky was given an office at the Giprovostokneft Institute, in the real estate development laboratory, to smoke his cigarettes and work as he pleased. He took an active part in public life, gave speeches at the National Front's noisy assemblies and at the thousands of meetings that became popular in Kuybyshev at that time. It seemed to him that a communist Renaissance was approaching, and that his time had finally come . . .

The Communist Alexey Razaltsky passed away suddenly on November 6, 1989. The restless anti-Communists Zhora Khomizuri and Vadim Yankov, each of his own accord, told me the sad news with great sorrow. It made me very sad, too. To be honest, I believed that if it were up to him, Razlatsky would truly have put all of us against the wall in front of a firing squad, but I was upset nonetheless. I guess a human being is not as simple as it might seem to a mind blinded by class theory. Shortly after that, on January 25, 1991, Kuybyshev got its old name back, Samara. And on December 26 of the same year, unexpectedly for many, the Soviet Union ceased to exist. *Sever* cigarettes, the kind that Razlatsky loved so much, were discontinued. They were replaced by filter cigarettes with the same name. Alexey Razlatsky's fame passed to his son, Alexey Alexeevich Razlatsky, a singer-songwriter and guitar player who wrote an anthem for the Samara soccer club, Kryliya Sovetov [The Wings of the Soviets], titled "Nashi Kryliya" [Our Wings]. They say that Razlatsky junior doesn't mind that there are players of different nationalities and races on the team. He accepts this fact with liberal understanding. And he doesn't have a mustache.

BUTOV

The great city of Odessa, the pearl of the Black Sea, was founded by Vytautas the Great, the Grand Duke of Lithuania, at the end of the fourteenth century. Soon after that, the Ottomans conquered the city and renamed it Khadzhibey (or Hacibey in Polish), incorporating it into the Yedisan province. In the eighteenth century, the Turks rebuilt Khadzhibey's fortress and renamed it Yeni Dünya [literally "New World"]. Khadzhibey became the *sanjak*, or administrative center, of the Silistre province. Through the efforts of Catherine the Great, Russia annexed this territory, and Odessa became the major port city of the "New Russia." In the course of a single century, Odessa became the fourth largest city in the Russian Empire, after Petersburg, Moscow, and Warsaw.

Odessa used to be famous for, along with other traditions, its criminal underworld (romanticized by Isaac Babel), its Jewish community, its political anecdotes from all eras, its citizens' discontent, its famous lust for freedom, and, as a result, its many dissidents. In our prison, this legendary city was well represented by the theoretical physicist Pyotr Butov. He was arrested on February 10, 1982, and the Odessa Regional Court sentenced him to five years of prison and two years of exile.

Pyotr Butov's contribution to the dissident movement was enormous. He inherited a unique library of anti-Soviet literature from Vyacheslav Igrunov, which he expanded and made available to readers, earning it a place in the annals of history. This library, a true miracle of the Soviet underground, consisted of both *samizdat* and *tamizdat* publications. Its catalog included Solzhenitsyn, Sakharov, Bulgakov, Platonov, Zamyatin, and Pasternak; periodicals beginning with *The Chronicle of Current Events* and ending with *The Chronicle of the Lithuanian Catholic Church*; a book collection ranging from George Orwell's *1984* to Andrey Amalrik's *Will the Soviet Union Survive Until 1984?*; and *tamizdat* journals ranging from Vladimir Maximov's *Kontinent* to *Posev*, the famous journal of the National Alliance of Russian Solidarists.

Over the course of Soviet history, there were only three such underground libraries—in Moscow, Petersburg, and Odessa. According to public opinion, the Odessa library was the largest, containing approximately 30,000 published items (books, journals, newspapers, posters, and so on), more than 20,000 titles, and 20,000 microfilms. The library had its own copying machines, its own microfilm developing laboratory, and even its own budget. It even used the Universal Decimal Classification (UDC) system. Library membership wasn't free—it cost one ruble a year, and, for a fee, the library would make copies. The library also published its own materials, for example, the yearly almanac *Deribasovskaya*.

After the collapse of the Soviet Union, the entire world learned about this library from a book by Lyudmila Alexeyeva, *The History of Dissent in the USSR*, published in Vilnius in 1992.[24] In that same year, I was invited to the Library of Congress to give a talk about Odessa's Igrunov-Butov underground library to an assembly of library directors from all over the world. Our colleagues from South America

---

[24] This book was first published in English translation, as Alexeyeva, Lyudmila. *Soviet Dissent: Contemporary Movements for National, Religious, and Human Rights.* Translated by Carol Pearce and John Glad, Wesleyan University Press, 1985. The book was published in Russia only in 1992.

were most interested in the subject, so the text was translated into Spanish and Portuguese, and, as far as I know, it helped dissidents to organize a similar underground library in Cuba. (In Cuba, the underground library was largely dedicated to media. They had a large collection of prohibited movies along with outlawed printed materials.)

Lyudmila Alexeyeva, the true queen of the liberation movement and the pride of Russian dissidents, explained that the secret behind the high quality of *samizdat* publications was directly related to the lack of proper equipment and facilities. Any nonsense can be printed, especially if you have money and connections, but if you're using a typewriter, you're bound to choose only something of real interest to you, something that you're willing to spend time on and take risks to reproduce. This is why *samizdat* truly represented the very best of literary, political, and social thought of that time.

The underground library under Butov's management lasted almost ten years and served thousands of people without jeopardizing its existence. Butov was an excellent administrator and a brilliant manager, and the library grew and blossomed during his tenure. Odessa's library gave birth to many legends, illustrating the fact that talented and devoted people are capable of anything, even in an evil empire. Unfortunately, this legendary library was destroyed in a fire—just like the Odessa summer theater had been. By arresting Butov and destroying the Odessa library, the Chekists added one more star to their epaulets. Butov liked to joke that the previous library directors had destroyed people's lives, but that he'd managed to get away with destroying only the books. I can just imagine how happy the Chekists felt when they found the library in the center of Odessa, in the secret basement of the house where Butov's girlfriend lived, and later when they brought volume upon volume of anti-Soviet literature up from that basement and threw them into the fire—an improvised auto-da-fé in the courtyard that lasted a whole week. The

Soviet press reported on this shameful act of destroying anti-Soviet literature, i.e., good books, and the information even found its way into the Georgian newspaper *Komunisti*.

Butov organized safe routes for importing anti-Soviet books from Europe and the US straight to the port of Odessa. Later he told me that he dealt only with the sailors, never trusting any of the "morale officers." He transferred almost all the anti-Soviet literature onto microfilm and kept the original books as the core collection. That's why the library hadn't suffered any serious losses until its downfall. On occasion they typed new copies, using thin paper like the paper used for cigarettes, one that could produce seven carbon copies at a time. We used the same simple method for printing our party's newspaper, *Samreklo*, or *Bell Tower*, which brought Butov and me even closer, establishing, on top of everything else, a special "technological comradery." When the Chekists found the library, they destroyed only its core collection, but the microfilms survived. And so, Butov's library exists to this day.

In 1983, Butov had already been arrested and transferred to a political prison when the Korean airplane tragedy occurred. He was so affected by the story that he thought about it constantly and decided to try and solve the mystery. He began by questioning the new inmates about the accident, asking about the time, the details of the flight, the history of that particular airplane, the passengers, the reaction of the Politburo, the position of the news broadcast *Vremya*, the West's reaction—in short, everything.

For Butov, the Flight 007 catastrophe was not only an act of sabotage conducted by the Soviet Union, but it was also a somewhat personal tragedy. On September 1, 1983, in the west part of Sakhalin Island, in the restricted airspace above the Japanese Sea, a Soviet interceptor plane shot down the Korean Airliner Boeing 747 as it flew from New York City to Seoul via Anchorage, Alaska. There were two hundred sixty-nine people on board (two hundred forty-six passengers and twenty-three crewmembers). All of them died, including twelve children under the age of twelve.

Initially, the Soviet Union denied any knowledge of the incident, but later admitted to shooting down the aircraft, claiming it was a spy plane. The Politburo stated that it was a deliberate provocation by the United States to probe the Soviet Union's military preparedness or even to provoke a war. The United States accused the Soviet Union of obstructing the search and rescue operations. Only ten years after the incident, yielding to pressure from the International Civil Aviation Organization, did Russia make the data related to the tragedy available to the public.

Considered one of the tensest moments of the Cold War, this incident escalated anti-Soviet sentiment all over the world, especially in the United States. As a result of this tragedy, the United States altered its tracking system for aircraft departing from Alaska and made the Global Positioning System (GPS) available for civilian flights in order to avoid such incidents in the future.

Right after the downing of the Korean flight, Ronald Reagan began calling the Soviet Union an evil empire. Here is what the President of the United States said regarding the Soviet Union: "While they preach the supremacy of the State, declare its omnipotence over individual man, and predict its eventual domination of all peoples on the earth, they are the focus of evil in the modern world."

More than a third of the passengers were Korean, and almost a quarter were American (one of them was a Congressman from Georgia, Larry McDonald). The remaining passengers were from Japan, China, the Philippines, Canada, Thailand, and the United Kingdom. There was a second aircraft that took off fifteen minutes later along the same flight path, but that second plane made it safely to Seoul.

At a secret meeting that took place in the small library room, with only ten inmates in attendance, Butov read us his report on the Korean aircraft. He finished his talk with the following words: "I don't know whether then Secretary General of the Communist Party, the 'poet' Yuri Andropov, who was sick in body and spirit (and who is no longer among the living), the Minister of Defense, the idiot General Dmitry Ustinov (who is also no longer among us), and the head of the State Security Committee, Viktor Chebrikov (who is still among us—who would dare kill him?!) knew that the aircraft that took off from JFK Airport in New York City on August 30, 1983, and that was shot down above the Japanese Sea by a Soviet missile was a symbol of the future fall of the USSR. The day when the USSR would cease to exist was not far off, and when it came, long-serving Politburo members would have to answer, along with many others, the following question: 'Do you recall the taste of children's blood?'"

In the prison life of inmate Butov, there was one episode that is still remembered by all of us. Once, Butov played Sherlock Holmes, tracked down a criminal, and meted out his punishment.

The story began suddenly. Out of the blue, the inmates began to notice that small items were disappearing. Nothing like this had happened in many years, but now it was happening all the time. The list of missing items made it rather difficult to come up with any system for their classification. Indeed, what kind of connection could possibly exist between Levan Berdzenishvili's nuts and his can of condensed milk, Rafik Papayan's single head of garlic, Johnny Lashkarashvili's twenty grams of butter, collected with great effort from his allotted ration, Zhora Khomizuri's fifty grams of egg powder, Misha Polyakov's one hundred grams of flour, and so on?

I brought this question to Odessa's pride and joy, the physicist and unparalleled Sherlock Holmes disciple Pyotr Butov (whose love of guns and violins connected him even more closely to Holmes).

"You're asking some strange questions, Mr. Georgia!" Butov said, gladly accepting the challenge. Just like his renowned predecessor, Butov often complained about the lack of crime during the first years of perestroika. "Truly, what can garlic and butter have in common? You can go now, Mr. Georgia, and come back in an hour—I'll have an answer for you."

One hour later, I came back accompanied by Zhora Khomizuri and Borya Manilovich. My choice of companions wasn't random. First, when it came to such petty thievery, the inmates, beginning with Pavelsons and ending with Bobkov, would eventually accuse Borya as he was the most obviously Semitic. In addition, Borya was very skeptical about Butov's crime-solving abilities, finding traces of anti-Semitism in many of his statements. Here I should note that Borya himself crossed a line when he said that Butov couldn't represent Odessa because, in order to represent that city, he should have a Jewish-sounding name—at least Butovich or, better yet, Butkevich.

"We do hope, Mr. Physicist Butov, the pride of Odessa, the greatest librarian and human being, that you will simply and straightforwardly investigate this case, find the offender, and restore justice. As you know, there are outstanding representatives of the South Caucasus among the victims," said the extremely eloquent Georgy Khomizuri, the one and only chairman of the Christian Federation of South Caucasian Nations.

"You put your trust in the right place, Mr. Geologist Zhora. I've already taken the first step in the investigation—I have discovered a profound connection among the stolen items."

"Are you, by any chance, referring to the fact that butter and garlic are edible items?" Borya inquired with a reverential tone.

"The butter was stolen from Lashkarashvili, was it not?"

"Yes, indeed. He has lung problems and his doctor allowed him five grams a day. He collected butter for four days, and the thief took all twenty grams!" Zhora said with indignation.

"Emotions won't help us here. Let's just remember that the butter was stolen from a sick person. Even more importantly, it was stolen from a person who wouldn't even think of hiding it."

"But wasn't garlic stolen from Rafael Papayan, who kept it in a secret safe?"

"Where would he get a safe in prison?" asked Zhora.

"I agree. Let's not call it a safe," Butov said. "But there is no doubt that the garlic was hidden rather well. And here we have the first clue: It's irrelevant to the thief how well the owner hides his things. He steals everything, even Papayan's well-hidden head of garlic—when, incidentally, no one in the prison had even seen a garlic clove in the last three months! And the thief has no problem stealing from a sick person, meaning he's free from any moral reservations or any national bias as well."

"What are you trying to say, Holmes?" I asked.

"That our thief is a remarkable psychologist."

"And how can you tell he has any knowledge of psychology?"

"Because of the thief's assessment that, even if he were to be caught and accused of stealing the garlic, no one would say a good word about Papayan, who had allowed his garlic, something as precious as gold, to dry out. And Lashkarashvili, who collects his butter instead of eating it, looks ridiculous to the thief. Presenting his victims as laughingstocks—that's the psychological weapon of our thief."

"So, if he steals butter, he's a pig, but if he steals garlic, he's a refined psychologist?" I asked, growing irritated.

"Is something going on that I don't know about?" Vadim Yankov asked as he entered the room. "The physicists and the philologists are discussing something, but there's no place for us poor mathematicians? Papayan's garlic is garlic, but my whole jar of clarified butter is not clarified butter?"

"Were you also robbed?" I asked, surprised, since Cos never saved anything. Whenever he received a package, he immediately consumed everything inside.

"According to my observations, Yuri Badzyo is the only man who hasn't been robbed yet because he carries his possessions with him at all times—*Omnia sua secum portat*, isn't that true, my dear Socrates?"

(Badzyo always carried his clock with him.)

"How were we supposed to know you had clarified butter?" Butov asked slyly.

"Why did you need to know about it? I knew about it!" Vadim yelled.

"The thief wants to shame you for eating clarified butter on the sly."

"Are you saying I should eat more obnoxiously?"

"No, but you should have let me try some," Zhora said.

"Help me find my butter, and I'll let all of you try some. One spoonful for everyone. But just one teaspoon. It's French butter."

"The thief is constantly at work. He's obviously a professional," Butov concluded.

"What's a professional thief doing in a political prison? Aren't his people next door? The thieves, murderers, and rapists are all over there."

"Well, we have one professional merchant here who used to sell Solzhenitsyn's *Gulag Archipelago* for ten rubles," Butov added. And it's true that, as long as I can remember, there'd been an endless dispute in Barashevo over whether we should consider Mr. Melnikov a dissident if he'd been selling anti-Soviet literature but didn't share the ideology of his products. Melnikov didn't consider himself a dissident.

"The thief is young," Butov suddenly announced. "And he was convicted under Article 70."

"How do you know?" we asked, clearly surprised.

"Papayan showed me his secret hiding place. You need to be young and in good physical shape to reach it."

Using this method of "deduction," we quickly singled out four candidates—Shabonas, Barkanas, Mironov, and Udachin.

"It's definitely not Shabonas," Butov said.

"How do you figure?" Yankov asked.

"He talks a lot, and he doesn't fit the profile of a thief," Butov concluded.

"Then there are three left—Barkanas, Mironov, and Udachin," I said.

"You Georgians have ironclad logic, but it's not Barkanas, either," Sherlock-Butov announced.

"And why is that, sir?" Manilovich asked, surprised. "Barkanas is as quiet as a mouse, and he has no health issues."

"He doesn't have any friends. Our thief is arrogant. He loves an audience and definitely has at least one close friend. He needs to show someone that he's smart and talented!"

"Doesn't Barkanas have any friends?"

"No, he doesn't. He's like a romantic poet, always alone."

"And he sleeps like the dead at night," added Yankov, Barkanas's neighbor in the barracks.

"So that leaves two—Mironov and Udachin," I concluded.

"They're both young, and both are in great physical shape. They're very capable young men. Mironov is interested in computers, and Udachin likes science fiction. Mironov is Levan's friend, and Udachin is Anderson's," Khomizuri informed us.

"Let me introduce you, my friends, to Udachin, our own goon and resident thief of political prison ZhKh 385/5-3," Butov announced almost solemnly. "This morning I noticed a small rash on his face. It looks like he's tried Berdzenishvili's nuts."

"The criminal has been found. What are we going to do with him now?" Zhora asked.

"What do we do? We need to go to the library and have a talk with his friend Anderson."

We went to see Anderson. Butov informed him of our investigation and its results. For some reason, Anderson was easy to convince, and he proposed a three-step conclusion to the drama:

> Udachin will publicly confess his crimes.
> He will return all the stolen goods.
> He will intentionally get into trouble and get sent to the hole.

This prediction was accepted, and everyone left. Only three of us remained near the library—Butov, Anderson, and I. All three of us knew that Anderson was in charge of a rather small but "ideologically correct" library. Anderson, however, didn't know that Butov, who was standing next to him, had created a legendary underground library of anti-Soviet literature, so large and complete, and most importantly, so ideologically incorrect, that for several years it gave the entire State Security of the USSR many sleepless nights. I also didn't know at the time that, many years later, I would be in charge of the Georgian National Library, the third largest in the USSR.

Udachin petulantly admitted to all his crimes. In the evening, the six of us (the investigators plus the wronged Papayan with his garlic—Anderson refused to share his food) were already eating *satsivi* with nuts while the controller Sureykin was escorting Udachin to the hole to serve fifteen days for disobedience and to allow him to reflect on the meaning of life.

Butov emigrated after his release. Now he lives in Germany and works as a physicist, while his colleague Vyacheslav Igrunov went into Russian politics. He's the deputy chair of the Yabloko party, though the party itself is in a serious state of crisis. And Korean aircraft don't even come close to the Russian border these days.

P olitical prisons, just like other Soviet prisons, had their own aristocracy—cooks, stockroom workers, librarians, boiler attendants, barbers, *banya* attendants, barracks attendants, movie projectionists, deliverymen, and so on. Many writers who have gone through the Gulag have written about it, including Solzhenitsyn, Ginzburg, and Shalamov. In the old days, before the Brezhnev era, when more than half of the Gulag consisted of people convicted under Article 58, all the "aristocratic positions" were filled by common criminals—murderers, thieves, and robbers—the "socially friendly" elements, if we use a broadly-accepted term from Marxism-Leninism. New times brought new prisons. Under pressure from the free world, the Soviets had to acknowledge, at least partially, that they did have political prisoners, and then had to build special political prisons for them. In the entire Soviet Union, there were only four political prisons—three were in the Perm region and one was in Mordovia, the famous Dubravlag. In these newly established political prisons, the "aristocracy" consisted of spies, war criminals, and traitors to the Motherland. In other words, if you were convicted under Article 70, the heir to Article 58 of the Criminal Code, you could never be a barber or a librarian even if, before your arrest, you were the best barber in the Soviet Union or the head of a large library.

Naturally, there were "aristocrats" in our prison too, such as the librarian Anderson, the cooks Maximovich and

Petrov-Senior, the barber Kukharuk, the boiler attendants Saar and Muzikyavichus, the *banya* attendant and movie projectionist (those were part-time positions) Lismanis, the stockroom worker Leikus, the barracks attendant Krainik, and others. In the old times, these "aristocrats" were disrespectfully referred to as *strawheads*, and Zhora Khomizuri continued this tradition into the new era.

Deinis Lismanis, the Latvian nationalist and social democrat, was arrested in November of 1980 and sentenced in a closed session of the Latvian Supreme Court to twelve years in prison as a traitor to the Motherland, i.e., the Soviet Union. Although accused of high treason against a land in which he had not been born, against a country that he considered an occupier and pillager, Lismanis did not take up arms to fight. After Latvia's occupation, he went into the underground and became a member of the Social Democratic Party, headquartered in West Germany.

I met Deinis Lismanis under rather peculiar circumstances. As soon as Dato and I arrived at the prison, we were welcomed with two things—dinner and a bath. As soon as I finished my dinner, I was taken to the banya. The local *banya* turned out to be an interesting place. The first thing I saw was "free" soap. I should explain here that in prison personal hygiene is as indispensable an aspect of our freedom as smoking. And if we were to continue the same analogy, when you're in a *banya*, you don't feel like a prisoner, you're not actually doing your time. Well, after I saw that "free" soap, I thoroughly lathered up my hair only to discover that there was no more water in the faucet. There were no other people in the *banya*, so no one could help me. The usual *banya* day was Saturday, but we'd arrived on a Thursday. The weather was hot, and there was no need for hot water. But you can't manage without water in a *banya*! Failing to find any reasonable solution, I wrapped an odd piece of fabric around myself and went out into the courtyard. I stopped the first passerby and asked him for help. That passerby explained that there was never any water in the faucet, that water was collected in a big barrel in the *banya*'s anteroom, the so-called pre-*banya* room, and all I had to do was to pour some water into my basin and, using a special ladle called a *shaika*, pour that water on my head with one hand while using the other hand for all other tasks. It wasn't very convenient, but the quest for personal cleanliness won out over all reservations. While I was searching for that big barrel of water, the man who was helping me had enough time to tell me a very funny anecdote about the *banya*. He told me the story with a noticeable Latvian accent, with prolonged vowels and sharp stresses either on the first or second part of long syllables. That man was Deinis Lismanis, a traitor, social democrat, and movie projectionist. "A Nordic type, a true Aryan, and a family man," as he liked to describe himself, imitating the narrator from the famous Soviet TV drama *Seventeen Moments of Spring*, written by the renowned Chekist Yulian Semyonov.

Deinis Lismanis was always in a good mood. No one could understand how he managed to be that way in a political prison, but the fact remains: No one ever saw him gloomy or in a bad mood. His cheerfulness was even infectious. Zhora believed that this was only a façade, Rafik thought he was shallow, saying jokingly that if it weren't for Lismanis's European appearance, we'd wonder if he wasn't Lismanishvili, Lismanidze, or Lismanauri (in other words, Georgian), Johnny thought he was cuckoo, Henrikh called him "spray-and-pray happy," Borya Manilovich considered him a natural anti-Semite, but only slightly, as was the case with all Balts, and Lismanis's polar opposite, the never-smiling Misha Polyakov, used to say that it would be interesting to get really drunk with him

There were other opinions as well. Yankov, for example, saw Lismanis as someone who rejected the all-Union struggle for democracy and looked upon him with suspicion. This fact, however, didn't stand in the way of their frequent conversations about *Faust*—Goethe was Lismanis's god. He knew German fluently, of course, and often recited long excerpts from *Faust*. Lismanis liked to joke that Goethe was God-the-Father, Thomas Mann, God-the-Son, and Schiller, the Holy Spirit. The Ukrainians tried to avoid him, finding his smile insincere and his open scorn for Russians just an anti-Slavic schtick. According to a common Ukrainian belief, the privilege to hate *Moscals*, their derogatory term for Russians, belonged solely to Ukrainians as the only lawful descendants of Kievan Rus.

Unlike the prison's Jews, who tried to avoid all activity on Saturdays—Grisha Feldman, for example, would prepare his *makhorka* cigarettes during the week and on Saturdays he'd run around the camp with one between his teeth and matches in his hand asking somebody to light it for him—Lismanis ruled the roost.

Saturdays gave Lismanis double dominion over our two islands of freedom—in the *banya* and in the dining hall where he'd show us a "new" movie. The movies that came to our prison, however, were never new. They were supposed to help correct our political views and thus lead to our rehabilitation. As a result, the movies were always about Comrade Lenin or Comrade Stalin, or about both of these comrades, or about other true comrades of those comrades, for example, Dzerzhinsky, or "Iron" Felix, the "intellectual" Frunze, or the all-Union head of state Kalinin.

I don't know why, but fate decided that I would meet by chance or have close relationships with many people that belonged to the world of cinema. First, one of my dearest friends was a film expert. Then once on Kutaisi Street in Tbilisi, I ran into Robert Redford (I still wonder what he was doing in that neighborhood—maybe he was looking for some car parts?). In Angers, France, at a dinner party for librarians, I met the actress Annie Girardot and gave her a short but information-packed lecture about *khachapuri*. (I recalled that once, on a Soviet TV show, when that actress mentioned *khachapuri*, the anchorman's mood, for some reason, went sour.) In the hallway of the Hotel Russia in Moscow, I bumped into the Italian producer Ettore Scola and Gina Lollobrigida, who was no longer young but could still turn her viewers into stone, just like Medusa. I was once on a flight from Moscow to Tbilisi with Lidiya Fedoseyeva-Shukshina and talked to her nonstop about the specificity of Shukshin's prose. In the international car of the Tashkent-Moscow train, I played cards with the actor Vyacheslav Tikhonov, who had already become Stierlitz. In Santa Monica, I happened to be in an elevator with Sharon Stone, who was tired and without makeup but still "enough for Holland" (a phrase used by the first and only president of the USSR, Mikhail Gorbachev, in answer to a Dutch journalist's question about how many nuclear warheads were left in Russia). Near the entrance to Warner Brothers Studio, I smoked a cigarette with Antonio Banderas, and when Catherine Zeta-Jones happened to pass by, I allowed myself to make a compliment that could have easily brought me an accusation of sexual harassment. Banderas had to explain that I was from the Caucasus, and that for Caucasian people, giving a compliment to a beautiful woman was basically like saying hello. (It's interesting that in English, one Caucasian means a representative of the white race, so he had to use the plural, Caucasians, or "double" Caucasian.)

Out of all these encounters that I could boast of, I was able to share only two while in prison—the one with Gina Lollobrigida and the one with Vyacheslav Tikhonov. The others happened later. With Lismanis, I, obviously, began talking about the very beautiful Gina, since boasting about a close acquaintance with the spy Isaev-Stierlitz in a conversation with an honest Latvian nationalist would not be *bon ton*. Back then we didn't have the word that we would use now to describe Deinis's passion—he was a real *fan* of movies, especially Italian movies. As soon as I mentioned Gina Lollobrigida's name, Lismanis got excited: "I wonder if you know, my Georgian friend, that Lollobrigida is the most American Italian actress, even more so than Sophia Loren? Lollobrigida was the biggest name not only in Italian cinema, but in world cinema of the fifties and the beginning of the sixties! And do you know what kind of period that was for Italian cinema? Do you know that she starred alongside such giants as Burt Lancaster, Yul Brynner, Frank Sinatra, and Sir Alec Guinness?"

"I only know that in real life, as they say, I, personally, have never seen a woman of such beauty," I said, beginning for the thousandth time to tell the story of me bumping into the animated group of Italians in the hallway of the Hotel Russia in 1975, when Gina Lollobrigida was about fifty years old.

"I wonder if you know, my dear Levan (he pronounced it Leevan, with the stress on the first syllable), that Gina participated in the Miss Italia beauty pageant in 1947?"

"No, I didn't know that, but I can imagine that she won decisively—she must've been only twenty years old back then."

"No, she didn't win! She didn't win! Another contestant won—Lucia Bosè (who starred in Guiseppe de Santis's *No Peace under the Olive Trees* and Juan Antonio Bardem's *Death of a Cyclist*)—and second place went to Gianna Maria Canale (who, by the way, was often compared with Ava Gardner). Lollobrigida came in third! How can we trust beauty pageants after that! We can acknowledge the beauty of Lucia Bosè, but Gina?!"

Lismanis watched all the movies from his projection room, occasionally providing us with unexpected commentaries, which some inmates found truly annoying, but which others found amusing and very entertaining. For example, when we watched the Soviet propaganda masterpiece *Wait for Me*, with

Valentina Serova, Konstantin Simonov's wife, in the leading role, the first time the actress appeared on-screen, Lismanis stopped the movie to announce:

"Here you can see the blonde beauty, Valentina Vasilievna Serova, the Soviet Marilyn Monroe, the sex symbol of the Soviet big screen in the thirties and forties. She was Stalin's favorite actress, and at state dinners, the leader of all the peoples of the world and cinema's greatest friend always invited this lady, along with Chkalov's wife, to sit next to him, since Valentina was the widow of the pilot Anatoly Serov, a hero of the Spanish Civil War. She later married that asshole Konstantin Simonov (Papayan, please, don't get upset), but it didn't stop the blonde beauty from having an affair with the general and future marshal Konstantin Konstantinovich Rokossovsky. The affair reached such a scale that, once during a state reception, Comrade Stalin asked General Rokossovsky: 'Do you happen to know, Comrade Rokossovsky, who the actress Serova's husband is?' 'The poet Simonov, Comrade Stalin,' Rokossovsky stammered. Then Stalin said: 'You know, I thought so too.' After that the future marshal ended all relations with his beloved. The actress lost herself in drink and died alone in 1975. Upon receiving this news, Simonov didn't interrupt his vacation in Kislovodsk, but sent roses instead. There were only three people, including her daughter, Maria Simonova, who paid their last respects to the Soviet cinema legend. Let's continue watching the movie now, my friends, and thank you for your attention."

Lismanis, as a rule, used to say terrible things while showing us such timeless Soviet masterpieces as *The Man with the Gun*, *Lenin in October*, and *Lenin in 1918*, which had become classics of Leninism. All his comments, however, were in Latvian, so Lismanis could always say that he was commenting on the skills of the actors playing Lenin. Sometimes the Georgians responded to Lismanis's joke, and in their comments,

delivered in Georgian, you could hear such innocent assess-
ments as *bastard, douchebag, son-of-a-bitch, cretin,* and other
comparable accolades. The Armenians didn't lag behind us in
this respect, interjecting a few beautiful phrases in the language of the immortal Gregory of Narek. In other words, with
Lismanis, watching these renowned masterpieces of Soviet
propaganda in lieu of real movies was fun.

Once upon a time, something unimaginable happened—for
a Saturday showing, we received a real film, Ingmar Bergman's
Autumn Sonata, starring Ingrid Bergman and Liv Ullmann. I
think the movie was shown first to the general public on the
outside, but it was such a flop, they decided to send the film to
the political prisons as a form of punishment: Here's your
beloved West and its incomprehensible masterpiece! To tell
the truth, the inmates didn't really like this rather difficult and
claustrophobic movie about a fraught relationship between a
mother and a daughter. But Lismanis kept pausing the movie,
pointing out the mastery of Sven Nykvist, Ingmar Bergman's
loyal cinematographer for twenty of his movies. Lismanis was
a true artist and could spot such details that the famous
Nykvist would probably have gladly hired him as his assistant.

Another time, we were honored to be sent a newsreel
along with the movie. Lismanis warned us that it wasn't a
movie, that it was only a newsreel, and that the movie would
follow. The newsreel was a short documentary, which showed
(don't forget, this was all happening in the era of perestroika,
at the peak of glasnost) unique footage that had been hidden
from the world for decades by Soviet Communists, as well as
by Western democrats. Anyway, the documentary showed
how the British, right after the end of World War II, released
Soviet prisoners from their occupied territory. Quickly realizing what was going to happen, Lismanis announced that
people with delicate nerves should leave the room as we
were about to see some horrifying footage. Of course, such a

comment compelled even those who were planning to skip the newsreel and smoke outside (we were not allowed to smoke in the dining hall) to stay.

A tall bridge, about a hundred meters above a river, appeared on the screen. The shot was taken from a distance, so you couldn't see anything clearly. As soon as the camera got closer, some dots appeared, and the dots were flying down from the bridge. The camera kept getting closer, and at some point, it became clear that those dots were people. People who of their own free will were jumping off the bridge into the river to meet their death. On the old, worn-out screen in the dining hall of ZhKh 385/3-5, Soviet prisoners of war were throwing themselves off a bridge over a deep gorge. Those people chose to jump off the bridge rather than fall into the hands of their own people, and there were women and children among them. Most of the prisoners tried to turn back, but the British welcomed them with rifles, killing them all on the spot. A terrible inhuman tragedy was happening on that bridge—and it was happening only a few months after the end of the cruelest war in the history of humankind. The Soviet prisoners from the British occupation zone knew that the Gulag was waiting, that a painful death lay before them, that the road back was cut off by the Allies' bullets, and that there was instant death in the deep gorge beneath the bridge.

Suddenly a small man appeared on the screen. He was running in the direction of the Russians with his hands in the air. The camera zoomed in for a close-up. Waving his arms wildly and yelling something, a small happy man was running toward his people.

All of a sudden, an inhuman scream shattered the dining hall: "Lismanis, stop the movie! No-o-o-o! No-o-o-o! Lismanis, stop!" Confused, Lismanis stopped the movie, and the inmate Timin, a small nondescript man who'd never said a word before, turned to his own image on the screen: "Where are you running to, you idiot?! Guys, that's me! That's me running back home only to spend forty years suffocating in the Gulag!"

Young Timin was looking at his older self from the screen. He was looking at all of us as if trying to understand what his future self, tormented in the Gulag, wanted from him forty years later. Lismanis turned off the movie projector. Meanwhile, the news of Timin being on the big screen traveled fast, and soon the entire prison burst into the dining hall. Everyone gathered in front of the screen—there was the warden, Major Shalin, Officer-on-Duty Sureykin, Deputy Commander for Morale and Welfare Lieutenant Arapov, the guards Trifonov, Kiselyov, and Trimazkin, and every inmate, without exception. Even Arkady Dudkin, who usually didn't watch the movies unless they were about the Battle of Berlin or the raising of the flag on the Reichstag, was there.

"Lismanis, start from Timin," Shalin ordered. And Lismanis started the film from the moment when a small dot separated from the crowd gathered on the bridge. Then the dot began to gradually increase in size until it transformed into the real Timin. Happy Timin was running, running toward the Motherland that he had so longed to see. He was running toward his twenty-five-year prison sentence, which in the Gulag was extended by another twenty years. He was running because he thought that, in the end, his Motherland would forgive him for his service in Vlasov's army, or at least they would talk to him in Russian.

The prison administration easily recognized Timin. Every one of them, beginning with Shalin and ending with Trifonov, broke into Homeric laughter and some inmates followed their example. It was a great show. In our dining hall that had been turned into a movie theater for a night, one half of the spectators could barely hold back their tears, their hearts gripped by grief, while the other half was dying of laughter. At first poor Timin tried to laugh too, but he couldn't. Then, suddenly, he passed out. We Georgians and Armenians, the members of the Christian Federation of South Caucasian Nations, took him outside to get some air, and our local Asclepius, Arnold Anderson, urgently revived him with his signature tincture, the non-secret ingredients of which were plantain and mint. The remaining secret ingredients were never revealed by the inventor of Soviet multivitamins.

"There's your renowned Winston Churchill for you!" Zhora Khomizuri exclaimed. "You know, Solzhenitsyn wrote about it, but I thought he was exaggerating."

"Winston Leonard Spencer-Churchill," said the omniscient Vadim Yankov, correcting him. "He was awarded the Nobel Prize in 1953, and it was in Literature, by the way."

"Sir Winston Leonard Spenser-Churchill was the biggest democrat of the twentieth century, the greatest politician of all time," Misha Polyakov said, completing the introduction. (By the way, according to a 2002 BBC research project, the British would consider Churchill to be the greatest Englishman ever, even more significant than Shakespeare and Newton.)

"No, Churchill wasn't the prime minister at that time, it was Clement Richard Attlee. Remember, the Labor Party won a sensational victory in the 1945 election," Borya Manilovich said, attempting to save the international legend.

"It's true, but, my dear Borya, the decision to return Soviet prisoners from the British zone to Russia was made with Churchill's blessing in February 1945 during the Yalta conference," Misha Polyakov said, reminding his fellow townsman of the bitter truth. "That means that, along with the illiterate, coarse, and angry donkey Uncle Joe, the responsibility for the tragedy of almost two million people like Timin falls on the chubby shoulders of the Nobel Prize winner, kind Uncle Winston, and the no less kind Uncle Sam—the handsome Franklin Delano Roosevelt—along with the entire noble, democratic, and humane West."

"When they're all behind a barbed-wire fence, they'll understand," Zhora said, reminding the naïve West of Solzhenitsyn's prediction.

"When there is a Red Flag above Paris," Borya added, showing no mercy for this international capital.

"There is enough red in their own flag. They love the Communists far too much," said Yankov, who'd never been fond of the French tolerance for communism.

"What are they supposed do when it was only their Communists and the Catholic Church that behaved decently during the war?" I said, trying to protect the French, for whom I've had a soft spot ever since childhood.

"Then they should choose the Church," Yankov said.

Lismanis came out from the dining hall and said: "Mr. Polyakov suggests that the general mess that is Russia is responsible for sending today's newsreel into a political prison, but I'm confident that the Soviet Communists have at most three or four years left. I don't get it, what are those idiots, Shalin & Co, laughing about? Very soon they'll have to guard themselves in Barashevo. First, the Soviet Union will collapse, then the international Communist movement will collapse, that is, all the Communist parties that are being fed by the Kremlin."

"What an apocalyptic picture," Yankov said with delight, unable to conceal his joy over the tragedy about to overtake the world's Communists. "All three of the Indian Communist parties will be liquidated!"

"There's no danger for China, North Korea, or Cuba. They'll enter the next millennium with communism," Zhora predicted. "But the Communist Parties of France and especially of Italy are in danger of disappearing. Soon *L'Humanité* and *L'Unità* won't be published anymore."

"Don't forget *The Morning Star*, my dear Zhora, the third-largest Communist newspaper in the world, after *Pravda* and

Renmin Ribao [The People's Daily]," Yankov said, taking a jab at the English Communists out of respect for Timin.

Unfortunately, I don't know anything about Lismanis's life today, and I have no idea what happened to Timin. But when the inmate Timin suddenly met the big-screen Timin, with the help of Lismanis, I saw the West in a different light. The West, which had seemed so picture-perfect and flawless, became alive and real, and I realized that it had always had its own shortcomings.

DATO

It's 6 A.M. on June 23, 1983. We're at home, at 17 Vedzini Street, Tbilisi. There are three of us—my wife Inga, my brother Dato, and I. All of us are sleeping. There are two staircases in our building: One leads to the landing we share with our next-door neighbors, the Yashvilis, and the other leads to the landing we share with the Kochoradzes. Our window faces this staircase, and I can hear some commotion coming from beneath the window. This noise wakes me up. From the window, I can see the Kochoradzes' staircase and the silhouettes of several serious-looking men. I quickly get dressed and wake up my wife. Meanwhile, we hear a cautious knock on our door.

I try to wake up Dato, but it's not a simple task. He came home late last night, usually sleeps very deeply, and in general doesn't like to get up early. He opens his eyes, but there is no reaction to my words: "Get up!" Then I say the magic phrase—"They're here!"—and he understands everything. I open the door, and about six people burst into our apartment while another six secure the staircase. Only twenty seconds have passed between my waking up and this invasion. The lightning speed alongside the prosaic, businesslike character of these events gave everything a surreal quality. What we'd been expecting for so many years had finally happened—just like waiting for death. And after that, our life-after-death began. The Georgian State Security drew a line that fractured our lives, dividing them into two periods—before and after 6 A.M. on June 23, 1983.

Colonel Gersamia was in charge of the uninvited guests. I already knew this man—he'd interrogated me once before. World history knows many famous brothers—Gaius and Tiberius Gracchus, Jacob and Wilhelm Grimm, Auguste Louis Marie Nicholas and Louis Jean Lumière, George and Andria Balanchivadze, the Kennedy brothers, the brothers Karamazov, Rocco and his brothers . . . but modern Georgian society knows only the Gersamia brothers.

In Soviet Georgia, these brothers had their own family business: One brother worked in the KGB, and the other was a judge. One brother arrested the criminals, and the other sentenced them—he had a strong preference for capital punishment. And there was no conflict of interest. Up to their last breath, both brothers boasted about their joint efforts, how together, hand in hand, they arrested and executed people, and that if they had the chance, they'd do it again and again— arresting and executing. After discharging their duties, they went proudly, hand in hand, into the next world. Their "glorious work" reached its peak in the eighties.

Such was the evil spirit that flew into our family home on the morning of June 23, 1983, presenting a search warrant and introducing us to two witnesses—who are the subject of a separate conversation. They lived in the far-off neighborhood of Saburtalo and, independently from each other, happened to be on a walk at six in the morning near Mtatsminda, where the KGB taskforce asked them to be witnesses to a search.

We'd waited for our arrest just as one waits for death, not seeing any life afterward, so when the uninvited guests came and proceeded to search our apartment, the fact that we were still alive came as a surprise and made us laugh. The shock and fear went away and our courage and sense of self-esteem returned and increased gradually in the presence of those people who, in carrying out their jobs, were so far from truth and honor simply because the very business they were in was so disgraceful.

They took Dato away while the search was still underway. Digging through our books for two hours without any result, these responsible and competent officers failed to uncover anything—I mean, if we were awaiting our arrest, why would we have kept any material evidence at home? By the end of their search, all they could find were two "scary" books— Grigol Robakidze's *The Snake's Skin* and Irakli Abashidze's book about Khruschev's travels through India, which the old Stalinist Gersamia considered anti-Soviet. I couldn't help but laugh, which made the colonel mad: "What are you laughing about? Do you think this is a time for levity for you brothers?" I think he was mentally comparing us, unworthy brothers, to "the esteemed Gersamia brothers."

"Why? Can't I laugh? Do I need to ask permission from the man who thinks that Irakli Abashidze's book is anti-Soviet?" I asked, continuing to chuckle.

"Now, young man, get dressed and follow us, if you please," the colonel commanded with an expression on his face that was very easy to decipher. One could read an entire sentence on this long-serving executioner's face—a somewhat modernized version of the final line of Florian's fable: He who arrests last laughs best.

They kept Dato until evening in the office of the head of the KGB's department of investigation, where the following individuals were present—the department head, Alexander Mirianashvili, the investigator Gia Tsintsadze, and a Russian Chekist from Perm. At 8 P.M. Dato was transferred to a cell in the basement with two other inmates. One of them was a young man arrested in connection with the "Jewish case"—a high-profile case that shocked the entire Soviet Union in the spring of 1983, when a whole army of Jewish businessmen were arrested throughout the country, unleashing fantastic rumors that they had exported all the Soviet Union's gold to Israel and filling the public imagination with new pearls of anti-Semitic Chekist folklore. The second inmate was a career criminal who'd already served nine years and liked to point out that it wasn't him but his partner who had cut off the head of their third accomplice. Later, the same gentleman happened to end up in a cell with Johnny Lashkarashvili. The presence of such a criminal in the KGB infirmary was strange, to say the least, and Dato, despite his youth, instantly figured this inmate out. In their cell, Dato undertook a traditional Georgian occupation—teaching, beginning with a series of lectures on the history of Georgia (in similar circumstances I would lecture on Latin and Greek mythology).

The series of daily interrogations began, but the results were upsetting. Over the course of six months, the KGB, with its team of investigators, couldn't get answers to any of its questions in the David Berdzenishvili case. Bravely and of his own free will, Dato claimed the right to be silent, a right that the state would grant its citizens only twenty years later. My brother never boasted about it. No one ever heard him say anything like: You know how brave I am. The KGB couldn't make me talk for six months!

Dato would come to all the interrogations, but he would answer only two questions:

"Are you going to give any evidence?"

"No."

"Are you going to provide an explanation for why you're refusing to talk?"

"No."

Once, his investigator, who had almost given up on my brother, asked him only for the sake of protocol whether Dato had anything new to say, and Dato answered yes, that he had some news. The investigator grew excited, gave Dato a cigarette, cleared his desk, and took out a pen to write down "the news."

Dato then told him he had a toothache. At that moment, he saw the real face of the usually polite and "kind" KGB officer.

To verify his suspicion about his cellmate, Dato used a simple test: He gave his cellmate obvious disinformation, and when in the course of an interrogation the investigator mentioned that nonsense, his suspicion was confirmed. The Chekists had to transfer their criminal informant from the cell. Before that episode, neither Dato nor his provocateur cellmate had slept for ten days. The KGB treated those they arrested and their own agents with equal cruelty, especially when one witty and intrepid inmate was able to uncover their agent.

When it was time for us to be transported, all the founders of the Georgian Republican Party—Vakhtang Dzabiradze, Vakhtang Shonia, and Levan and David Berdzenishvili—were sent as a group to the Rostov prison. After Rostov, we were separated: The two Vakhtangs were sent to Perm, while Dato and I went to Dubravlag in Mordovia. After our arrival in Barashevo, my role as the responsible older brother was established. My main task was to keep the young and rebellious Dato out of trouble, but I can't say that I achieved any real success in that mission.

The workday in prison began at seven in the morning and lasted until four in the afternoon. Most inmates used the lunchtime as a marker—one o'clock in the dining hall. We all tried to finish our daily quota by then because that way we would have free time after lunch, which we could use to prepare ourselves for our future freedom—by writing letters, reading books, creating an illusion of privacy, and reflecting. Some inmates saw the workshop as a real hell. It's true that the job of a sewing machine operator required certain skills, and for people lacking such talent, handling a sewing machine was a very challenging business. Zhora Khomizuri, who hated sewing machines, our workshop, and everything associated with collective labor, suffered most acutely in our prison. In his opinion, the sewing workshop—its unheard-of cruelty, the horrifying nightmare of it all—was created by Chekists to get even with dissidents for their days and years spent with a typewriter.

"It's simple," Zhora used to say. "A typewriter, a typing machine, a machine . . . from that machine to a sewing machine . . . an eye for an eye, a machine for a machine—this is their diabolical and well-thought-out plan. I think this idea could have only come from Beria. Even Stalin couldn't have come up with something so evil!" Zhora continued without showing any pity for his fellow countrymen.

From the beginning, Dato didn't like sewing very much. So he told me that I'd have to complete his quota since he'd never be able to master the skill and would have to spend all his time in solitary. But then he began watching experienced sewers. He learned from Polyakov how to concentrate on the work, he picked up different sewing tips from Papayan, he learned organizational skills from Anadenko, and he figured out the secret of attaching the thumb of the mitt with the help of Butov. As a result, my brother eventually became a very skillful sewing machine operator.

Dato sewed very fast. The sewing experts—Butov, Anadenko, and Papayan—were able to finish one hundred pairs by noon. Sometimes I could keep up with them, but Dato broke all the records and finished his quota by 11 A.M. As he explained, the mitts he produced were not of the highest quality ("I sewed on the borderline of the rejects," he explained), but they were within the norm. One day Dato outdid himself, significantly improving on his own record. When at 10:15 A.M. he finished his quota and stopped working, the sweatshop ex-champion, Odessa dissident Pyotr Butov, submitted a written complaint to the prison administration, claiming that Berdzenishvili-junior was turning out low-quality products. Butov was a real Soviet dissident, and as such he upheld Soviet laws and took a personal interest in the quality of the products the inmates manufactured for their Motherland. I must mention here that at the same time that we were working in the sweatshop, next to us in the female political prison ZhKh 385/3-4, the women inmates were doing the same; as our invisible neighbor, the renowned Russian poetess and dissident Irina Ratushinskaya recounted in her book *Grey Is the Color of Hope*; they were very concerned about the quality of their products—because the simple Russian people, builders not Chekists, would be using their work mitts.

As any inmate who respects himself and others would do, Pyotr Butov provided Dato with a copy of his complaint. Inmate Butov operated openly and, as he believed, honestly.

All the political prisoners in Barashevo were very confused by Butov's unexpected action—lodging an official complaint. The "democrats" broke into two groups: One faction, led by Anadenko, justified Butov's action. The other faction saw his complaint as a denunciation of one prisoner by another and considered such an act immoral and unacceptable. Zhora Khomizuri, an elder in the Christian Federation of South Caucasian Nations, was in charge of the second faction, which sought to protect the moral code of the inmates, and his position was very strict. In a speech, he even mentioned the poet Nekrasov and his famous lines: "You do not have to be a poet, but you are obliged to be a citizen." However, in order to shame his opponents, he changed the lines to: "You do not have to be a Chekist, but you are obliged to be a snitch."

Being referred to as a Chekist and a snitch upset Butov tremendously. He considered it a capital offense and for a long time broke off all contact with us, the inmates from the Caucasus. This event found its proper place even in Barashevo's language: Johnny Lashkarashvili, a big fan of linguistic experimentation, suggested the Georgian neologism *butiny* to commemorate the controversy surrounding Butov's complaint. The phrase "It's a *butiny!*" became especially popular.

The Odessa dissident and patron of the largest underground anti-Soviet library, Pyotr Butov, couldn't have predicted the consequences of his actions—as the seed of this destructive complaint had been thrown into very fertile soil. Even before these events, the prison administration had given Dato the cold shoulder—we felt it as soon as we arrived at the prison. The local administration was heavily influenced by the Georgian KGB, which couldn't forgive Dato for his six-month silence at the pretrial detention center when he refused to give any testimony, driving the Chekists mad. Representatives of the Georgian KGB also visited us in Barashevo, "warmly welcoming us," then, so as not to give the wrong idea, openly threatened us by saying that our case was not over yet. "Gorbachev and Shevarnadze come and go, but the KGB was, is, and always will be!" The KGB was not a frequent visitor to our prison. Only a few were so honored, and after their visit our "political capital" in the prison instantly increased. (Later, the KGB would honor the Petersburger Misha Polyakov with a visit.) It was the Chekists who explained to the prison warden, Major Shalin, that despite a relatively light punishment, the founders of the Georgian Republican Party, especially the younger Berdzenishvili, were very dangerous people and warranted special attention and supervision. The administration reacted to Butov's unusual missive and assigned someone named Flor Vasilievich to the case.

Flor Vasilievich was a free man. Nevertheless, for years, without budging, he'd worked in our sweatshop alongside the inmates. He had a God-given, unalienable right, which gradually turned into an obligation as the years went by. Every night he would leave the prison, buy a half-liter of the cheapest vodka, go to his one-room cell in an apartment building on the other side of the prison gate, and drink half of his vodka alone, while snacking on half a pickle. After that, he would think about the vanity of this world, asking himself about the meaning of life, only to search and fail to find a satisfying answer. Such deliberations would tire him, and he'd fall asleep right there at the table, only to be woken up the next morning by the radio and that enemy of sweet Morpheus, the unrelenting anthem in a major key. This anthem was created in 1943 through a collaboration between the composer Alexander Alexandrov and the poets Sergey Mikhalkov and Gabriel El-Registan. Later in 1977, the anthem was revised by the same Sergey Mikhalkov. The revisions undertaken by the renowned author and father of two filmmakers consisted entirely of removing Stalin's name from the lyrics.

With the anthem blaring, Flor Vasilievich would wake up, eat the remaining half of his pickle, and go straight to the prison to wash his face in the "smoke shack" along with the inmates. Then, at half past six, again with the inmates, he'd drink the special prison tea, also called government tea or the tea of the people's commissars, which was, more precisely, just boiling water with the color of tea, and he would never miss the free breakfast. Flor Vasilievich had his breakfast, lunch, and dinner with us inmates, and he wore the same clothes we did, the same boots and foot cloths. In this way, he managed to save "big" money, which he spent on everyday necessities—*makhorka*, matches, and vodka. Flor Vasilievich was undoubtedly a happy man. He organized his life so well that he didn't want for food, drink, or interaction with interesting people, he had a completely sufficient degree of freedom, and he didn't exhaust himself with overly agonizing reflections on the meaning of life.

In the ZhKh 385/5-3 prison, Flor Vasilievich was the head of the Technical Quality Control Department. We inmates sewed mitts for construction workers, and Flor Vasilievich checked their quality. For that he would take a mitt and check whether the stitches were at the permitted distance from the edge and of the proper length (the longer the stitch, the faster the mitt could be made), whether the distance between the two parallel seams fell within the permitted distance, whether the rubber palm was correctly sewn on, and whether the thumb had been properly attached. From a stack of ninety-three pairs, he'd take three or four of these work mitts, measure everything with a ruler, and if he found no unlawful deviations, he'd affix a seal and move on to the next stack. If it happened by chance that he found a defect, he'd mark the entire stack as rejected and the worker wouldn't make his quota. And that was Flor Vasilievich's entire job.

On the third day after Butov's complaint, Flor Vasilievich meticulously examined Dato's pile and rejected it. My sewing machine was strategically situated: From my workspace, I could easily observe Dato, Dmitro Mazur at his layout machine, our pattern shop, and, most importantly, Flor Vasilievich. So, as soon as he rejected Dato's pile, throwing the mitts on the floor, I quickly made my way to the technical quality control shop. I tried to get there before Dato, fearing that my brother, with his unrestrained behavior, might attack Flor Vasilievich and make a real mess of things.

"What's the problem, Flor Vasilievich?" I asked, trying to remain as calm and polite as possible.

"I'm very glad you came by instead of your brother," Flor Vasilievich said happily, realizing that his conversation with Dato wouldn't have been easy.

"What does he want?" asked Dato, who had suddenly shown up in the shop. The inmates began to gather around us.

"Stay out of it, Dato," I said, warning my brother. "I'll take care of it calmly and quietly."

"The quality of the work mitts produced by inmate Berdzenishvili does not satisfy the technical requirements,"

Flor declared with a phrase that he had probably spent all night memorizing. "That's why I can't accept his stack."

The administration's plan was simple: Flor wouldn't accept Dato's quota today, or tomorrow, or ever. For not fulfilling his quota, Dato would be denied the right to shop in the prison store, then to see his family, then they'd transfer him to solitary, and from there—to a maximum-security prison. Then, finally, he'd receive an additional sentence. I clearly saw this path etched on Flor Vasilievich's face.

"Why are you doing this, Flor Vasilievich? My brother is almost a child, don't you have children of your own?" I asked, raising my voice.

"The quality of the work mitts produced by inmate Berdzenishvili does not satisfy the technical requirements," Flor said, repeating the unforgettable phrase in a shriller voice.

"And I'm telling you that my brother's mitts satisfy the technical requirements," I said in a voice that I wasn't especially fond of—you could clearly hear in it the metallic tones of the Caucasus region.

"Here, see for yourself," Flor said, giving me one of Dato's work mitts, on which the two seams were . . . well, not exactly parallel.

"What is the permitted distance between the seams?" I asked.

"From two to five millimeters," Flor declared victoriously.

"Can I borrow your ruler, Flor Vasilievich?"

"Please," Flor said happily because now the conversation was turning away from the touchy subjects of children and morals to that of technical details, where he was like a fish in water.

Flor brought a ruler and measured the mitt. Then he took another one from the pile and measured again. Then another one. And another. For half an hour Flor measured the work mitts, trying to find an obvious flaw. An unimaginable miracle was happening right before our eyes: All the work mitts produced by Dato met the technical requirements even though at first glance none of them appeared to be sewn correctly.

A weight fell from my shoulders. Now they wouldn't be able to increase Dato's sentence. The KGB was powerless. I thought that we were actually following our father's parting words, which he said to us during our trial (making the judge very angry): "Try your hardest not to get your sentences increased!" And here we were. We had listened to him and we were trying!

The situation calmed down, and when everyone decided that the incident was over, I gathered the mitts that, as it turned out, were correctly made, rolled them into a huge and heavy ball, and literally, without any metaphors, threw them at Flor Vasilievich's head.

Polyakov and Khomizuri dragged me out of the workshop. Flor Vasilievich ran to the administration building and submitted a complaint to the effect that "Berzenishvili-senior threatened to kill my children and then hit me on the head with his younger brother's products."

This incident had the following consequences:

I was denied the right to use the prison store.

Both Dato and I were denied the right to ask for up to two rubles a month to spend on stationery supplies, such as postage stamps, envelopes, notebooks, pens, pencils, and erasers.

It was explained to Flor Vasilievich that his children were never in any danger, especially since he didn't have any.

Pyotr Butov came and brought us a bottle of sunflower oil, as if to say that since you were denied the right to use the prison store, please, take my modest contribution. He never apologized to Dato.

Khomizuri and Anadenko, after long discussions, achieved a compromise: In the future, any inmate's complaint involving another inmate must be submitted first to the all-inmate secret committee.

Dato began boasting endlessly about how well he sewed his

work mitts, and he carried this rather dubious belief with him into the next millennium.

My brother had always been a rebel. It was his idea to start fighting for the right to compose letters in our native language, which we won after a long struggle and began sending letters home in Georgian. Obviously, everyone could exercise this right, and this is how the political prisoners began to correspond in their native languages.

In our prison, the number of visits was strictly regulated. In the course of a year, we were allowed one personal visit from one to three days and two two-hour-long visits around a table with a guard present. Once my wife arrived for a two-hour-long visit and was allowed to see both of us. Dato immediately began fighting for double the time—that is, to extend our meeting from two hours to four because there were two of us, and each of us had a right to his own two hours. He even threatened that if the administration denied the request and our rights were not observed, we'd refuse the visit. We won this battle, even though I was very afraid that they'd cancel our visit altogether, and my poor Inga would leave Barashevo without seeing me. That's what had happened to Zhora Khomizuri's wife, Nina Melkumova.

My wife never missed any visits. All my family members used to come to visit us—our mother, my elder brother and his wife, as well as my wife's brother and sister. As a rule, my elder brother Fridon (aka Mamuka, aka Fore) would bring the entire group to Barashevo.

In another fight initiated by Dato, we established the right not to sweep the prison grounds with a broom, even though the administration had the right to demand this from the inmates. Even on his last day in prison, Dato started a fight. When the guards wanted to transport him quietly to Tbilisi, he demanded to say good-bye to me, and he won.

The year my brother Dato spent in Barashevo was a year of many battles and skirmishes. The administration, after adding the classic line "the inmate did not mend his ways" to his record, demanded that Dato be kept under police supervision. So, after Dato had served his time, he was denied the right to live in Tbilisi, and with that the KGB blessed him with new battles. A political leader emerged from those battles—a man who was able, on his own as a member of the small Republican Party of Georgia, to be nominated as a representative of the city of Batumi, win the election, and become a member of the Georgian Parliament. His signature, along with those of other representatives, can be found at the bottom of the Act of Independence of the Republic of Georgia.

From prison, Dato was transferred to the capital of the Mordovian ASSR, the city of Saransk, and then, escorted by three officers, he was taken to Moscow by plane. In Lefortovo Prison, he was thrown into a huge cell and left there alone. Dato finally walked out a free man from the KGB isolation unit in Tbilisi. By that time, he weighed one hundred thirty pounds. He was so skinny that when he made it home, our friend didn't recognize him and began asking my wife about Dato in his presence: When is he coming back?

The day Dato walked free in Tbilisi—I didn't have any supporting evidence, but I sensed that it had happened—I brewed some very strong tea in a special one-liter thermos using my remaining tea supply, made wonderful sandwiches with Volna fish pâté, and invited guests to the feast. Zhora Khomizuri was the toastmaster and Misha Polyakov, Heliy Donskoy, Borya Manilovich, Johnny Lashkarashvili, Rafik Papayan, and Vadim Yankov were in attendance. Pyotr Butov came without an invitation and apologized. That day, June 21, 1985, was very special for another reason. In a certain sense, I, too, was set free on that day—free from the responsibility for my brother. I spent an additional year and a half in the Barashevo prison after that.

Now About Myself

O nce when I was little, my mother took me with her on a road trip. My mother was a Georgian language and literature teacher at a school in Batumi. Of course, it wasn't the school that my brothers and I attended, but it was nonetheless in our small seaside city. My mother read in the *Komunisti* newspaper that somewhere in Russia, in the Northern Caucasus, near the city of Mozdok, there was a Georgian village called Novo-Ivanovka, and so she organized a three-day student expedition there. My mother's pupils traveled throughout Georgia, visiting its most remote corners, and now the itinerary was outside our Motherland, so it felt like we were travelling abroad!

When I got on the bus, many children wanted me to sit near them, and they all expressed their wish rather loudly. Of course, this wasn't because of me—I was just a chubby little boy, who, according to mean people, never kept his mouth shut, but in the opinion of my family, I was a boy with strong communication skills, which eventually helped me become a professor, a journalist, and even a politician. All my mother's pupils wanted to sit next to me because I was their favorite teacher's son, and so I, without saying a word, walked to the back of the bus and sat alone. The bus took off but stopped soon to pick up a few more students, and a very beautiful woman got on with her daughter. The mother was beautiful— when I would talk about it later, everyone would correct me: What are you talking about? You're exaggerating! There wasn't

SACRED DARKNESS · 225

any gorgeous woman on that bus!—but her daughter was the most beautiful girl in the entire world. And that girl walked to the back of the bus and sat next to me. She took a seat near a window—my wife generally prefers window seats in every form of transportation. When we book plane tickets, we order her a window seat and the one next to it for me. They say it's impossible to find the love of your life at such a young age, being almost a child, but that's what happened . . . During the three days of that excursion, I talked very little because I already knew that I was in love, and I knew that it was for the rest of my life, forever, until my last breath.

When we were on our way back home from our expedition, from the top of Tsikhisdziri Mountain I saw our hometown surrounded by the Black Sea, and my heart stopped—I couldn't imagine my life without her, my Inga.

In August 1978, right after our wedding, I took Inga to Tbilisi where I was working in the Greek and Roman library with a monthly salary of forty-seven rubles and fifty kopeks. I was renting a little studio apartment on the sixth floor of an apartment building in the Vake neighborhood, which had a view of the Vere River. As soon as my wife entered the apartment, she understood that it was also the headquarters of an underground party and a print shop with publishing equipment. I've never hidden anything from my wife. From the day I met her, I was sure that she'd never say to me: "I'm sorry, darling, I found someone else!" Where did such confidence come from? I can't answer that. I purchased our first typewriter, a Ukraine-2, near the metro station named after Lenin, in what was called the Novyi Department Store, where they asked to see my passport, took a typing sample of all the letters (the KGB didn't rest, not even in stores), and registered the typewriter in my name. In the box marked "intended use," they wrote "scholarly work." Then I took this very heavy typing machine (it weighed the same as at least five laptops) to

Kolkhoznik Square, where the deaf-mute artisans changed the font to Georgian. In that same place, I bought my second typewriter, a Remington, which already had a Georgian font. Those two typewriters comprised all our technical equipment for publishing illegal literature, especially our magazine *The Bell Tower*. Inga became the first and, for a long time, the only woman member of the underground Georgian Republican Party.

But even earlier, on May 21, 1978, Vakhtang Dzabiradze, Vakhtang Shonia, my brother Dato, and I founded the first Georgian underground party and named it the Republican Party. Regardless of the new party's name, the mere fact of its existence was taken as anti-Soviet because there was a one-party political system in the USSR and so any non-Communist party was illegal. But on that day, we argued for a long time, until four o'clock in the morning, about what we'd name our creation—"A name, a name, my party for a name!"—we wanted that name to express our mutual dream, the independence and freedom of our Motherland, the Republic of Georgia. Dato was only seventeen years old at that time, and in order to give him an opportunity to join the party that he had actively helped to create, we added a special amendment to the freshly written charter, which allowed Dato to become a member without the right to vote until he reached legal age.

The first issue of our magazine *The Bell Tower* included six articles, some of which were written collectively—as, for example, "The Appeal of the Georgian Republican Party to the Georgian Nation," which opened with: "Brothers, sisters, fathers, and children!"—and some were written by individual members (at that moment, there were only four members in our party, including one member without voting rights). With the addition of my wife, the party acquired a professional editor, stylist, proofreader, and a caring mother.

Four years later, on a winter day, I left home with a thick

folder under my arm—I was carrying my dissertation about Aristophanes to a typist—when I saw a casual acquaintance getting out of a car and walking toward me. I knew that he worked for the KGB.

"Where are you going?" he asked me.

"I'm carrying my dissertation to a typist," I answered, trying to continue walking.

"Hold on a second!" he said, stopping me. "If you're in a hurry, we'll give you a ride!"

"There's no need for that," I said. "It's nearby . . . "

"We're nearby too," he said with an iron voice. "Get in the car!"

This is how I got arrested, and the next six months I did indeed spend nearby—one hundred meters from my house—but the next three years I spent very far away.

"The accused organized a criminal group, which they called 'The Republican Party,' and by joint agreement made a decision to publish *The Bell Tower*, an illegal mouthpiece of their false party for the dissemination of anti-Soviet materials. In accordance with the decision of the panel of the Supreme Court of the Georgian Soviet Socialist Republic . . . "

From Barashevo Prison ZhKh 385/3-5, I wrote Inga every month—to write more often wasn't allowed—but those were long letters, filled with love. She wrote me even more often, and I read each of her letters many times over. My parents, brothers, their families, Inga's parents, and our friends—all these people were with me in the Barashevo prison, innocent victims of my crime, sentenced to waiting. And the most innocent among them was a little girl, whose name I couldn't pronounce without tears—my daughter Tamuna. I was able to take all those letters with me after I was released, and they formed a long epistolary saga about the survival of love. Somehow it happened that all those letters were lost, but I've stopped being upset about it. All that's left is memory, clear and bright as a single short letter: "Darling, I've found you, and I'll be with you always."

About the Author

Born in 1953 in Batumi, a city on the Black Sea, Levan Berdzenishvili is the author of numerous books on ancient comedies, modern society, and Latin.